EPITAPH
ROAD

DAVID PATNEAUDE

EGMONT
USA
NEW YORK

EGMONT
We bring stories to life

First published by Egmont USA, 2010
443 Park Avenue South, Suite 806
New York, NY 10016

1 3 5 7 9 8 6 4 2

www.egmontusa.com
www.patneaude.com

Library of Congress Cataloging-in-Publication Data
Patneaude, David.
Epitaph Road / David Patneaude
p. cm.
Summary: In 2097, men are a small and controlled minority in a
utopian world ruled by women, and fourteen-year-old Kellen must
fight to save his father from an outbreak of the virus that killed ninety-
seven percent of the male population thirty years earlier.
ISBN 978-1-60684-055-9 (hardcover) — ISBN 978-1-60684-070-2
(reinforced library binding)
[1. Sex role—Fiction. 2. Virus diseases—Fiction. 3. Fathers and
sons—Fiction. 4. Science fiction.] I. Title.
PZ7.P2734Ep 2010
[Fic]—dc22
2009025118

Book design by JDRIFT DESIGN

Printed in the United States of America

CPSIA tracking label information:
Random House Production • 1745 Broadway • New York, NY 10019

To my steadfast writing and running buddy Sydney,
who only occasionally questioned my judgment.

ACKNOWLEDGMENTS

My immeasurable thanks go to the mostly unsung but highly talented people—especially agent Elana Roth and editor Greg Ferguson—who were so instrumental in making this book possible. I also couldn't have written the story without the continued support of my wife, Judy, and the rest of my family, immediate and extended, whose names alone could fill several pages. But you know who you are. And I can't forget to acknowledge the bad guys and buffoons who were partly responsible for inspiring this tale. Last but not least, I want to thank my mom, a world-class reader, who lived almost long enough to add this book to her collection.

And then we can fly to the moon.

—Charlie Winters, August 7, 2067

AFTER

Charlie frowned as muted sunlight leaked through the ragged umbrella of evergreen boughs overhead. Someone had discarded a red plastic Coke pouch in the middle of the trail. Under his breath, he gave that someone a name: "Pig." He stomped the pouch flat and stuffed it in his backpack. Two days into the hike and already one big compartment was crammed with trash.

"What are you gonna do when you run out of room, Charlie?" The loud voice was a clue, but his nose confirmed that his kid sister, Paige—three years younger but constantly mothering him anyway—had closed the gap between them. Her insect repellent was called Morning Coffee; it stank like Midnight Vomit. But antibug concoctions—foul or not— were a necessity now. Mosquitoes and their pesky cousins ruled. Their natural predators—frogs, salamanders, snakes, turtles, native fish, birds—were parading toward extinction. In the right climates, in the right seasons, in the right amounts, warmth was a good thing. But the earth, and a lot of its inhabitants, had overdosed on it.

"There's plenty of space in *your* pack," he said.

"I don't do garbage." Paige was only eleven—princess age—but when she wasn't being a mother she was being a queen.

"Sure you do," Mom said, glancing back at them without slowing. "But let's get the litter on our way back. We need to keep moving." Her voice sounded pinched. She'd seemed stressed ever since daybreak, when she stashed her radio abruptly and announced that they had to break camp right away. Now the radio was out again, clenched in her hand, its earpiece plugged snugly into her ear.

"What's the hurry?" Charlie asked. It wasn't even noon, and no one was waiting for them at the lake campsite. Still covering ground, Mom studied his face. She pressed her hand against his forehead. "Do I look sick?" he said.

"A little pink. Too much sun." She accelerated, practically speed-walking. Charlie and Paige hurried after her. The trail emptied them into a clearing of sickly die-hard shrubs and grasses. Here and there, rotting stumps clung to parched dirt. Barely pausing to look up, Mom pointed. In a deep crease in a far-off peak, a skinny splotch of snow remained, the dingy disgusting color of a skull.

"Can we hike up to it?" Paige said. "Can we touch it?"

"Yeah," Charlie said. "And then we can fly to the moon."

Paige ignored him. Mom shook her head. They marched on into the next stand of trees, where they came to a lightning-downed cedar, its trunk sawed flat to form a long bench.

"Lunch," Mom grunted. She let her eyes wander to his face again. He'd caught her at it a half dozen times already. How many had he missed?

"*What?*" he said.

"Yeah," Paige said. "Why do you keep *gawking* at *Charlie*?"

Mom shrugged off the questions and her backpack. They sat. Charlie and Paige pulled out flatbread, cheese, and trail mix from their packs and began eating. Mom set down her radio. She'd been obsessed with it since last night, but whenever Charlie asked her why, she ignored him or changed the subject.

The radio sat by her on the log now, earpiece detached, volume low, but he heard what sounded like a newswoman's voice. And there was something unsettling in that voice.

Before Mom could react, he snatched the radio and, twisting away to hold it out of her reach, upped the volume. *Deaths* was the first word he picked out. *Plague* was next. He stopped chewing.

"No continent has been spared," the woman said in a British accent. Her voice sounded hollow, dreamlike. "Nearly overnight, millions of men and boys . . . have dropped dead. As I speak, millions more are dying. Their bodies . . . are piling up . . . *everywhere*."

While she paused, Charlie's imagination broke loose. Pictures swirled in his head. On the radio, in the background, a gentle female voice said, "Go on."

"Old men, young men . . .

". . . babies."

Hesitation. Throat clearing.

"Privates and generals, clerics of every stripe, doctors and lawyers and scientists and writers and musicians . . .

". . . pilots . . . their passengers."

Dead air. A paralyzing chill held Charlie in place while his mind flew. This must be some kind of hoax. A radio play, maybe. *War of the Worlds,* a hundred-and-something years later. But Mom's stricken face told him it was no hoax, no play. Paige's had lost its freckled color; her eyes overflowed.

"The horror is indescribable . . . ," the woman said. "The British prime minister is dead, as are most of the members of Parliament. The exception: women. The American president is dead. His cabinet is skeletal."

Long delay. Deep breath. Charlie tried to breathe. He *couldn't.*

"Most of the U.S. Congress are gone . . . except for female legislators. In nearly every nation . . . leadership has been decimated." She sighed and went on. "Anarchy flares . . . but flames out. Looters, murderers, barbarians don't live long enough for sustained individual assaults. But the overall effect is unrelenting chaos."

The woman's words accelerated. "Worldwide, males have tried to flee cities, but highways are impassable. Airports, seaports, railroad stations, bus depots are all shut down. Deadly fights erupt over bicycles and motorcycles and boats. Men have barricaded themselves in their houses and gunned down anyone who gets close to them or their sons."

"What about Dad?" Charlie asked. Dad had put off leaving home for an extra day so he could finish up a work project, but Seattle—home—would be one of those cities where the ways out would be impassable or shut down.

Mom left his question hanging in the still air, and the newscaster continued. "In every country, emergency services are scarcely limping along. To a large degree they have relied on men, and now there simply aren't any. . . ."

Mom and Paige bookended Charlie on the log bench. He felt Paige's tears spill warm onto his shoulder; he heard more words spill from the newswoman. "Medical officials have crucial words of warning: If you're a male . . . and you're showing *any* sign of respiratory distress—coughing, shortness of breath—do *not* expose anyone, particularly males, to your symptoms. No one knows how this plague is spread . . . but it appears to be airborne, highly virulent . . .

". . . and horrifyingly quick."

Charlie managed a breath. In. Out. "I'm okay," he said. "I'm *okay*."

The newscaster went on. "If you're a symptom-free male, isolate yourself. Females apparently aren't dying . . . but they could be carrying. Avoid anyone you see just as you'd avoid a man with a bomb . . . and a wild gleam in his eye. This epidemic seems hellish, but its genesis is organic—a bacteria or virus or—

"Oh, God!" the woman cried.

A faint ominous hum crawled out of the radio. The

surrounding forest was hushed, as if even the branches of the trees were listening.

The woman's voice returned, a haggard hoarse murmur. "I'm signing off . . . for now. My producer has collapsed on the control-room floor. Two coworkers are trying to help him. . . ." The station went silent.

A moment later, music—something classical, piano and strings—replaced words. Senses numbed, Charlie didn't recognize the melancholy notes at first.

Then he did. "Brahms's Lullaby." *Go to sleep.*

The music faded away. It died. Silence, unbroken, followed.

"That's not real," Paige said as Charlie searched for other broadcasts. He couldn't get even a whisper on any band— satellite, AM, FM, shortwave.

"I'm afraid it is," Mom said. She knelt in front of them, grasping their hands. In Charlie's hand, hers felt cold and clammy and small. But strong. Willing him to stay put. She must have seen in his eyes what he felt inside—an urge to take off back down the trail, to see for himself what was happening at home, to find Dad.

"How?" Paige said.

Mom shrugged. "We may know soon."

Charlie repeated his question, previously left dangling: "What about *Dad*?"

"I've been praying he got out before everything went crazy," Mom said.

"He was supposed to leave home *Sunday*," Charlie said. *"This morning."*

"Wasn't everything crazy *this morning*?" Paige said.

"Yes." Mom gave a bare nod of acknowledgment. "Yes."

"What about *Charlie*?" Paige said, putting words to his worry.

"Charlie's safe here, sweetie." Mom's eyes didn't leave him.

"How do you *know*?" Paige moaned.

"I don't believe we're infected," Mom said. "And no one is likely to catch up with us. If we meet people heading back, they won't have been exposed, but we'll avoid them anyway. If necessary, we can survive for a year up here. Or longer. For as long as we have to stay."

A year, Charlie thought. A year was *forever.* No, *dying* was forever. Would a year even be enough?

◆ ◆ ◆

MONDAY, AUGUST 8, 2067:
VOICES ON THE RADIO REPORTED A BILLION DEAD.

TUESDAY, AUGUST 9, 2067:
TWO BILLION.

Charlie knew Dad could have arrived at the lake Monday night if he'd hurried. He *didn't* arrive. He could have appeared Tuesday. He *didn't* appear.

Wednesday morning, Charlie found the big paw prints of a bear crisscrossing the dirt near the remains of the fire, and he chose to consider the bear a good omen, a stealthy advance

7

scout for Dad. But good omen or not, Dad *didn't* come.

As dawn broke on Thursday, Charlie propped himself up on an elbow and peered through wisps of mist across the lake, still faintly hoping to catch sight of a familiar hiker coming up the trail.

Something moved on the opposite shoreline. Charlie got up and crept to the water, keeping his eyes on the small opening in the trees two hundred yards away. Again, he saw a blur of motion, dark. But it wasn't a man. Not even a person. It was a bear. Big, blackish-brown, lumbering.

A cool wind snuck through the trees. It slipped past Charlie and across the lake, stirring up the surface fog. A few moments later, the bear rose on two legs and turned in Charlie's direction, raising its big cartoonish head.

Charlie waved. He hoped the bear would wave back. A raised paw, at least. He wanted another sign. But the bear stood immobile, using its nose to check out Charlie and maybe Mom and Paige, too. *Friend? Foe? Breakfast?*

Finally, the bear dropped back to all fours. It moved nonchalantly along the shoreline, away from the trail, and disappeared.

News had continued to dribble in from the radio. As of last night, two-thirds of the world's male population was dead. Three billion souls gone. And the plague was continuing to worm into every pocket of humanity. No kind of medical intervention had any effect on the disease, which seemed to run its lethal course in less than twenty-four hours, from the first symptoms to the final tortured breath.

In many countries, disorder reigned. In others, new governments were forming as the constitutional orders of succession spiraled down to the first woman. In the United States, that was Secretary of State Candace Bloom.

President Candace Bloom, now.

President Bloom and what was left of the executive branch were working tirelessly to keep the country from disintegrating—propping up what remained of the three branches of federal government; cooperating with foreign countries; going forward with individual states to make sure courts and law enforcement agencies still functioned; triaging and handling all crises; coordinating medical care; activating what was left of the National Guard and other military units; initiating and orchestrating the mass cremation and disposal of tens of millions of bodies; bringing together medical researchers to solve the mystery of the contagion before every male in the country and on the face of the planet was wiped out.

Charlie returned to the campsite and got his fishing rod. He waded out, over the rocks and sand, through the mud, and began casting. Mosquitoes buzzed his head, but his repellent was still working.

In the quiet, in the solitude, his imagination ran wild, to places dark and borderless. He tried not to imagine where Dad might be.

That day, he caught seven cutthroat trout, fat on bugs. That night, he circled the lake and left three on the opposite shoreline for his friend the bear.

Ten more days crept by. In the mountains, little changed. Morning wind spoke in the trees, morning clouds gathered, then dispersed in afternoon sunshine, night came, a little earlier each time, stars shone and faded, rain fell, morning arrived again. Hearts ached, day after day.

Dad didn't come. No one came.

Around the globe, cautious reports surfaced that deaths had halted. But the male of the human species had come face-to-face with extinction. The estimate of the dead: more than four billion, or 97 percent of the male population.

Most of the survivors lived in remote backcountry. Others were on the move—nomads, refugees, passengers and crews on ships at sea, space station occupants, moon colonists—while some lived in cities but were forgotten enough or resourceful enough or ruthless enough to avoid human contact.

A handful of males had been exposed but had not fallen ill. A small number turned out to be transgender—female by birth. Others either dodged the disease or were immune. If so, no one knew why.

A few survivors had happened to choose this time to backpack into the wilderness. *Lucky*, the newswomen called them. Charlie wasn't so sure. He felt grateful to be alive, but to him, *lucky* would be Dad walking into the campsite, thin and unshaven and bedraggled from two weeks of avoiding a monster, but alive.

Alive. That would have been *lucky*.

On the far side of the sturdy branch-and-bough lean-to that Charlie and Paige had painstakingly woven together after the first night of rain overwhelmed their tent, Mom and Paige still slept, if fitfully. Paige's nightmare-fueled whimpering had awakened Charlie. Sunrise wouldn't happen for a while, but there was enough light for him to locate the radio.

As he switched it on, he foolishly half hoped for music, but this morning, as always, news filled the airwaves and the plague was all the news. No crime sprees, no crooked politicians, no environmental disasters, no weather, no sports. He imagined empty stadiums. No players. No fans.

Because no plague-related deaths had been reported in almost two days, scientists believed the disease had run its course. For now. Newborn boys were no longer dying. Ships were returning to port. Within hours of one another, the Americas, Europe, Africa, Asia, Australia, and New Zealand all officially noted the cessation of deaths.

Charlie's stomach rumbled. Their rations of food had dwindled. They were all sick of trout, although no one said anything. It was fifteen days, now, since the first deaths occurred. Sixteen days since they'd left home. They wouldn't have to survive here for the year or more he and his mother and sister had feared, but it seemed like they already had. He turned off the radio and rolled onto his back, waiting for Mom and Paige to wake up.

It was time to go back. And face the music. Even if there wouldn't be any.

I wouldn't even ask to see his face;
I'd settle for the music of his voice from down the hall —
a three a.m. cry for his mother's milk.

—EPITAPH FOR LUKE HONEY (MAY 6, 2067–AUGUST 7, 2067),
BY MARIA HONEY, HIS MOTHER,
NOVEMBER 2, 2068

CHAPTER ONE
JUNE 16, 2097—THIRTY YEARS LATER

Glum and restless, I stared out through the living room window as rain ticked sideways against the glass and flowed steadily down. In the late-afternoon murk, the glossy streaks of wet looked like narrow metal bars. This wasn't a prison, but the nonstop Sunday downpour made it feel like one. Outside, the sprawling carpet of grass drank in the cloudburst. I could practically see the individual blades growing, which meant more work for me. But not today, a bad day for mowing lawns. Or hopping on my bike and heading off to somewhere—anywhere—more exciting.

Maybe the rainfall was trying to tell me something. Because what I should have been doing was getting ready for my trials. Confined by the weather to this big old house, with most of its other residents in their rooms or otherwise quietly keeping to themselves, I had only one excuse for not studying: Mom had asked me to meet her here. She was going to make time in her busy schedule for a "visit" with me. How could I have refused?

Anyway, I had a reason—besides just getting a chance to talk to her for a change—to meet with her. I had my own topic to chat about. It was a topic I believed she'd been avoiding.

I heard the office door open, and a moment later she appeared. The two other women in the room glanced up and went back to their reading. She smiled and plopped down on the couch next to me and for a moment joined me in gazing silently out the window. Her mascara looked clumpier than usual, maybe to mask the fatigue in her eyes. It wasn't working.

"How are you, Kellen?" she said finally. She rested her hand on mine. It felt comfortingly familiar but irritating at the same time.

"Terrific," I said. "Smooth summer so far. We won our game yesterday. I got two doubles."

"That's wonderful."

"Too bad you weren't there."

"I wanted to be."

"Three," I said, silhouetting three fingers against the gray daylight.

"What?"

"Three. Games. You've been to three. I've played eleven."

"Work keeps getting in the way. We've had . . . complications. But they're temporary. Things will be back to normal soon."

Normal. "Normal" meant she would've gotten to four or five games. Her job with PAC—the Population Apportionment Council—was her top priority. I was number two. "It's okay." I'd raised a subject. Not my main subject, but a start. I'd made a point, maybe.

"It's not okay. I simply don't have a choice."

I shrugged. She *had* a choice. She had smarts, degrees, experience, other employers sniffing around. She would've had no problem finding a different job. But I was done with this topic. I freed my hand from hers and pretended to straighten a sock.

"How are your studies going?" she asked, getting to what I figured all along was her motive for our "visit."

"Have you talked to Dad yet?" I said. "About me going to see him?"

"I've been so busy. And you need time to prepare for your trials."

"My studies are fine. You said you'd get him a message. Or talk to him about it the next time he called."

"What about your history class?" Mom said, not wavering from the topic of my education. "What do you think of Ms. Anderson as an instructor? Is she getting you the essential material? I've heard she can be . . . unconventional."

Anderson? She was *unconventional*, maybe, but in a good way. "She's doing great. I'm doing great. Why?"

"I want you to think about something," she said, lowering her voice.

"I'm already thinking about something."

"This is more important than your travel plans, Kellen. What I want you to think about is your trials. Your *life*, in other words."

"Travel plans? You think I'm just interested in *travel*? What I'm interested in is seeing *Dad*. I want to spend time with him. I want to see how he lives. I want to see how *guys* live."

"And what I want is for you to consider something really vital," she said, plowing ahead. "I want you to consider seeking help if you get close to your exam date and don't feel completely confident you can pass with flying colors."

"Help studying, you mean?"

"Dr. Mack knows the chair of the regional trials board."

Dr. Mack. Rebecca Mack. Mom's big boss. The head of PAC. She wouldn't just *know* the chair of the PAC trials board, she probably had the final say on the woman's appointment to the position. The chair, whoever she might be, was no doubt firmly under Rebecca Mack's thumb. She would fold if Dr. Mack pressured her, even just a little.

I fidgeted with my other sock. "What about Dad?"

"I know this feels as if I'm stepping on your toes, Kellen, but I just want what's best—"

Her e-spond chimed. She got to her feet and moved to the window, eyes out on the gloom and splash. "Heather Dent," she said into the mouthpiece, just loud enough for me to overhear. "I'm home," she said. "I was just talking to Kellen. We've hardly had time—"

A pause. "Nothing new," she said after a long moment of listening.

Another pause, then: "Four days. We may not hear from her again."

More listening. A glance at me. "It's all in motion on this end. I'm monitoring everything." She snuck another look at me. I tried to put on a bored expression. "And there?"

She hesitated, listening. "If you need me," she said. Then: "Let me check." With her back half turned to me, she fingered her display, studied the feedback, and resumed her conversation. "The earliest flight will get me to San Diego about eight. I'll be on it."

She returned to the couch but didn't sit. "Give me a hug," she ordered.

A hug. Her cure for everything. "You're leaving again?"

"I have to. But Paige will be here."

Aunt Paige. Aunt Reliable. "How long this time?"

"A few days. We'll talk when I get back."

"Sure." I got up and let her put her arms around me. I let her stand on her tiptoes and kiss me on the cheek. Then she was off, hurrying across the room and angling for the stairs.

An angry *rat-a-tat-tat* sound pulled my attention away from her and toward the window. Hail had replaced rain. While strong gusts of wind threw the hard white ice pellets against the glass, I stood and watched and wondered what was going on.

I longed for the cavernous ache to ease
as frost bloomed white on the lawn and
small schoolgirls trudged back and forth
in their colorful coats,
but night after night, still heartsick,
I stood at the bedroom mirror and examined
my naked belly,
growing plump and tight and blue-veined
with the startling bulk of our son, Jimmy,
a treasured comfort now,
but in those acutely empty days mostly a reminder
of you and what might have been.

—EPITAPH FOR JAMES CABLE
(SEPTEMBER 3, 2036–AUGUST 6, 2067),
BY LAUREL CABLE, HIS WIFE,
NOVEMBER 3, 2068

CHAPTER TWO

JUNE 19, 2097

I listened to the two new girls—Tia and Sunday—outside my bedroom door, giggling, talking loud, like spectators at the zoo waiting for feeding time. Besides their names and ages—fourteen, same as me—most of what I knew about them was that they were cousins and they hadn't spent much time around boys. When we'd met the day before, they couldn't keep their eyes off me. Of course I'd been a curiosity my whole life, so I was pretty much used to the animal-on-exhibit treatment by now.

The girls had just moved from a small town in Nebraska where the male population was in single digits. The big rooming house my mom and aunt owned had vacancies, and it was near the University of Washington, where the girls' moms were starting new jobs. From halfway across the country they'd negotiated a package deal that meant they could keep their families together.

Coincidentally, Nebraska also happened to be the birthplace of my grandfather, Joshua Winters. So in my mind the girls had something going for them already. Besides the cute factor, that is.

Silently, I got up, slipped into shorts and a T-shirt, and yanked open the door. *"Hey!"* I growled, and the taller, blond-haired girl—Sunday—almost went backward through the hallway wall. I hadn't surprised the dark-haired one, though. Tia just looked at me as if she was bored, meeting my gaze in a little contest. Then she laughed. It was a great laugh, from somewhere deep inside her chest.

"You're funny for a boy," she said. "Most of the boys I've seen have long faces."

"I wonder why," I said. The irony in my voice was supposed to remind her of the reason for her long-faced boys. Everyone knew the cloud we lived under. The bug that had caused Elisha's Bear—the name some female Bible scholar, and then the world, had given the monstrous plague of

2067—had visited three more times since then. So far the outbreaks had been away from North America, away from cities, never involving more than a few thousand males, and throwbacks at that, but who could predict when or where the next one would arrive?

"He *ain't* funny," her cousin said, shaking off her collision with the wall. "He scared the crap out of me."

"Sorry," I said, although I wasn't. "But you woke me up. And *ain't* isn't a word."

"Sorry, *professor*, but I spend my time on the things that count—the stuff we'll be tested on in our trials. And grammar *ain't* one of 'em."

"Our trials *ain't* until September," I said.

"Spoken like a true slacker," Sunday said.

"Before your aunt left for work," Tia said to me, throwing her cousin a little frown, "she told us you'd show us the neighborhood. We *were* hoping it would happen *this morning*."

"I have a history session," I said, "in an hour." School was out for the summer, but history was a year-round subject, separate from the rest of the curriculum. Unlike grammar—or creative thinking—history was a major piece of our trials. *Disregard the past, suffer the future,* the oft-repeated saying went.

"We know," Tia said. "We're registered, too."

"We'll keep you company," Sunday said.

"I have plenty of company already." All the time. Everywhere. My aunt. My mom. A dozen official or unofficial watchdogs.

"But we can go with you?" Tia said.

"If my aunt said you can, then you can. But when I'm ready to leave the house, you have to be ready, too. I don't like being late."

"We're set to go," Tia said.

"So you really *do* care?" Sunday asked me.

"I have to," I said. Passing the trials was important to me—at least the practical me—because it would keep my options open. If I decided to stay within the confines of PAC-dictated society once I got to be an adult, I'd have educational, career, and citizenship opportunities (like voting, for instance) not available to people—guys, especially—who didn't make the grade.

We took off on our bikes for the Learning Center, which was located on the Seattle waterfront. I pedaled hard, keeping to the wide but busy bike trail at first but weaving in and out of car and bus traffic, attracting the usual stares, glares, and honks, once we left the trail downtown. I thought Sunday and Tia might show their nerves in big-city traffic, but they looked comfortable on their tandem, Tia doing the steering, like one well-oiled four-legged machine, like they'd been riding together forever, and they stayed on my tail. They had some incentive—they didn't want to get lost.

They pulled up closer. "*Why* do you have to?" Sunday yelled over the traffic noise, but I didn't follow her question.

"*Care,*" she said. "Why do you have to *care*?"

"For myself," I yelled back at her. "And my mom expects it. If I don't ace my trials it'll damage her hard-earned PAC image. And there's pressure from my aunt Paige, too. But she's thinking more of me. She wants me to be a doctor."

"Do you?" Tia said. "Want to be a doctor, I mean?"

"I wouldn't mind," I said. "It's one thing PAC allows us guys to do."

"I'm gonna be a doctor, too," Sunday said. "A vet, though. No crap from people. Lots of gratitude from the patients."

"Environmental science," Tia said. "The oceans, maybe."

I wondered for a moment if that job was on the guy-approved list. I actually had my eye on something else, though—a different job, a different life. But unless I wanted to attract dark looks and more "visits," I couldn't mention it to either Mom or Aunt Paige—or anyone, really. I couldn't talk about leaving all this "civilized" stuff behind, taking off for the hinterlands, trying out the loner life, being like my dad. Working with him.

Experiencing freedom.

A small blue car, a neglected-looking Lectra-Cell, passed uncomfortably and probably intentionally too close to me. From under its hood rumbled the simulated sound of an old, barely muffled internal combustion engine. Most vehicles on the road, powered by some form of noiseless electric motor, were equipped with collision-avoidance sound systems designed to let people know they were nearby. Sometimes, instead of fake engine sounds, cars broadcast music, crowd noises, nature recordings, a medley of assorted stuff.

In the crowded traffic we were in now, instead of distinctive sounds, I heard a jumble of noise, loud and obnoxious enough to cause an instant headache and a longing for solitude.

For the hinterlands.

But it wasn't loud enough for Sunday and Tia. Just to annoy me—I was 99 percent sure—they turned on their own sound effects, jangly-clangly ice-cream-vendor music and some guy singing an antique song about a bicycle built for two.

My bike wasn't equipped to produce fake noise. I liked it that way.

We arrived at the center, a glass-faced thirty-story building that was once—pre-Elisha (PE)—crammed top to bottom with law offices. In the lobby, I headed for The Grounds-keeper, an espresso stand run by a girl named Petey. She'd failed her trials three years earlier but planned on trying again in another year. She'd asked me more than once if I wanted to study with her, but I'd been putting her off. I thought a boy-crush was involved in her offer, and I'd already had my bittersweet experience with an older girl.

She raised her head at our approach. Her cool day-of-the-week sunglasses were in the shape of fat Ws. "Company today, Kellen?" she said. She had a hoarse, sexy voice, the remnant of an infection she'd suffered as a little girl. That same infection robbed her of her eyesight, but she seemed to do okay without it. Effortlessly, she began putting together my mocha—whole milk, extra shots, extra chocolate, extra hot.

I introduced her to Sunday and Tia. Petey's blindness wasn't obvious, and I wondered if they noticed. When she finished with my drink she stepped out from behind the counter to hand it to me up close. She held on to the tall paper cup even after I had my fingers wrapped firmly around it, touching hers, and she leaned nearer. Her nose practically brushed my shirt while she inhaled deeply, as if walking up and sucking in someone's scent was the most natural thing in the world. As if we were two dogs meeting in the park. Then she leaned back and let go of my coffee and smiled. "Don't you just love the smell of this boy, girls?" she said.

I no longer wondered if Petey's blindness had gone unnoticed.

Tia and Sunday exchanged an amused look. They followed me to the elevator and we rode it to the seventh floor, where our classroom overlooked Puget Sound, blue and sparkling in the morning sun. Through tall windows we could see fishing boats moving north and south, ferries east and west. I could tell the girls were impressed, although Sunday pretended not to be.

They found their desks, a couple of previously vacant ones next to mine, with shiny-new SUNDAY and SEPTIEMBRE— Tia's given name—labels taped to the top surfaces. By design, I was surrounded by girls. There was one other boy in the class, a long-faced guy named Ernie, but he sat far away, inside a triple picket fence of more girls.

Ernie and I didn't talk much. Anxious over his upcoming trials, he spent most of his time studying and the balance of it worrying. Like the rest of us, he'd have to wait another four years to undergo a more difficult battery of tests if he flunked the first time around. Like the rest of the boys, he was facing longer odds to begin with. In an average year, 87 percent of girls passed their trials. For boys, the number was 72 percent. And it was no secret that the difference was accounted for by the scores in the oral exams. Women gave them. Women scored them. Boys floundered.

And then there was the whole aftermath thing, even if you passed. For girls, the career choices were limitless. For boys, they were pared down and capped and dead-ended. Thus, Ernie's chewed-down fingernails and chewed-up pencils and long face.

Despite Mom's continual fretting, I tried not to worry. Aunt Paige said she had confidence in me. She said the questions were common sense, and I was a sensible kid. If she wasn't worried, why should I be? I listened (usually) while I was in class, I took notes, I remembered some of the stuff—the big stuff, anyway—I read and studied archives on the Net and watched movies and looked around a lot, at what was and what used to be.

According to everyone I'd talked to, the main thing to do when I underwent my trials—the oral parts anyway—was to impress the examiners with my knowledge and sensitivity, to look sincere when I was doing it, and to exhibit my awareness of how EVERYTHING (almost) HAD IMPROVED SINCE WOMEN TOOK OVER THE WORLD. And that didn't seem too hard. I was a guy, but it would have been foolish to deny pre-PAC history. It would have been silly to deny the improved condition of society under PAC governance. And I didn't want to.

Could anyone in his right mind have made a case for going back to a world of poverty and hunger and crime and disease and greed and dishonesty and prejudice and war and genocide and religious bigotry and runaway population growth and abuse of the environment and immigration strife and you-get-the-leftovers educational policies and a hundred other horrors?

Not me. But a little less regimentation would have been good.

"What's the instructor like?" Tia whispered at me.

The bitchy girl in front of her—Dawn was her name—turned and made a face. "Anderson?" she said before I could reply. "Booorrring."

"Not really," I said. "She lost her dad and two brothers to the Bear. Her words have barbs; they dig in and stay."

Tia nodded, but Dawn gave me a look, like *What do you know? You're a GUY.* She held her tongue, though, because she knew I'd call her a fish and she'd call me a bastard and I'd tell her at least my dad's not a glass tube full of frozen semen waiting to swim upstream and I'd have the last word.

I'd have the last word because in this culture a bastard with an identifiable living, breathing father had slightly higher standing than a fish, whose dad was most often some well-selected but mysterious donor.

Dawn flashed me a final eye roll and turned away to face the front of the room. Anderson still hadn't appeared.

Instead of readying myself for her arrival and what she might have in store for us, I stared out at the water and thought about Dad and his life. I wondered for the millionth time how our lives would be different if Elisha's Bear hadn't come.

According to my lessons and all the other stuff I'd heard and read, it took only a couple of years for women to figure out how much better off they—and the world—were without men around to keep things in a downward spiral.

Wars ceased. Crime, especially crime against women and children, dropped dramatically. Illegal-drug demand plummeted. Gangs disappeared. Prostitution and pornography all but evaporated; females low on self-esteem, high on drugs, or attached to the end of some creep's short leash had to make other choices. Prisons emptied.

Once political leadership—all women—was reestablished, priorities changed. Money no longer used for fighting wars and lobbying for wars and profiting from wars got routed to health care, medical research, education, social programs, the environment, alternative transportation, and renewable fuels.

The United Nations gained power. Countries merged. Within a decade, North America, with its capital in San Diego, had become one nation; South America one; Africa one; Europe and Asia (Eurussia, Indochina, Mediterranea) three; Australia, New Zealand, and their neighbors (Oceania) one. In all these new countries, UN and national laws prohibited men from holding positions of power or influence in the public or private sector. The women in control decided that men had had their opportunities.

So now, even if a guy passed his trials, the best he could hope for was a chance at a nonthreatening profession (teacher, salesman, therapist, engineer, actor, architect, doctor, dentist, baritone, etc.) with one tentative toe in the shallows of mainstream society. If he passed major scrutiny, he could be a sperm *donor*. If he jumped through more hoops, he could be an official *dad*.

One of the first things the newly powerful United Nations did was establish PAC. It was staffed by female representatives—political leaders and scientists—from every country. Its job: population control and restriction of male births. The Council decided that no more than five percent of the population should be male. The surviving men of the world had little voice and no choice in the decision.

The science existed to make the apportionment mandates work. It involved parent selection and test tubes, artificial insemination, gender-determining implants, and sterilization. Lured by the promise of money from PAC, many males volunteered to be sterilized. If they'd failed to take or pass their trials, they had no choice. Others fled to the boondocks, backwoods, and mountains, where colonies of men—throwbacks and loners—were pretty much left alone.

Anderson finally walked in. The chatter ended abruptly. Her reddish cottony hair was a mess, as usual. She tossed her bike helmet on her desk and faced us. "New victims?" she said, spotting Tia and Sunday. She clicked on the overhead screen and scrolled through the class roster. At the bottom, Septiembre's and Sunday's names showed as additions.

"We just moved here," Sunday announced. "We're nearly fifth-levels. We already have our Provisional Minders' credentials. We'll be ahead in this class."

"You'll be behind," Anderson said matter-of-factly. "I don't dawdle."

Sunday opened her mouth and shut it again. Tia smiled. Sunday sat taller. "We *ain't* gonna be behind," she said.

"Aren't," Anderson replied.

"That's what I said."

Anderson shook her head and muttered something about constrained educational focus while I thought about Sunday telling me a little earlier in the day that she was only interested in stuff that would be on our tests.

"Let's get moving," Anderson added energetically, and the class roster disappeared from the screen, replaced by a video of a peaceful vista—a bay city filmed from the water, from a distance. A graceful suspension bridge angled from left to right.

I sat up and leaned forward. I recognized this place from old photos. An ageless bridge, tall buildings, hills in the background. It was San Francisco.

I knew what was coming.

Without warning, the sky erupted in a giant flash of light. The buildings—all of them—seemed to lean for a moment. Then they instantly disintegrated. Some simply vaporized, others shed debris like scales, and pieces flew toward the camera and in every other direction. The sound was thunderous, then gone. Waves rolled out across the water, sprinting unnaturally. The bridge bucked and heaved and ripped apart, whipping vehicles into the air and bay. And behind the destruction of the skyline, an eerie column of energy rushed skyward. As the camera drew back, the column slowed, and a cloud mushroomed out of its crown.

Anderson clicked off the screen. "A date we must never forget," she said. "On July 4, 2054, just over thirteen years before Elisha's Bear struck, a powerful nuclear device—a bomb—was detonated in the heart of San Francisco, destroying that city along with parts of Oakland and smaller nearby communities. Its immediate effects were felt as far away as San Jose, and its cloud drifted east, dropping poisonous fallout on populations across the United States and eventually around the world."

Across the room, Ernie cleared his throat timidly. He hunched down and began tapping his e-spond furiously. I felt sorry for him.

"A minister named Clyde Long," Anderson continued, "an advisor to President Napper, said it was God's retaliation for the sinfulness of that city. He predicted the end of the world was near.

"On July 6, based on secret intelligence, the United States launched a submarine missile attack on Beijing, wiping out that city and most of its thirty million inhabitants. Within two hours, China attacked with its own missiles and destroyed Los Angeles.

"On July 7, a Taiwanese group claimed responsibility for the San Francisco assault.

"On July 8, U.S. bombers dropped two nuclear bombs on Taiwan. Later that day, a group in the Philippines said they were in fact the terrorists behind the initial attack, that neither Taiwan nor any other country had anything to do with it.

"With half of California destroyed, the world on the edge of all-out nuclear war, Taiwan and China at last united against a common foe, and ninety percent of the U.S. population demanding his ouster, faulty intelligence or not, President Napper was impeached and removed from office in a single day. His vice president, James Corson, took over.

"The world held its breath, began cleaning up after the destruction, and started burying what remained of the seventy million dead and caring for the dying. Everyone waited for the next move. Others joined in Clyde Long's prediction.

"But the countries involved teetered back from the precipice. The United States promised China and Taiwan financial compensation. An effort was made to track down the terrorists.

"Life hobbled on, but painstakingly. The United States, Taiwan, and China were deeply wounded, and the healing that took place formed ugly scars. Despite all that has happened in the interim—Elisha, most notably—small but undeniable remnants of the 2054 terrorism, incompetence, and sheer buffoonery are with us today. Men are no longer in charge, but the distrust and wariness they spawned lingers in places around the globe. To this day, there are women who are unwilling to sit around a campfire holding hands with certain strangers and singing 'We Are All Sisters Under the Skin.'"

Dawn made a fake snoring noise but kept her eyes wide open, trying to look innocent.

Anderson wasn't fooled. "I'm boring you again, Dawn?"

"That wasn't me." She looked in my direction.

Anderson ignored the implication. Unlike many women, she liked boys. She liked me. She liked men. Ernie, who lived with his mom in the same rooming house as Anderson, told me she often rode her bike to the hinterlands to meet up with a loner boyfriend. Rumors swirled that she was a bit of a loner herself, not exactly in step with the party line. I'd seen evidence of the rumors in her teaching and attitudes. I recalled Mom's word: *unconventional.* At the time, it didn't sound like a compliment. "Why don't you come on up, Dawn?" Anderson said. "Since you know it all, we'll have you answer any questions the class has."

She waited while Dawn, red-faced, pushed herself out of her desk and headed for the front of the room as someone snickered and I hummed the funeral dirge under my breath but loud enough for her to hear it. She gave me a look, but I stared guiltlessly ahead.

Dawn turned and faced the class, keeping her distance from Anderson, but Anderson sidled over and put her arm around Dawn's shoulders like they were old buddies.

"Fire away, boys and girls," Anderson said. What would she have said if Ernie or I hadn't been here? *Boy* and girls?

I raised my hand, and Dawn reluctantly nodded at me. She had no choice. No one else had a hand in the air. "Did they ever figure out who really set off the bomb?" It was a legitimate question and one I was certain Dawn couldn't answer.

She narrowed her eyes at me. "That wasn't covered."

Tia waved her arm and attracted a pointed finger from Anderson's free hand. "New girl?" Anderson said, amusement warming her eyes.

"It's in the study guide for this lesson," Tia said, standing. "You were supposed to read it."

"Yeah, we already had it," Sunday blurted out.

"So what's the answer?" Anderson asked Tia, trying to ignore Sunday. "I'm sure Kellen—and the rest of the students—would appreciate knowing."

"At least fifty-seven nations, and possibly as many as ten radical groups, had nuclear weapons by 2054," Tia said as if she'd memorized the words. I had a feeling she'd have no trouble with her trials. "Thirteen different groups ended up claiming responsibility. No one ever determined for sure which one of those was the culprit. Or even if it *was* one of those."

"Thank you . . . ," Anderson said. She touched her remote and the class roster reappeared on the overhead. "Septiembre."

"*Tia*," Tia said, sitting down.

Ernie raised his hand. "What happened to 'em?" he said.

"Who?" Dawn said.

"Not who. *What*. The bombs. What happened to 'em?"

Dawn stared at Ernie's long and curious face. She looked at the floor. She gazed at the ceiling. She glanced at Anderson, who let her stew.

Sunday raised her hand, observing classroom etiquette this time. Dawn nodded. Sunday stood. "After the California and Asia disasters, nothing happened to stop the production and proliferation of bombs," she recited mechanically.

"But after Elisha's Bear came, nuclear weapons were sought out, dismantled, and piecemealed. Components were destroyed. Raw materials were collected and neutralized. Effective monitoring agencies were established. Nuclear reactors were torn down and outlawed. The last atomic weapon was found and demolished in 2072. Chemical and biological weapons had long since been eradicated."

Sunday sat down. Tia bumped fists with her.

"*Now* who's the junior professor?" I said under my breath.

Sunday frowned. "There ain't no more bombs," she broadcast in her loud Sunday voice, departing from the script in her head, showing me she was no junior professor after all.

Anderson lifted her eyebrows. A small grin lit up her serious instructor face. She glanced at the attendance list. "I apologize, Sunday. Your grammar is crap, but you and Tia *are* ahead of us. And you're willing to speak your minds. Thank you both for your answers."

Grin gone, she looked at Dawn. "The bar has just been raised in this class, young woman. Continue to snore your way along, and you'll fail to get over it. You'll be qualified to pick up cigarette butts at the bus depot."

Dawn slunk back to her desk. On the way, she managed to aim dark glares at Sunday, Tia, and even poor Ernie. She reserved her ugliest look for me. "Bastard," she hissed, driven by humiliation to risk my comeback.

Fish was on the tip of my tongue for an instant.

"Throwback hag," Sunday said. Tia smothered a laugh. Dawn turned her back on us and I let it go. Her shoulders already sagged with the twin burdens of being different and inferior, and I knew how that felt.

Anderson continued on with the lesson. My mind strayed off course while I thought about what she'd discussed so far and the image of the bomb ripping San Francisco apart.

My dad, Charlie Winters—Mr. Lucky, he called himself sometimes—dodged the near-holocaust when he was just a baby, and then survived Elisha when he was about my age. Later, he passed his trials, and he and Mom, once they got together, received authorization to have a baby. Dad, like most men who hadn't been outright sterilized, was surgically implanted with a hormone-excreting gadget to drastically reduce the chances of him producing a male infant, but he managed to do it anyway. I showed up nine months later—an instant marvel, I'd been told.

But Dad didn't stay around for long.

When I was five, he decided he was tired of living under

the government's constraints. And he no longer wanted to be in Seattle, the city where Elisha had sucked the breath out of his own dad—my grandfather Joshua.

Dad had tasted life before the restrictions. And now that marine life had returned to the Olympic Peninsula waters, he yearned to be there. He moved to a place called Afterlight, a mostly male commune.

Throwback was the term used for people living in the small loosely organized collectives scattered around the world who preferred living their lives closer to the way lives were lived PE. Dad, though, wasn't under an illusion that things had been better in the old days. He mostly just wanted to be let alone. To be what some people called a *loner*. He restored an old commercial fishing boat and rechristened it—what else?—*Mr. Lucky* and began fishing the Strait of Juan de Fuca for salmon, halibut, and cod. The boat became his home.

Sometimes I got to spend time with him when he came to the city to sell his fish. He'd call me, and I'd bike to the dock and meet him for lunch. Afterward we'd take a walk or he'd give me a ride on *Mr. Lucky*. He'd always let me drive from high on her flying bridge, and when the cool, salted wind hit my face, I'd dream about having my own boat someday, being my own boss, and not being under someone's—nearly *everyone's*—thumb.

I wondered—when Mom finally let me go see him and he took me out on the water again—would he still let me skipper *Mr. Lucky*? Or was that part of my life gone?

If I had a son—or daughter—and I decided to leave the city, I'd take him or her with me. If I absolutely couldn't take the crap, I'd try my hardest to take the kid.

Mom seemed to have conveniently forgotten her promise that I could visit Dad for the first time this summer, but I wasn't going to stop riding her about it. A promise was a promise. And I wanted to go soon, before I had to begin cramming for my trials. I'd have to travel with babysitters—*Minders* was what the government called them—but I was used to that, kind of.

A soft buzzer sounded, marking the end of class, and I gazed across the room toward the windows as everyone began packing up. With the addition of Sunday and Tia, there were now two males and thirty-seven females in the history class, a close reflection of the population at large. The Council had done an efficient job of maintaining the nineteen-to-one ratio, even as the world's population continued to shrink toward a goal of two billion. A smattering of the throwbacks and loners out in the hinterlands and the few fertile women they attracted had babies, including boy babies, but there weren't enough fringe people to make a difference, especially with recurrences of Elisha keeping them in check.

Anderson transmitted the next day's take-home assignment—excerpts from a PE watchdog Web site—to our e-sponds, and we headed for the door. Sunday and Tia were surrounded by other girls, their newly formed fan club. Dawn hurried out by herself. In a classroom where it was cool to be smart, she'd made a curious choice.

Ernie, in the center of his own group of girls, caught up to me at the elevator. "Good question, Ern," I said, and he smiled a little. But he looked especially nervous. When we'd first gotten into Anderson's history class together I tried to get him to hang out with me some, but he had way more excuses—the trials, his mother's health, and, I was almost sure, my mother's PAC connection—than he had time for me.

"You, too, Kellen."

The girls in his group milled around, casually brushing up against us with their shoulders, elbows, hips. They didn't look at us. They pretended it was accidental. The contact, not just at school but everywhere, bothered me at first, but I'd gotten older, and accustomed to the uncomfortable yet comforting feeling that girls were so close to me, that they wanted to be.

Aunt Paige said not to get a big head over it, that girls were curious about anyone with different body parts, and getting close kind of satisfied that curiosity. I knew she was right. Ernie, with his sad face and unsociable ways, was proof of that.

When we passed through the lobby on the way out, I got a little too near The Groundskeeper and Petey. Somehow, in the midst of all the smells surrounding her, she picked out mine. Or maybe she just assumed I was somewhere in the pack of departing kids. Maybe she was showing off for the new girls. "Safe journeys, Kellen," she sang out to me in her gravelly, sexy voice. She inhaled, big, and held it in as

I walked by. She smiled. I couldn't see her eyes, but I knew they were twinkling with mischief.

"You, too, Petey," I said.

"That's disgusting," Tia said as we approached the door, but she was trying to hide a grin.

"This ain't Nebraska," Sunday said. "It ain't 2066."

We got on our bikes and headed for home. I told them to lead the way, see if they could avoid getting lost, pass the Seattle geography test, and I was sure they could, but they were content to cruise along beside me.

When we got to the house, a strange car was parked in the driveway. I peered through its windows, looking for clues to its ownership. Two briefcases sat on the backseat; one of them looked familiar.

Tia and Sunday didn't care about the car or its contents. They were already on the front porch, opening the door. Just on the other side stood two women. One of them, old but tall and unbent, I didn't recognize. The other one was a surprise.

Forty-two years safeguarding his flock,
but when the baddest bear came, her eyes fell on him.

—EPITAPH FOR THE REVEREND DESHAWN TIMMS
(JANUARY 18, 2000–AUGUST 8, 2067),
BY LUCILLE TIMMS, HIS WIFE,
NOVEMBER 6, 2068

CHAPTER THREE

A few days, Mom had told me when she left, and for once
she'd been accurate. Her trip didn't stretch out to a week or
two or three. She spotted me, pushed past Tia and Sunday,
and hurried down the steps. I met her halfway, and we tried
to out-crush each other. It was a draw, but I was sure I'd get
her next time. I was getting bigger and stronger; she was
getting skinnier and older.

She kissed me on the tip of the nose and both cheeks,
something she'd learned on her travels to some foreign land,
no doubt, a remnant of the Russian or French cultures. I
half expected her to kiss my hand next. "I'm so happy to see
you, Kellen," she said, not letting go of my arm but allowing
me to start for the house. "I missed you."

"Me, too," I said, even though I hadn't been that thrilled
with her the last time we "visited." And I hadn't really had
time to miss her. Three or four days or whatever it had been

was a short absence for my globe-trotting mother. She said she was happy to see me, but her eyes didn't look happy. They still looked tired. Once more, I wondered what was going on.

We reached the front door, where Tia, Sunday, and the old woman were hanging out. I should have been embarrassed at Mom's public display of missing me, but I wasn't. I'd been under the microscope for so long, I'd quit caring.

"Septiembre and Sunday, this is my mom, Dr. Heather Dent," I said. The majority of kids—and I was in the majority—shared their mothers' last names. Marriages, on the rare occasions they occurred, tended not to last. A lot of married men, even though they'd passed their trials and maybe had a kid, succumbed to the multiple temptations to wander, in every meaning of that word. Single dads were even less likely to stick around. Moms were the constants in kids' lives.

"*Tia,*" Tia said.

"I love your names," Mom said. "Sunday and Septiembre. How beautiful."

"*Tia,*" Tia repeated.

"And this is Dr. Rebecca Mack," Mom said, nodding toward the old woman, and I found myself instantly zeroing in on her. Up close her crumpled tissue-papery skin made her look older, but her eyes reminded me of the fierce, watchful eyes of an owl I once did a face-to-face with at wilderness camp.

"Sunday," she said, shaking Sunday's hand warmly. "Septiembre." Another friendly handshake, even though I was sure Rebecca Mack caught Tia's eye roll at the use of her full name.

"Rebecca, this is my son, Kellen," Mom said, and it was my turn for a handshake.

This one was even warmer. And for an old woman, she had a grip. She hung on tight while she smiled and said, "I've heard so much about you, Kellen. Your mother thinks you walk on water."

"Nice to meet you," I lied. Besides being Mom's demanding boss, Rebecca Mack was the chairwoman of PAC, the organization dedicated to *keeping me* from walking on water. Closing in on eighty years old, she was still running the worldwide show.

What was *she* doing here? I wondered, but I didn't ask. I knew what was okay by now, and asking about Mom's work definitely wasn't.

I remembered Anderson once referring to the old lady as "Mack the Knife," which prodded me to do a Net search. I'd discovered that "Mack the Knife" was a once-popular song originally written for a 1920s play called *The Threepenny Opera*. That was about as far as my curiosity took me. I chalked up the nickname to the good doctor maybe having a background as a surgeon before moving into her current line of work. It was as good a guess as any.

We went inside, where the air felt heavy and lifeless, the colors looked murky. Mom and Rebecca Mack headed to the study, talking in low voices. The girls invited me to do homework with them at the kitchen table, but I was ready for breathing space. I carried my backpack to my room, turned on some music, and hit the button on my e-spond to load the assignment onto my desk display. In an instant the words HISTORY LESSONS, COURTESY OF PAC ARCHIVES, EXCERPTED FROM JUNKYARDDOG.BITES, showed up on the big screen. But the vision of San Francisco evaporating was still stuck in my brain, replaying itself again and again. It shoved everything else to the fuzzy edges of my mind.

I touched the PRINT command on the screen and my printer began spitting out the information while I sat and started spooling slowly through the stuff on the display. I noticed the heading again.

HISTORY LESSONS, COURTESY OF PAC ARCHIVES, EXCERPTED FROM

JUNKYARDDOG.BITES

Now I was focused enough to wonder what PAC had to do with Anderson's assignment. I puzzled over the question for a moment, but then I dove in. It looked like a big batch of heavyweight facts, and I didn't have all day to devote to studying. I wasn't going to obsess over this. I wasn't Ernie.

SEPTEMBER 15, 2035, JUNKYARDDOG.BITES—CHICAGO POLICE AND

FEDERAL AUTHORITIES REPORT THEY HAVE NO SUSPECTS IN THE

ASSASSINATION OF CONGRESSWOMAN AND LEADING PRESIDENTIAL

CANDIDATE CHERYL BAUER LAST WEEK.

DECEMBER 11, 2035, JUNKYARDDOG.BITES—EXECUTIVES OF CROWN INDUSTRIES, THE NATION'S LARGEST CONGLOMERATE, HAVE DISSOLVED ITS RETIREMENT BENEFITS PLAN, EMPTYING THE ACCOUNTS OF TEN MILLION EMPLOYEES AND RETIREES.

JUNE 8, 2036, JUNKYARDDOG.BITES—A U.S. JUSTICE DEPARTMENT STUDY REVEALS THAT FOR THE FIRST TIME, THE NUMBER OF EIGHTEEN- TO TWENTY-TWO-YEAR-OLD MEN IN PRISON, JAIL, OR UNDER THE JURISDICTION OF THE COURT SYSTEM EXCEEDS THE NUMBER IN COLLEGE.

AUGUST 2, 2036, JUNKYARDDOG.BITES—A MALE CALIFORNIA CONDOR NICKNAMED HAN SOLO, THE LAST KNOWN MEMBER OF A SPECIES SAVED FROM EXTINCTION MORE THAN A HALF CENTURY AGO, HAS DIED.

NOVEMBER 21, 2036, JUNKYARDDOG.BITES—INDIA, SURPASSING 1.5 BILLION PEOPLE FOR THE FIRST TIME, NOW HAS AT LEAST A BILLION OF ITS CITIZENS LIVING BELOW THE POVERTY LEVEL. HALF OF THEM ARE IN EXTREME POVERTY AND FACING STARVATION.

FEBRUARY 4, 2037, JUNKYARDDOG.BITES—GLACIER NATIONAL PARK TODAY WAS RENAMED GOING TO THE SUN NATIONAL PARK. ITS LAST GLACIER HAS MELTED.

True once, but when I was ten, Mom and I took the flash train to Montana. A new glacier was forming on a high peak at the park. People had come from all over the country to admire it, as if it were a newborn baby with the cutest nose ever. Mom cried when she saw it. Tears of elation, she said.

APRIL 2, 2037, JUNKYARDDOG.BITES—OVER THE PAST DECADE, REPORTED INCIDENTS OF RAPE IN THE UNITED STATES HAVE INCREASED 176 PERCENT.

MAY 10, 2037, JUNKYARDDOG.BITES—HOOD CANAL, A ONCE-PRISTINE BODY OF WATER ON WASHINGTON STATE'S OLYMPIC PEN-INSULA, NO LONGER SUPPORTS MARINE LIFE. A LONG SERIES OF FISH KILLS HAS LEFT NOTHING LIVING IN ITS OXYGEN-DEPLETED, PLASTIC-POISONED DEPTHS. WORLDWIDE, FISH POPULATION NOW STANDS AT 5 PERCENT OF 1900 LEVELS.

Hood Canal. I thought about my dad, the fisherman. Mr. Lucky. What would he have done if the fish hadn't made a comeback?

MARCH 23, 2039, JUNKYARDDOG.BITES—CITING FAMILY FEARS LINGERING FROM THE ASSASSINATION OF PRESIDENTIAL HOPE-FUL CHERYL BAUER PRIOR TO THE 2036 CAMPAIGN, SENATOR SUSAN ABRAMS TODAY WITHDREW FROM THE 2040 PRESIDEN-TIAL RACE.

JUNE 3, 2044, JUNKYARDDOG.BITES—EXPLORATION TEAMS HAVE FOUND VAST OIL RESERVES UNDER ICELAND'S CRUST.

JANUARY 27, 2045, JUNKYARDDOG.BITES—PRESIDENT MONTY STRONG ANNOUNCED TODAY THAT EVIDENCE OF WEAPONS OF MASS DESTRUCTION HAS BEEN UNCOVERED IN ICELAND.

FEBRUARY 16, 2045, JUNKYARDDOG.BITES—WITH THE APPROVAL OF THE LEGISLATIVE BRANCH AND A SHRUG OF THE MEDIA'S SHOULDERS, THE UNITED STATES AND A CONSORTIUM OF OTHER OIL-POOR-BUT-HUNGRY COUNTRIES TODAY INVADED ICELAND.

NOVEMBER 3, 2048, JUNKYARDDOG.BITES—PRESIDENT MONTY STRONG WAS REELECTED TO OFFICE EARLIER TODAY WITH AN UNEX-PECTEDLY, AND SOME SAY SUSPICIOUSLY STRONG, SHOWING IN MID-WEST STATES.

OCTOBER 17, 2049, JUNKYARDDOG.BITES—WITH POPULATION DENSITY AND SPRAWL BOTH REACHING CRITICAL MASS IN THE UNITED STATES, TRUE GRIDLOCK HAS SET IN. COMMONPLACE ARE HUNDRED-MILE, FOUR-HOUR COMMUTES AND CLOUDS OF TOXIC EMISSIONS BLANKETING CITIES AND SUBURBS AND HOVERING OVER RURAL AND WILDERNESS AREAS.

AUGUST 3, 2050, JUNKYARDDOG.BITES—IRAQ HAS JOINED OTHER MIDDLE EASTERN COUNTRIES IN FURTHER TIGHTENING RESTRIC-TIONS ON FEMALES' RIGHTS IN MARRIAGE, DRESS, EDUCATION, VOTING PRIVILEGES, AND ELIGIBILITY FOR PUBLIC OFFICE.

SEPTEMBER 6, 2051, JUNKYARDDOG.BITES—THE SOON-TO-BE-DEFUNCT SOCIAL SECURITY ADMINISTRATION PAID OUT ITS LAST

RETIREMENT BENEFIT YESTERDAY. STATES ARE GIRDING UP FOR A COLOSSAL INFLUX OF WELFARE APPLICANTS; LAW ENFORCEMENT AND EMERGENCY AGENCIES ARE SCRAMBLING TO PREPARE FOR A WINTER OF CRIME, VIOLENCE, AND DEATH; CHARITABLE ORGANI-ZATIONS ARE PLEADING FOR DONATIONS AND VOLUNTEER HELP.

I recalled last semester's history class. Female political leaders, lawmakers, and social workers reestablished Social Security in 2073, when they wrote the constitution for the new country of North America.

MARCH 28, 2053, JUNKYARDDOG.BITES—WITH SUPPLIES OF OIL IN THE ENTIRE MIDDLE EAST WANING, THE REGION HAS TURNED TO A MORE RELIABLE INDUSTRY: DRUGS. THE BIGGEST IMPORTER, DESPITE THE FACT THAT ITS JAILS AND PRISONS ARE CRAMMED WITH PEOPLE CONVICTED OF DRUG-RELATED CRIMES: THE UNITED STATES.

JULY 4, 2054, JUNKYARDDOG.BITES—OUR WORST FEAR HAS BEEN REALIZED.

I pictured the morning's lesson—San Francisco shedding its skin, the mushroom cloud rising above the city like a gloating grim reaper, surveying his handiwork.

JULY 5, 2054, JUNKYARDDOG.BITES—MADMEN BLAME IT ON THE VICTIMS.

JULY 6, 2054, JUNKYARDDOG.BITES—THE MADNESS CONTINUES.

JULY 8, 2054, JUNKYARDDOG.BITES—WHEN WILL IT END?

JULY 10, 2054, JUNKYARDDOG.BITES—PRESIDENT NAPPER'S ONE-DAY IMPEACHMENT TRIAL HAS CONCLUDED WITH HIS REMOVAL FROM OFFICE. VICE PRESIDENT JAMES CORSON ASSUMES THE PRESIDENCY.

JANUARY 21, 2059, JUNKYARDDOG.BITES—PRESIDENT CORSON'S ORDER FOR THE INVASION OF MEXICO WAS BASED ON A TERRORIST-INFESTED VISION FROM GOD, HE CLAIMS. HIS ORDER TO DEFOLIATE AND OCCUPY A FIVE-MILE-WIDE STRIP OF MEXICAN TERRITORY STRETCHING ALONG THE ENTIRE BORDER HAS COUNTRIES TO THE NORTH AND SOUTH OF THE UNITED STATES IN AN UPROAR.

I shut down my computer and pushed back from my desk. I was having a hard time coaxing the air out of my lungs, as if I'd just crashed into a wall chest-first.

Where was the world headed before Elisha?

I exhaled finally.

To hell, I decided.

CHAPTER FOUR

I'd had enough of being alone. I walked down the hall and banged on Sunday and Tia's door. No answer. I went downstairs and found them still in the kitchen, still locked in on junkyarddog on a wall display linked to Tia's e-spond.

"I thought you almost-fifth-levels already had this stuff," I said.

"Not all of it," Tia said. "Not in this context. You never know what they'll throw at you in your trials."

"Being nearly fifth-levels doesn't guarantee us anything," Sunday said, continuing to scribble notes in her journal.

She was right. The Worldwide Scholastic Boards administered elective achievement tests, which were nothing more than benchmarks to tell you how you were doing in preparation for your trials and eventually college. So far my best score was just above level four, but that didn't mean I couldn't do better with a new retake. Or ace my trials.

I shook my head. "You two ever do anything besides study?"

Tia smiled. Her eyes were still on the screen. "Sure."

"We like to dance," Sunday said. "How about you? You ever dance with a girl?"

"Everything I've *ever done* was with a girl," I said. "I can dance. But I don't like it much."

"Baseball?" Tia said. "You like that? We used to play on a team in Nebraska."

"Catcher," I said. "I wanted to pitch, but the league won't let guys pitch."

"We could hit you," Sunday said. "We can hit any boy's pitching."

"Let's see," I said, remembering that they'd barely been around boys. How good could their competition have been anyway? I headed for the basement as Tia darkened the display, giving it one last look. The girls followed me. I switched on the light at the bottom of the steps and grabbed three mitts, two bats, and a bag of balls off a shelf. We went back up. There was no sign of Mom or Rebecca Mack.

On the way out we passed a couple of women—more housemates—coming home after work. We now had a total of thirteen living here, counting Sunday, Tia, and their moms. A houseful.

I was the lone guy.

Luckily, everyone cooked and cleaned up after themselves, mostly. Two women did the major housework a couple of times a month and cooked dinners three nights a week for reduced rent, and I helped with housekeeping—my specialty was windows—and did most of the outside stuff—mowing, weeding, watering—for spending money. For a while I helped with the group cooking, too, but complaints surfaced about my other specialty—oyster pizza—so I was transferred out of the kitchen.

I glanced at the lawn on our way to our bikes. Still thriving on Sunday's rainfall, it needed a haircut. I'd better get to it soon or Mom would forget how glad she was to see me.

And speaking of Mom, as we passed the half-open parlor window, I heard her voice. It was raised, but another voice rose to meet it. Aunt Paige's. She'd come home early. A physician, she usually worked long hours in a downtown clinic. She almost always found me to say hello, but not this time.

"How did you find out?" Mom said.

I didn't get on my bike. I stopped at the edge of the driveway. Like twin shadows, Sunday and Tia stopped next to me.

"Never mind," Aunt Paige said. "It's dangerous. You're overstepping—"

She paused in mid-sentence. I looked up at the window. Mom was staring out. Her face looked flushed. She saw the three of us, slid the window shut, and disappeared. Rude. No way to treat an accidental eavesdropper. I gave a bat and mitt to each of the girls, hung the bag of balls from my handlebars, and pretended to monkey around with the placement of my mitt. But my tactics got me nowhere. The closed window was doing its job. Or maybe Mom and Aunt

Paige had continued their discussion at a lower volume else-where.

We got on our bikes and headed down the bike path. "What was that about?" Tia said.

"I don't know," I said.

"That was your aunt's voice, right?" Sunday asked.

"Right."

"She's your mom's sister?" she said.

"My dad's."

"She and your mom don't get along?" Tia asked.

"They usually do," I said. I held two fingers in the air, no space between them. "They're close." I pedaled harder. I wasn't much for conflict. I wanted to leave this one—whatever it was—behind me. But it stuck to me like the sweat that was materializing between my shoulder blades. What *had* they been talking about? *What* was dangerous? *What* was Mom overstepping? Was it the mysterious thing that had been weighing on her? Did it involve me?

The park was huge, stretching from Sand Point Way to the western edge of Lake Washington and north and south along the shoreline for two miles or more. We turned in at the entrance road—Northeast 74th, officially, but because of where it led and what it bordered, everyone called it Epitaph Road.

Next to me Tia and Sunday slowed. I followed them to the curb, where they stopped, straddling their bikes. What stretched out in front of us must have been impressive to the girls from small-town Nebraska: a wide expanse of grassy fields and playgrounds and trees and gardens, and to the left of all that another vast span of green, this one scattered with tall white crosses and punctuated by a soaring black monolith.

"What is this place?" Sunday asked.

I tried not to smile. At last I knew something they didn't. This bit of local history wouldn't have been covered in their test prep. "I had to do some research on it once," I said, "but it *ain't* going to be included in your trials. I don't think so anyway."

"You're *Kellen* me, professor," Sunday said. I ignored her.

"We don't care if it's included," Tia said. "We want to know."

"I can talk and ride at the same time," I said, and pushed off, coasting down the slight hill. The girls moved up next to me.

"This was a military base during World War Two," I said. "Then it was converted to a combination government facility and park toward the end of the last century. After Elisha, a big part of it was converted again, into the site for a graveyard."

"The crosses," Sunday said.

"Yeah, but they're not just markers," I said. "I'll start at the beginning, though."

I felt their eyes on me. Even Sunday was quiet. All I could hear was an occasional chirp of a bird and the distant soft noise of gas-fed flames, real or imagined. "A giant hole, ten stories deep and as big as three soccer stadiums, was bulldozed out. For days, dump trucks and garbage trucks, draped in black, arrived at the gravesite, weaving through crowds of mourners, dumping tens of thousands of bodies, some cremated but most not, into the hole. Cremation took too long."

"What about the crosses?" Sunday said.

"Did she take her pill today?" I asked Tia.

"You're getting under my skin, Kellen," Sunday said.

"Go on with the story," Tia, the adult in the group, said.

"Other trucks had other destinations," I said, taking my time. The field of crosses and the monolith were growing closer. "Barges at the waterfront, desolate areas in eastern Washington and neighboring states where holes had been dug, freight trains heading east, north, south."

"We had burial sites in Nebraska," Sunday said. "Outside Lincoln there's a huge one where a cornfield used to be."

"Maybe some Seattle dead ended up there," I said, trying to be civil and adultlike, before going on.

"After nearly a week, this grave was almost filled. I've seen photos showing a lake of bodies. The workers—almost all women—stopped with ten feet to go and topped off the hole with dirt. More dirt was added over the years as the bodies decomposed and settled."

I glanced at Sunday, giving her a clue: *Here comes the part you're so interested in.* "Work crews sank white metal pipes deep below the surface to collect and burn the methane gas from the decaying. If you stand near the pipes, you can see that they extend above the grass fifteen feet or so."

"But they look like crosses," Tia said.

"Yeah," I said. "Somewhere along the way, someone got the idea to attach a horizontal bar to each of them. So now we've got flaming grave markers."

We reached the monolith. It stood at the closest edge of the field, next to a walkway into the graveyard. Now I could hear the gas burning for sure. I stopped to give the girls a better look. "It's a monument," I said. "Thirty feet tall. Carved from black granite, smooth on all five surfaces. Weatherproof displays are imbedded in the stone at eye level, one on each side."

"Displays?" Sunday said.

"The monolith is the one tombstone for the whole grave-site," I said. "Touch the screen and you can get to the entire list, the names of every person identified before the trucks started rolling—men, boys, infants, a few women."

Many of the names were followed by words of remembrance—epitaphs—written by loved ones. My grandfather's name—Joshua Winters—was on the list. I'd found it many times. After it my grandmother and her children—Dad and Aunt Paige—wrote:

> *We watched for you, every breath a prayer,*
> *while days became shorter and nights became colder*
> *and hope became heartbreak.*
> *But only the bear came.*

Dad had told me the story of this bear—the huge tracks

through their campsite, the stare-down—or smell-down—across the water, the gift of fish. I sometimes wondered if that same bear was still alive and wandering the hills of the Olympic Peninsula. But I never looked up any facts on bears. I'd rather not know their life expectancy; I'd rather imagine the bear, gray-muzzled now, maybe, cruising the shoreline of that lake for berries, searching along the water's edge for another free and easy meal.

The lesson was over. We moved on. Beyond the tombstone, and the wide but low hill of crosses, lay a grass field, fir trees here and there. We circled around the graveyard on our bikes to a spot where there weren't many people, where a small backstop stood and patches of dirt loosely defined an infield.

Under one nearby tree, five women and three little girls shared a picnic lunch. Closer to the lake, a dozen or so girls about my age and one boy, probably younger, played soccer. They'd set up red cones on both ends of their little field and arranged brightly colored pieces of clothing to mark the sidelines. Ordinarily, I would have gone over and asked them if I could join in. But I had a challenge to meet.

I stared at the flames licking out of the tips of the crosses, remembering the times I'd ridden my bike to Epitaph Road at night just to watch the flames light up the sky. They were harder to see in the bright sunlight. "My grandpa's down there somewhere," I said. "I like to think those flames are his. Part of them anyway."

"The brightest part, probably," Tia said, and I gave her a look, figuring she was giving me crap. But she smiled, shiny-white against her brown skin. And I got this sudden warm feeling.

I got off my bike. "You guys ready to show me what you've got?"

Sunday pointed at her impressive bicep. "Say your prayers." I was thankful for my long-sleeved T-shirt.

She and Tia carried the bats and two gloves to the back-stop. I took my glove and the bag of balls to the mound, fifty or sixty feet out from home plate. While Tia and I played catch, tossing the ball back and forth harder and harder, Sunday took practice swings, timing my throws. She looked like she knew how to swing a bat; Tia could definitely throw a ball.

Tia crouched down behind the circle of dirt that represented home plate. Sunday stepped in, the bigger bat perched on her shoulder.

"You should be wearing a mask," I told Tia. "You'll catch one in the teeth." *Beauteous teeth,* I thought to myself.

"I'm okay," she said.

"You're sure?" Sunday said.

"No worries," Tia said.

I shrugged. I wasn't going to throw easy just because Tia was back there. I toed the dusty ground, looking for a decent place to set up. Finally, I faced the batter, wound up, and let one go. It was a little outside. Sunday watched, uninterested, as it flew by. I threw another, almost in the dirt. She wasn't tempted. I was trying too hard.

I backed off on my third one, and it was going to be a strike. I watched it heading for the heart of the plate.

It didn't get there. Sunday squinted and jumped all over it. The ball screamed over the shortstop spot and well into left field. She didn't smile. She stood there, poised for my next one.

I picked up another ball and fired it hard. She swung, harder, but missed this time. The ball plopped into Tia's mitt.

I kept throwing, Sunday kept swinging. Sometimes she connected, sometimes she didn't. Finally, I blew three in a row past her and she gave Tia the bat and headed for the outfield to retrieve balls. She wasn't ready to sacrifice her teeth.

Not choosy, Tia took cuts at just about everything I threw her—high, low, outside, in—so I did better against her, the misses slamming against the weathered wood of the backstop. But she connected from time to time. She hit the last one deep, over Sunday's head, and raced around the bases, laughing. She beat the throw home, but I tagged her anyway. As she squealed and squirmed away, I caught sight of the smooth coppery skin of her stomach. The tiny external tip of her PAC-mandated birth-control implant protruded from her belly button like a piece of silvery jewelry.

They let me hit, taking turns pitching. I was rusty at first but then started nailing some. Sunday threw hard; Tia was more accurate.

We quit, finally. All in all, we were pretty even. They'd proven they could hit me, could throw a ball past me; I didn't know what I'd proven. Maybe that my league should allow me to pitch, that I was nothing special, not even in baseball.

We were leaving the park when a long procession of women and girls paraded through the entrance on foot, moving toward the burial mound, humming something familiar and mournful that hovered above their heads like a dripping gray cloud. They all wore long crimson gowns; they all held tall, unlit white candles and candlesticks in front of them like altar girls. Their leader, an older woman, barefoot, carried a big wooden cross with a candle mounted in the top, stepping out by herself, her long gray hair flowing behind her.

We stopped our bikes to let them cross the street. The women ignored Tia and Sunday but smiled at me. The younger girls waved.

"Fratheists?" Tia said once we were back on our bikes and moving.

"Yeah," I said.

"I've heard about them," she said, "but I've never seen any before today."

"Not exactly mainstream," I said. "But what is, anyway?"

"PAC," Sunday said. "Apportionment."

Tia got this strange look on her face, but instead of commenting on Sunday's remark, she launched into something kind of unrelated, as if she was trying to cover up her thoughts. "Right after Elisha, mainstream churches did well," she said. "Some people believed a kind of half-baked Rapture had occurred. Nothing else happened, though, and there was almost no clergy to hold things together. Before long, faith in traditional stuff cooled. Church attendance spiraled down. Buildings stood empty."

"Omaha has Fratheists," Sunday said. "My mom has a friend who lost her dad, granddad, brother, and two uncles to Elisha. She drives three hours one way to go to the Fratheist service." Which made sense to me. I'd come across this local group before today, and I'd been curious enough to do some research. What I'd found out was that Fratheists worshipped God, but they did it through prayers to the souls of the men and boys who had perished in Elisha. Friends, fathers, grandfathers, uncles, nephews, husbands, sons, grandsons.

Brothers.

According to the Fratheists, all of the dead were our brothers, and now messengers to God.

Several times a week, Fratheists made a pilgrimage from neighboring churches to Epitaph Road, where they lingered among the crosses until darkness came. They reached high to light their candles from the flames and then marched away, chanting hymns with candlelight playing on their mournful, radiant faces.

Some people believed they were responsible for ghoulish acts involving the mass gravesite. From time to time, walkers crossing the burial field early in the morning would find signs of grave disturbances: big squares or rounds of cut turf, loose soil below, as deep as the layer of dirt and perhaps beyond, into the bodies themselves. But no one had ever caught the Fratheists doing anything creepier than just hanging around and lighting their candles.

"They like you," Sunday said.

"Because I'm a guy," I said. "Someone has to."

Woe to you who long for judgment day . . .
That day of the Lord will be darkness, not light.
It will be as if a man fled the fury of a lion,
only to encounter the wrath of a bear.

—AMOS, 5:18–19
—EPITAPH FOR NATHAN GRIGSBY (JULY 12, 2002–AUGUST 8, 2067),
BY CHELSEA GRIGSBY, HIS WIFE,
NOVEMBER 16, 2068

CHAPTER FIVE

On the way back, Tia wanted to stop at the library. Sunday and I went along with it. I pretended I was doing Tia a favor, but I'd had a long attraction to libraries. And I needed some books for required reading.

We left our bikes and baseball gear at the door, but as usual, even though we were in library-visit mode now, the female patrons—almost everyone—gave me unswerving stares as soon as we got inside.

It was a big structure, converted from an old police station and jail. Since Elisha's arrival, governments had been able to shut down most station houses and lockups, converting them to libraries, schools, residences, office buildings, and storage. Tia headed for the research room; I headed for fiction. Sunday surprised me by following along.

"What's Tia up to?" I asked as we began meandering through the stacks of books. I made mental notes, titles I wanted to come back to on another day, to read for myself.

"Hush-hush," Sunday said. "She's checking out some kind of theory she's dreamed up, but she won't even tell *me* what it is."

"A theory?" I said. "You don't have any idea what it's about?"

"We were just looking at the junkyarddog stuff and she got all serious. Then quiet." She shrugged. "Be right back." She headed for a nearby lav. A silhouette of a toilet—no woman, no man—on its door.

I'd seen old photos taken at a time, PE, when there were separate restrooms for women and men in public places. Now that was no longer practical. Everyone was expected to make do with locks and floor-length stalls and respect for everyone else's privacy. The urinals still in existence attracted curiosity and giggles and occasionally flowers, but not a lot of urine.

I spotted a book I needed and pulled it from its shelf and leafed absentmindedly through it, letting my fingers get a feel for the pages. It was an old story, written more than a hundred years ago. But a mandatory read before we got through the summer and took the trials. *Slaughterhouse-Five,* by a guy—a *guy*—named Kurt Vonnegut, Jr. It was skinny. I decided I should get it read soon. I had to show Mom or Aunt Paige or whoever was in charge of me when the time came to visit Dad that I was ahead on my assignments.

Sunday returned, wiping her hands on her shorts. "No towels," she explained.

"Does Tia think she's some kind of professor, too?" I asked her.

"She really could be," Sunday said. "She's curious. She wants to figure out how we got to where we are."

"You and Tia?"

"Society. All of us."

"Don't *you* want to know?" I asked.

"I'm learning. This is our second time through some of this stuff. I can be patient. Tia, she's hungry. She's like you, with an extra load of history riding on her shoulders—a real dad somewhere, and a gramps. The two of them were sailing the South Pacific together in a small sailboat when Elisha hit."

"She sees them?"

"Never. They're loners, living up north. Outside of Fairbanks someplace. She was excited to move out here and get closer to them."

A couple of aisles over I found another book on my list: Ray Bradbury's *Fahrenheit 451*. For an old book it looked interesting. This copy had been printed in 2074—twenty-three years ago—but it was still in good condition, probably because most people checked out the electronic versions of books. I preferred the real thing. I liked the way I could fold over the oversized cover flap on this one to mark a place. I liked the way I could fan through the pages and create a small breeze that smelled of paper and ink and an old brick building with tall streaked windows and polished dark wood floors and worn oval rugs.

Sunday was still just shadowing me, not picking up anything. I decided not to ask her if she had already read all the required stuff. I didn't want to get discouraged. And humiliated.

We moved to the shadowy corner of the library where nonfiction was shelved, where I located one of the two titles I was still looking for: William Shirer's *The Rise and Fall of the Third Reich*. I'd still be reading this one when I started shaving. Beyond thick, it felt like it weighed five pounds, minimum, enough to give me an instant hernia. Traditionalist or not, I was tempted to see if there was an e-version.

Next I found Rachel Carson's *Silent Spring*. The only woman among this assignment's authors, and another ancient book, but several copies of this title sat on the shelf. Sunday took one finally.

"What about Tia?" I said.

"She's read it," she said. "Over and over."

I felt myself smiling.

Sunday looked around us. The dim and airless space between the stacks was empty. "You ever make out with a girl, Kellen?"

Talk about a change of subject. I swallowed. "I'm afraid of girls."

"No, really. Have you? That girl at The Groundskeeper, maybe?"

I was torn between a smart-ass answer and an honest

one. The second choice won out. "A year or so ago. This older girl named Merri lived in our house for a while. She tried out some things on me."

Merri Nuyen. My first love. Or something like that. She moved into our house with her mother, a brilliant scientist with lungs that didn't work so well but eyes and ears that always did, especially when it came to Merri and me. Merri and her mom took off abruptly after just a few weeks, leaving me with a temporarily broken heart. Semi-reliable buzz around the house was that they'd gone to the hinterlands.

"How did it make you feel?"

I didn't have to think for long. Those feelings hung on for months after Merri left. "Excited. Nervous. But she—and her mom—didn't stay. They left in a hurry."

"Do *I* make you nervous?"

I glanced around, trying to look casual and unembarrassed, wondering if there was a graceful way I could make an escape.

"*I* wouldn't leave," she added, and her eyes—the color of brand-new fir needles, I suddenly noticed—told me she meant it.

I studied those eyes, thinking. She was cute. She was nice in a pushy kind of way. I shook my head. "*Tia* makes me nervous."

Sunday didn't look insulted. Maybe she wasn't; maybe she was a good actor. She grinned. "I'll have to tell her."

"No. Please. I'll get over it."

"You might not. Smart girls stick with you."

"Merri was smart. I got over her."

"Okay," she said. "Keeping a secret ain't difficult for me." She moved a little ways away. "But let me give you a little tip. When you talk to Tia, use her name. Girls like that. Even smart ones. It makes us feel special. Not one of the crowd."

"Thanks for the advice," I said kind of sarcastically, but in truth I was grateful for any information about girls in general and Tia in particular. Being vastly outnumbered by females hadn't helped me understand them any better.

"No problem," Sunday said. "Let's go see what she's up to."

We found Tia in the reference room. After my confession to Sunday, I felt different—something beyond nervous—about being this close to her cousin. I tried not to stare at her, but now she suddenly had this aura thing going for her, and I couldn't ignore her at the center of it.

Sunday gave me a knowing grin, but she didn't let Tia see it. "You about ready, Tia?" she said.

I mentally kicked myself. *I* should have asked that question. "Find what you're looking for, *Tia?*" I added. Her name felt good rolling off my tongue, especially with the little emphasis I gave it. Sunday pretended not to notice, but I was sure she was proud of how smoothly I'd worked in the use of the name.

"I guess." Tia smiled at me. She hit PRINT on her touch pad and signed off. She had a stack of four or five books on the desk, and she picked them up and moved to the printer to collect her pages.

On our way out of the room, a woman stepped out of the shadows and straight into my path. She stopped in front of me, arms folded across her chest. If it hadn't been for her scowl and the shiny silvery badge that said SECURITY pinned to the stiff poop-colored fabric of her shirt, I would have said she was attractive.

"I've had my eye on you," she snarled in my direction, and although at first I hoped she was talking to someone else, her glare didn't waver, and she was the law, at least in these parts. Most crimes had become rarities, but petty thievery, including sneaking stuff out of the library, remained a problem. I'd never been interested. Guys who were caught pocketing library materials faced an extra helping of trouble.

Finally, I pointed to my chest and raised my eyebrows: a question the cavewoman might understand.

"*You*, man-sweat. I see what's under your arm. That book doesn't leave this room."

I was speechless, searching for words. Sunday wasn't. "You're talking to Mr. Law-abiding, Sheriff," she said.

"And I'm *not* talking to *you*," the security cop said without looking at Sunday. She still had me in her sights. She took a big breath, puffing herself up further. Her chest strained against her uniform. I tried not to stare. I didn't want her thinking I found anything about her attractive.

"Kellen's not a thief," Tia said reasonably. "All of his books are okay for checkout."

"Mind your own business, brown eyes," the sheriff said. She still had me locked in her steely stare. "How about you, hairball?" she said to me. "You don't talk? You a dummy?"

. It had taken me a while, but at last I figured out her problem. She didn't know anything about me, so I guessed a chronic case of male-phobia was fueling her fire. Still, though, she would have needed something to set her off. I slipped *The Rise and Fall of the Third Reich* from the stack under my arm. I held it within inches of her face, so she couldn't miss the title. "Is this the one you're worried about, skunk-sweat?" I said. I opened it so she could see the scan code on the inside of the cover.

She turned a nice satisfying shade of red. "Pissant," she said, but she moved out of my way.

"Butt-wipe," Sunday said as we resumed walking.

"Bigot," Tia said over her shoulder.

I was quiet until we were out of the reference room and on our way to the exit. I pictured the guard spotting me, profiling me, hanging close like a scent-challenged blood-hound. "I'll bet both of you she's not a Fratheist," I said.

The girls humored me with laughter. They must have felt sorry for me. Most of the time I wasn't subjected to male-hate, but right now the idea of someday heading off to the hinterlands looked more appealing than ever. Maybe they saw it on my face.

I tried to think of a way to coolly use Tia's name again. Then a doubt hit: Maybe Sunday was trying to sabotage me. Maybe Tia didn't like her name worn thin from over-use. Maybe she liked being one of the crowd. But she *had* smiled.

We scanned out the reading material and escaped into the sun and warmth. Feeling grateful to the girls for sticking up for me, I insisted on stuffing all our books in with the balls and hanging the bag on my handlebars. It was an off-balance ride the rest of the way home, but we all managed to get there in one piece.

"Thanks for helping me out with the book cop," I said as we parked our bikes on the side of the house. "Sunday. And *Tia*."

"You're an okay guy, Kellen," Sunday said, as if she'd never brought up the subject of making out with me. "She was an embarrassment."

"We're on your side," Tia said with another smile. "Really." I got nervous again.

The parlor window was open once more, but no sound escaped. We went inside and got rid of our stuff. The old house breathed quietly. I inhaled the good aromas of cooking coming from the kitchen, where the two helper-women were preparing our Thursday dinner. I was reminded of my chores.

I went to the backyard, dragged the lawn mower—prehistoric but earth-friendly—from the ramshackle shed, and attacked the lawn, building up a sweat, breathing in the smell of fresh-mown grass. Not quite a match for dinner on the stove, but not bad. I raked the lawn clean, pulled new weeds from the flower beds, threw everything in the compost bin, and returned the mower to its home.

Peonies grew tall against the sun-soaked boards of what

we called the "wayfarers' wall," the nearest-the-house side of the shed, where over the years my housemates—and I—had written random thoughts when moving in or out or on appropriately—or inappropriately—inspired occasions in between. Hellos, good-byes, one-liners, poems, dissertations, sayings, quotes, political statements, lyrics from songs, rants, recipes, prayers.

When I was six years old and just starting to read, one of the newer arrivals at the house, an angular, freckled college student with a nice smile that featured liquid brown eyes and shiny red lipstick, surrendered to suicide in her room. Pills, I heard much later. The day after she died, I was the first to discover her good-bye note among the wall's other writings. Instantly, its words were engraved deep into my brain, even though at the time I didn't grasp all their individual or collective meanings or even their pronunciations.

I am cursed by a full and relentless imagination. What was. What could be. Wishes. Dreams. Possibilities. Reality pales. It is vapid and vacant and empty of promise. I reject it.

Later that day, I scribbled down the words in my beginner handwriting on a scrap of paper, and after the policewomen left, and the assistant collectors from the Office of the Early Departed took away the body of the college student, someone painted over the message. It was almost as if it had never appeared.

Almost.

The suicide lowered a dark cloud over our whole house. I remembered the sad faces and the quiet that settled

71

everywhere. To encourage their remaining housemates to get their feelings out, Mom and Aunt Paige came up with the idea of stocking brushes and jars of paint and water-proof markers in a cabinet just inside the shed door. Next to it they placed an eight-foot stepladder to reach less-accessible and still-blank spaces on the wall.

The writing incentives did their job. Or maybe tradition and doggedness and more optimistic points of view would have shrugged off the chill of the college girl's farewell message anyway. Regardless, before long the writing resumed.

When I was eight or so, after I realized Dad had really meant it when he told me he wouldn't be coming back to stay, after I discovered that thoughts and impressions could be translated into something called poetry, even if it was just beginners' poetry, after I found out it was okay for me to make a contribution to the wall, I climbed the ladder and claimed a virgin spot in the upper left-hand corner. There I wrote:

> *Across the deep water, a man, tall and plucky,*
> *stows his anchor and sails the sea.*
> *He stands at the helm of his boat, Mr. Lucky,*
> *looking for fish but thinking of me.*

Wishful imagining, maybe, but Dad's exit didn't keep me from believing that deep down he loved me more than his fish or his freedom, that he'd prefer to have me standing next to him at *Mr. Lucky*'s wheel. That someday he'd come back and reel me in like a trophy salmon and take me home with him.

I crouched at the far right end of the wall now, spreading apart the long stems of the flowers. I'd chosen the spot when Merri, the one-time object of my affection, was still living in our house. I thought she might discover this perfect place—inconspicuous but accessible.

Inside the red outline of a heart, I wrote my initials and hers:

KD AND MN.
FOREVER.

Kid stuff. Immature. Naïve. I knew it, even as I'd painted it on the wall, but I didn't care.

For weeks afterward, I checked the weathered boards for some kind of acknowledgment from her. But nothing showed up. I quit looking. The day before she left, though, I noticed a cryptic piece of writing in what I'd come to believe was my private domain: the spot on the high left corner of the wall I'd staked out at an early age and marked with additional pieces of writing over the years. The trespassing couplet simply read,

Long winding highway,
may it take a homeward turn.

I didn't know what it meant. I didn't know who wrote it.

But it must have given me some encouragement, because the day after Merri and her mom ran off, something made me look at my semi-hidden heart-note one more time.

Inside the heart was an arrow, pointing from Merri's initials to mine, and next to my word *Forever,* the words *And beyond.*

Although it occurred to me that someone else could have written it, the writing looked closely similar to the highway note, and I chose to think Merri had made the additions. The thought gave me comfort, even though her departure made me sad.

The heart and initials and words—already faded—were still there. I left them now and cut a big bunch of peonies and carried them around to the front of the house.

Inside, I dropped off my fistful of flowers in the kitchen and headed for the stairs, passing the study on the way. The door was closed. I paused, listening. I heard a woman's voice, just one. One side of a phone conversation, it sounded like, but the words didn't filter through. Just the inflections and tones and attitude. It was the old lady, Rebecca Mack.

I got upstairs and walked down the hallway to the big bedroom Mom and Aunt Paige shared. Another closed door. There was an epidemic of them. I heard voices. They sounded agitated or angry or something. I didn't care. I knocked.

Mom came to the door. She didn't open it all the way. Now she didn't look happy. I saw Aunt Paige's reflection in a wall mirror. Her face was flushed.

"What's going on?" I said.

"I'll talk to you later," Mom said.

"How long will you be home this time?" I said.

"Why?"

"You were going to tell me about Dad, when I could go see him."

"Not for a while."

"You said *soon*. In *a while* I'll be all involved with my trials. Right now I'm ahead on my reading and everything."

"We'll talk after dinner." She shut the door in my face. I heard the latch click. I stood there for a moment, wanting to pound through the brittle old wood. Instead, I went to my room and sat on my bed, boiling inside, fingering through *Slaughterhouse-Five*.

After a moment I realized I was mutilating the poor pages. White-knuckled, I slammed the book shut and tossed it on the floor. I wasn't in a mood to read. Mom had practically promised me I could visit Dad, and now she was backing out? *Why?*

I slid a chair into my closet. In its ceiling was a trapdoor to the attic. I stood on the chair, pushed the door aside, and pulled myself up. The low, cramped space was warm, and I began sweating immediately. The weak dust-flecked light came only from vents in the walls.

The attic ran the length of the house. I knew it like I knew my own room. I'd spent a ton of time up here, taking a break from the constant attention, listening to conversations from time to time when the feeling arrived that something was about to affect me.

Like now.

The key thing was being quiet. I was already on my belly. I pushed, pulled, and slithered my way toward Mom and Aunt Paige's room, a few inches at a time, until I was there.

I held perfectly still. Their voices rose like smoke, bumping into the ceiling below me, wafting through.

"You're being terribly thickheaded," Mom said. "But let me say it one last time. We don't *have* a choice. Our own operative—beyond reliable—reports that they're in the final phase."

"They're too close to Seattle," Aunt Paige said. "And civilization. You can't guarantee the quarantine won't be breached. And then what?"

"The alternative is unthinkable," Mom said. "We can't allow their work to see the light of day. Especially with the latest analysis from PAC Intelligence."

"You're talking about my *brother*, who once meant *everything* to you. You're talking about your *son*."

"I've made arrangements for Kellen to go east," Mom said. My heart pounded in my chest. I hoped it wasn't reverberating through the boards. I was going *east*? *Why*? When was she going to tell me this wonderful news? What about Dad? My trials? My *life*?

"We've got to warn Charlie," Aunt Paige said. *Charlie.* My *dad*.

"We can't. We can't consider it. He's involved. He'd warn the others."

"His involvement is minimal. We can make up a lie to get him out of there."

"He's not stupid, Paige. He'd suspect."

"No, he *wouldn't*." Aunt Paige's voice shook. "I'll think of *something*."

I heard a knock on their door, footsteps across the hardwood floor, and Mom's voice: "Rebecca."

"Can we talk?" Rebecca Mack said. Her distinctive, demanding voice moved into the room. "Alone?"

"Paige knows," Mom said. "She's been playing detective."

"I'm hardly a detective," Aunt Paige said. "I don't know what Heather has told you about me—if anything—but I'm a doctor. Public health. The Council sends me advisories on potential mass fatalities and bulletins on quarantine activity, even when the deaths and quarantines are virtual, just part of supposedly mock exercises. I'm sworn to secrecy, of course, but between the notices, the scurrying around I've witnessed lately, and a small amount of investigation on my own, it wasn't that difficult to put together a fuzzy picture of something on the horizon."

"You'll tell *no one*," Rebecca Mack said.

"I have a brother in harm's way," Aunt Paige said.

"Of course," Rebecca Mack said. "Kellen's father."

"I lost *my* father," Aunt Paige said. "Uncles, cousins, a grandfather. I can figure out a way to lure him away without raising his suspicions."

"You—we—can't take the risk," Rebecca Mack said. "And your losses were hardly unique."

"There will *be* no risk," Aunt Paige said.

"Paige," Mom said.

"If you persist in this idea," Rebecca Mack said, "we will need to place you in custody until the event's . . . *conclusion.*"

"*Custody?*" Aunt Paige said.

"Yes," Rebecca Mack said. "Lock and key and no way to communicate."

The room was silent for a moment. Then footsteps sounded. The door slammed.

"Well, you've got me alone," Mom said.

"Can she be trusted?" Rebecca Mack said.

I waited for Mom's answer. My head spun. What was going on? For some reason, I wished Tia were up here with me, listening to this. I had a feeling she'd figure it out. "I don't know," Mom said finally.

"Come downstairs with me," Rebecca Mack said. "I need to show you something. And we have to make a call."

I waited for the door to close, then belly-slid back toward my room. I was sweating more now, breathing harder. Even all the way up here, I could smell dinner cooking. But my stomach felt knotted. I was no longer hungry.

Even though Dad
always tried his hardest not to give away
his feelings, I'm pretty sure he loved Charlie best.
But that didn't make me super sad, really, because
Charlie is the firstborn and a boy and he looks a lot
like Mom and he's the best brother in the whole world,
even during those tearful times when he's being colossally
stubborn and bossy and rude (I especially don't care about
any of that stuff now, because Elisha's Bear makes him
nervous and not himself most of the time). The sad
part, actually, is that I'll never get another chance
to make Dad see that I might have been
second to come around, and I might
be a girl, but I'm okay, too.

I really am.

—ENTRY IN THE DIARY OF PAIGE WINTERS,
DECEMBER 17, 2067

CHAPTER SIX

I found Aunt Paige in the backyard by herself, pacing barefoot back and forth near a bed of sweet peas and rosebushes. A fragrant sugary scent saturated the air, at odds with the foul thoughts filling my head. She didn't seem to notice that one of the thorns on the yellow rose she was holding had pricked her first finger. A trickle of half-dried blood wound around it like a thin red ribbon.

Not certain what exactly to say, I stood there a minute, silent, before she noticed me. She forced a smile. "How are you, sunshine?" she said.

"I heard you," I confessed.

"What?"

"I heard you and Mom and Rebecca Mack talking. I was in the attic."

She smiled again. This one was small but authentic. "Up to your old tricks."

"What's going on?" I said. "What do Dad and I have to do with it?"

"Forget what you heard," Aunt Paige said. "You'll be taken care of." She paused. "And so will your dad."

"You won't tell me?"

She got close. She grasped my shoulders and looked me in the eyes. "Listen, Kellen. I have to go away for a day or two. But you can't say anything about it until after everyone knows I'm gone. And you have to do exactly what your mom tells you to do, go where she wants you to go. No matter what, don't try to see your dad."

"What about the *custody* thing?"

"An empty threat. Don't worry about it."

"When will you go?"

"You'll know when you don't see me."

"Where?"

"I can't say, buddy. If you think you have it figured out, though, keep it to yourself."

We went in for dinner. Tia sat down next to me at the big table, and I wondered if Sunday had let something slip. But neither of them acted like anything had changed. I breathed in, mostly smelling myself, wishing I'd thought to take a shower after a couple of long bike rides and baseball and lawn-mowing and crawling around in a hot attic. But I'd had other things on my mind, and Tia was nice enough not to say anything. She even shifted on her chair, getting a little nearer.

Two of our housemates were elsewhere, so there were twelve of us, counting our guest of honor, surrounding the table. The conversation was cordial, but it felt artificial. Mom introduced Dr. Rebecca Mack to everyone she hadn't met. She didn't say who Rebecca Mack was, but I had an inkling everyone knew.

Across the table from me, Aunt Paige told a joke about an old-lady patient who wanted to know the location of her heart. Along with the rest of us, Rebecca Mack chuckled at the punch line, but I wondered if she appreciated the humor. I wondered if my aunt was purposely trying to get under this old lady's skin.

After dinner, everyone carried dishes to the kitchen and went their mostly separate ways. Mom and Rebecca Mack returned to the office. Aunt Paige headed upstairs. Tia and Sunday asked me to go with them on a bike ride.

I was tempted. The sun had just dropped below the roof-tops across the street, perfect conditions for biking, and I could impress the girls—Tia, maybe—with my knowledge of the city. I certainly hadn't impressed them with my pitching, but I told them no. Something was about to happen, and I wanted to be there when it did.

I grabbed *Slaughterhouse-Five* from my room and slipped into the quiet of the backyard. Beyond the glass of Mom and Aunt Paige's upstairs window, the light was on but the shades were drawn. I found a chair and began reading. The story grabbed me and pulled me in, but after twenty pages I looked up. The light was off.

I walked around the side yard to the front. Aunt Paige's little car, a green Volt-Age Midget, was gone. A strange gray micro-van cruised down the street and slowed at our house. Tinny country music wept out from under its hood. On its side was a familiar logo—a green globe behind silhouettes of a giant woman and miniature man—above the letters *PAC*. The driver—a red-faced, pig-nosed woman—looked at the house number and pulled up to the curb.

She and her partner, younger and thinner with skin the color of milk chocolate, got out, eyed me for a moment, and walked to the porch. They knocked, but no one answered.

"You live here?" the driver asked me. Her blue uniform jacket angled open. She had handcuffs hanging from her wide leather belt. A PAC cop. The enforcement arm of the Population Apportionment Council. I'd heard about them and their strong-arm tactics, but they kept a low profile most of the time. The Council preferred to pay people to comply with sterilization and other regulations.

If the time came, would I accept their money and conditions? Hide? Head for the hinterlands? If I didn't pass my trials, I'd have a decision to make.

I nodded.

"Is Dr. Rebecca Mack on the premises?"

"She was here for dinner. I think she's still around."

"Can you get her for us?"

"I'll see if I can find her." I left them standing on the porch and went inside. I rapped on the office door, still closed.

Mom opened it. "We're in the middle of something, Kellen," she said, but she didn't need to tell me that.

"Some PAC cops are here," I said. "Looking for Dr. Mack."

"Oh." Mom swung the door wide. Rebecca Mack was already on her feet, scurrying toward me. She swept past and toward the front door, Mom in her wake, me tagging along.

Dr. Mack asked the cops to come in. "She's upstairs, I believe," she said. She turned and saw me. "Can you take these officers to your aunt's room, Kellen?" she said.

It wasn't really a question, although for a moment, half numb with disbelief, I considered disobeying the command. I didn't want to be a part of this, whatever shape it took. But then I remembered Aunt Paige's dark window, her missing car. "Sure," I said, and led them up the stairs.

I knocked. Relief eased my pulse when no one answered. I pushed open the door and turned on the light. It was obvious nobody was there, but the cops went to the closet and bathroom, making sure. The young one—BLEVENS, her name tag said—even peeked under the bed. Brilliant.

"Where else would she be?" the older one—STOUDT— asked me.

"I don't know." I didn't mention Aunt Paige's car. If she'd made her getaway, she needed a head start.

The cops pushed past me, so I followed at a distance. As I descended the stairs, I heard them telling Rebecca Mack and Mom that Aunt Paige wasn't in her room.

"Search the house," Dr. Mack ordered.

Mom touched a key on her e-spond and held it to her ear, waiting. "She isn't answering," she told Rebecca Mack as I got downstairs. Mom left, and I heard her moving from room to room. She went upstairs and returned, ignoring Dr. Mack's glare, and hurried outside.

In a moment she was back. "Her car's gone." She looked at me. "Did she say anything to you, Kellen?"

I started retelling the joke Aunt Paige told at dinner, the one about the old lady and her heart.

Mom gave me the vile eye. "About *where she was going.*"

I decided I was out of favor, suddenly. "No," I said. "I didn't see her after dinner. Maybe she went back to work or something."

"I don't think so," Mom said.

"Why does it matter?" I asked. "Why are you—they— looking for her?"

"We need to find her, Kellen," Rebecca Mack said. "It's important. Are you sure she didn't tell you anything?"

"Why would she?" I asked. "I'm a kid—a guy—with a runaway mouth."

She gave me a long look, but I resisted flinching. I stayed

in character: wiseass kid whose mother—but no one else—thinks he walks on water. "You're right," she said finally. "Why *would* she?"

The two cops returned empty-handed. The cuffs clanked uselessly on Stoudt's belt. She and Blevens walked to the front porch with Mom and Dr. Mack, mumbling and muttering. I stared at the back of Mom's head. I was having a hard time digesting the idea that she could have a role in putting Aunt Paige behind bars. Or locked doors, at least.

When Mom and Rebecca Mack returned, they went straight back to the office. I stood in the foyer, imagining them sending out advisories and all-points bulletins like the police in the old cops-and-robbers movies. I imagined them adding Aunt Paige's name to the list of most-wanted criminals, posting her picture with front and side views on the Net.

From the stuff I'd overheard, I thought I had an idea of where she was going. She wanted to warn Dad about something. Which was good, I guessed, except Rebecca Mack and Mom knew what I knew and more. They knew *why* the fugitive criminal wanted to warn Dad.

So they'd be on her trail. They'd be watching the ferries and roads. They'd try to find Dad and wait for her to show up. I didn't know why they wanted to keep her from talking to him, but I knew they were serious about it.

Reflexively, I reached in my pants pocket and fingered my e-spond. But I couldn't call or message him. He didn't have a phone of any kind. He preferred it that way, and where he lived and worked, the service was sketchy anyway. He didn't own a computer, either, so e-script was also out of the question.

I couldn't reach him. Aunt Paige couldn't reach him. It was in person or nothing. But even if I'd been able to talk to him, what would I have said? *Hey, Dad, I'm hereby giving you an official warning, but I don't know what it's about or what you can do about it.*

CHAPTER SEVEN

It was nearly dark by the time Tia and Sunday returned. I'd migrated to the front porch, and although I resisted shouting *Hey!* this time, I surprised them when I walked out of the shadows. "You missed some excitement," I said. I told them about the cops and Aunt Paige. I didn't tell them about my eavesdropping or where I thought the escapee was heading. I wanted to share, but I wasn't sure how far to go.

"I'm gonna go check my mail," Sunday said. "Sorry about your aunt, Kellen." She gave me a little wink, like *Here's your opportunity, knocking.* She went inside, leaving the door open, and ran up the stairs.

Tia stayed. "It's nice out here," she said. "Is Dr. Mack still around?"

"In the study with my mom."

"She gives me the creeps." Tia sat down on a low canvas chair. I could barely see her face, but I noticed a glistening layer of perspiration on her forehead, a remnant of her long bike ride. My fingers itched to test the warmth of her skin. But all I managed to do was pull over another chair and sit next to her.

"Me, too," I said.

"Do you know she's famous?" Tia said.

"I guess. She's got a big-time job."

"But I mean she's *really* famous. She was around when this whole thing began. After Elisha, when the governments were just trying to figure out how to pull everything together and move along, she and a few other women took their ideas everywhere, pointed out what had changed for the positive, talked about how to make that change permanent, planted their philosophies and strategies deep, got them adopted for the long haul."

"Does this have something to do with your new theory?" I said.

"It's not exactly *my* theory. But yes."

"You won't tell me what it is?"

"I should do more research. And the bike ride gave me time with my thoughts, but I should do more thinking, too."

"What if *I* tell *you* something?" I said. "Tia."

Her face turned to me in the shadows. I could smell her— shampoo or soap or something. Not sweat. Whatever, it was light and fragrant and intoxicating. I breathed deep and held it in. "Something important?" she said.

"You decide." I told her the rest of my story—the accidental overhearing, the attic eavesdropping, my conversation with Aunt Paige.

"Your dad's a loner, right?" Her voice was alive.

"Yeah."

"But he's living near a population of throwbacks?"

"Afterlight's the name of the community. On the Olympic Peninsula."

Tia stood. "Your aunt's computer is in her room?"

"Still there. I saw it when the cops came."

"You think your mom's still in the study with Rebecca Mack?"

"I don't think they're coming up for air."

"Let's look." She pulled me from the chair. Her hand was warm.

"What about your theory?" I said as we rushed into the house.

She didn't answer. We cruised past the closed office door slowly enough to decide that Mom and Rebecca Mack were still in there, then climbed the stairs two at a time but quietly.

Tia sat down at Aunt Paige's computer while I paced, one eye on the open doorway, one ear alert to sounds of someone coming our way. I heard voices, but I recognized them as a couple of our housemates whose room was at the end of the hall.

When I got over to the desk, Tia had a screen up, but it was a page of medical records, headed with the photo of a young woman. "Give me a minute," she said. "Your aunt has files everywhere."

She thought a moment, tapping a pencil on the wood surface of the desk, then attacked the touch pad so fast her fingers blurred. In an instant, another screen appeared, but she touched a prompt and jumped to another.

This one was some kind of bulletin. CONFIDENTIAL, it said in bold letters across the top, which made me even more nervous than I already was. I slipped over to the door again, listening and looking, and hurried back to the desk.

"This is what your aunt was talking about," Tia said. "The quarantine advisory."

I crouched down to peer over her shoulder. She didn't move to give me room, so I was forced to get nearer. Which gave me something else to think about.

I speed-read the notice. Tia was right. It was an advisory sent out by the Council to doctors, hospitals, government officials, law enforcement agencies, emergency response teams, the National Guard, the Coast Patrol, all of them based in Washington, Oregon, and British Columbia. "They make it sound like a drill," I said, still reading.

"Your aunt didn't think so."

No. And why would the PAC cops be after her if it were just a drill? I got to the specifics. Nearly the entire peninsula, from the southern tip of Hood Canal north to the Strait of Juan de Fuca, from Puget Sound on the east to the Pacific Ocean on the west, would be quarantined. No traffic of any kind—highway, logging road, trail, ferry, private boat, aircraft—would be allowed in or out for a minimum of two weeks.

"Done?" Tia said.

"Yeah."

She scrolled to the next page. I found what I was looking

for: a date. The "drill" was to be initiated on June 21. Less than two days away. No wonder Aunt Paige was in a hurry.

Tia logged out. "Come on," she said, and I followed her down the hall, relieved to be away from my aunt and mom's room, but not relieved about anything else.

Sunday was sitting on her bed, making faces into her e-spond, when we walked in. Her idea of messaging apparently involved dramatics. "You want me to leave?" she said innocently.

"No," Tia said, not looking at me. We took turns telling Sunday what I'd overheard, what happened with Aunt Paige and the PAC cops, what we found on her computer.

"She went to warn your dad, you think?" Sunday said. Her e-spond was forgotten.

"I know she did," I said. "But I don't see how she'll get to him. They'll be waiting for her. She's driving, and there's really only one road in."

"Maybe she'll leave her car," Tia said.

"And hike?" I said. "She doesn't have time."

"I don't get the whole quarantine idea," Sunday said. "It sounds like they're expecting an outbreak of something contagious and deadly."

I realized I didn't get it, either. Exactly what kind of catastrophe could scientists forecast so confidently?

"Elisha's Bear," Tia said.

"But how can they predict *that*?" I said.

"You wanted to know my theory," Tia said.

In my dreams, you are always alive, and young.
I feel your hands on me.
I awake and curse the morning.

—EPITAPH FOR RAUL "SONNY" SANCHEZ
(APRIL 12, 2023–AUGUST 9, 2067),
BY GUADALUPE SANCHEZ, HIS WIFE,
NOVEMBER 22, 2068

CHAPTER EIGHT

"Both of you were curious," Tia said, moving to her desk, touching her computer to life. Sunday and I hovered. "I wanted to do more research so we'd know for sure, but let me show you what I've found so far."

"When did you come up with this?" I said.

"While we were still in Nebraska we had a teacher—remember Hernandez, Sunday?—who encouraged independent study. And I found some stuff doing a PE history project that just seemed too neat and coincidental. I didn't know what to do about it, though. I just kind of let it go.

"Then today in class the San Francisco video and discussion stirred up my interest again. Not the information itself, so much, but the fact that Anderson was so into it. And when I looked at our take-home—the junkyarddog stuff—I got the impression she was trying to tell us some-thing important."

I felt like asking a million questions, but I didn't want to risk looking dumber than I already felt.

Tia turned to face her computer display, where excerpts from that day's take-home—excerpts I hadn't yet read—suddenly appeared. "Did you look at the whole lesson?" she asked me.

"No," I admitted. "Half, maybe. My brain got full."

"Where did you leave off?" Sunday asked.

"We'd just invaded Mexico. But I've got the whole thing printed out. Hold on."

I raced down the hall and back. When I returned I had the printout in my hand. I liked having an assignment on paper. I liked looking at it, folding it up, sticking it in my pocket, carrying it around, unfolding it whenever I wanted. It was the book thing, all over again. Maybe I really *was* a throwback.

But Tia wasn't impressed. She stayed focused on her monitor. "You stopped right before it got interesting," she said to me. She scrolled up and stopped at an entry while I found it on my printout. Sunday crowded in close. Whatever we were looking for, she must have missed its significance the first time.

MAY 12, 2061, JUNKYARDDOG.BITES—MCDONALD'S CORPORA-TION REPORTS TO ITS STOCKHOLDERS THAT THE COMPANY NOW HAS A PRESENCE IN EVERY COUNTRY IN THE WORLD, WITH A

TOTAL NUMBER OF 59,886 RESTAURANTS. NOT TO BE OUTDONE, STARBUCKS CLAIMS MORE TOTAL CUSTOMERS.

FEBRUARY 12, 2062, JUNKYARDDOG.BITES—EARLY THIS WEEK, POACHERS WERE INTERCEPTED TRANSPORTING NEARLY A THOUSAND MALE NORTHERN OWL MONKEYS (*AOTUS TRIVIRGATUS*) FROM VENEZUELA TO A LARGE LABORATORY ON GRAND CAYMAN ISLAND, NOW MOSTLY DESERTED BECAUSE OF OCEAN ENCROACHMENT. A SPOKESWOMAN FOR THE LAB CONTENDS SHE WAS UNAWARE OF THE POACHING, AND THAT THE LAB, AN ARM OF AN ORGANIZATION CALLED BRIGHTER DAY, IS INVOLVED IN VALUABLE RESEARCH ON A VARIETY OF ACUTE, INFECTIOUS, AND HEREDITARY DISEASES, SUCH AS INTERSTITIAL PNEUMONIA, MYOCARDITIS, LEGIONNAIRES' DISEASE, EBOLA VIRUS, AND HEMOPHILIA.

BADAKHSHAN PROVINCE, AFGHANISTAN, APRIL 17, 2067, JUNKYARDDOG.BITES—A REMOTE VILLAGE OF 354 PEOPLE IN THIS POPPY-GROWING REGION REPORTS THAT OVER A PERIOD OF TWO DAYS, ITS ENTIRE MALE POPULATION DIED OF APPARENT CARDIORESPIRATORY FAILURE. AN UNEXPLAINED CORRELATION TO DRUGS IS SUSPECTED.

BADAKHSHAN PROVINCE, AFGHANISTAN, APRIL 21, 2067, JUNKYARDDOG.BITES—THREE MALE WORLD HEALTH ORGANIZATION RESEARCHERS SENT TO THE VILLAGE TO INVESTIGATE THE DEATHS DIED WITHIN A DAY OF ARRIVING. TWO ACCOMPANYING FEMALES ARE HEALTHY AND ATTEMPTING TO ISOLATE THE CAUSE OF THE DEATHS, ALTHOUGH A COMMON WELL IS SUSPECTED AS THE INI-

TIAL SOURCE OF THE MYSTERIOUS BUG OR TOXIN. THE AREA HAS
BEEN QUARANTINED INDEFINITELY.

ISLAND OF NUKAPU, SOLOMON ISLANDS, JULY 5, 2067, JUNKYARD-
DOG.BITES—A FEMALE ELDER ARRIVES BY BOAT FROM REMOTE
PUERTO VERDE ISLAND TO REPORT THAT THE MALES ON HER
ISLAND AWOKE HEALTHY ON JULY 4, BUT BY NIGHTFALL ALL 223
OF THEM WERE DEAD. "DAYLIGHT TOOK THEIR BREATH AWAY,"
SHE SAYS.

I suddenly realized I wasn't breathing. I was cold, even
though the bedroom was sticky-warm. I didn't know where
this was going, exactly, but I knew it was somewhere dark
and suffocating.

PUERTO VERDE ISLAND, JULY 7, 2067, JUNKYARDDOG.BITES—
A TEAM OF WOMEN INVESTIGATORS ARRIVES AT THE ISLAND TO
DELVE INTO THE CAUSE OF THE DEATHS. AFGHANISTAN DEATHS
STILL UNRESOLVED.

PUERTO VERDE ISLAND, JULY 10, 2067, JUNKYARDDOG.BITES—
FEMALE ELDER REPORTS THAT ON THE DAY BEFORE THE DEATHS
(JULY 3), A LONE EUROPEAN WOMAN DOCKED HER SMALL SAIL-
BOAT IN THE ISLAND'S HARBOR. SHE DEPARTED EARLY IN THE A.M.
OF JULY 4.

BADAKHSHAN PROVINCE, AFGHANISTAN, JULY 12, 2067, JUNK-
YARDDOG.BITES—A VILLAGER REMEMBERS TWO STRANGERS—

WOMEN WEARING TRADITIONAL DRESS—STOPPING FOR WATER ON APRIL 14, THE DAY BEFORE THE DEATHS BEGAN. RESEARCHERS REPORT NO SIGN OF POISON OR CONTAMINATION IN WATER SUPPLY OR BODIES.

NEW YORK, JULY 16, 2067, JUNKYARDDOG.BITES—SOFT DRINK GIANT COCA-COLA ANNOUNCES THAT ITS NEWEST SPORTS ENERGY DRINK, STUDFAST, WILL BE INTRODUCED TO CONSUMERS IN A HUGE MARKETING BLITZ THREE WEEKS FROM TODAY. REPRESENTATIVES OF COCA-COLA'S MERCHANDISING PARTNER, GLOBAL PERSPECTIVES, WILL DISTRIBUTE TRIAL SIZES OF THE DRINK AT BASEBALL AND SOCCER GAMES, GOLF AND TENNIS TOURNAMENTS, AUTO AND HORSE RACES, AND OTHER HIGH-PROFILE SPORTING EVENTS TAKING PLACE WORLDWIDE ON AUGUST 6. IN THE UNITED STATES ALONE, FIVE MILLION FREE SAMPLES WILL BE HANDED OUT.

JULY 23, 2067, JUNKYARDDOG.BITES—SECRET DOCUMENTS AND SOURCES INDICATE THAT A CLANDESTINE OFFSHORE ACCOUNT TRACED TO PRESIDENT RAMSEY HAS RECEIVED A BILLION-DOLLAR DEPOSIT THROUGH SERPENTINE CHANNELS LEADING BACK TO THE CHINESE GOVERNMENT. THE PURPOSE: TO BUY HIS EFFORTS TO PUSH THROUGH TRADE AGREEMENTS FAVORABLE TO THE CHINESE AND DEVASTATING TO THE U.S. WORKER.

JULY 24, 2067, JUNKYARDDOG.BITES—IN A SWEEPING SERIES OF ARRESTS TODAY, THE DEPARTMENT OF HOMELAND INTEGRITY TOOK INTO CUSTODY JUNKYARDDOG BLOGGERS JILL AND BETSY COWAN

AND THEIR FULL-TIME STAFF OF RESEARCHERS AND WRITERS. THE COWAN SISTERS, FOUNDERS OF JUNKYARDDOG.BITES, A LONG-ESTABLISHED GOVERNMENT, BUSINESS, AND ENVIRONMENTAL WATCHDOG WEBSITE, HAD RECENTLY UNCOVERED AND POSTED A—

"Two weeks later, Elisha struck," Tia said. "That's a fact. It's history. But why did Anderson choose to show us these events leading up to it? I began checking into it when we were at the library. I couldn't figure out what McDonald's and Starbucks had to do with it, so I started with the lab on Grand Cayman—the Brighter Day facility—and the story about the male monkeys. I dug into old records from Brighter Day that showed its statement of purpose, organizational chart, and rosters of employees."

She touched the screen and a display of photos and names appeared. The heading read BOARD OF DIRECTORS, 2065. Which was when men still walked the earth in large numbers, before they'd become dinosaurs.

But everyone on the Brighter Day board of directors was a woman.

And in the middle of the top row was a remotely familiar face and immediately familiar name: Rebecca Mack, M.D., Ph.D.

"Dr. Mack," Sunday said. "Oh, crap. *Dr. Mack.*"

"Check out the second row," Tia said.

I did. I didn't recognize any of the photos, but at the far right, under the picture of a middle-aged, attractive woman, was another familiar name, one from the history books.

Candace Bloom, the fifty-fourth president of the United States. The secretary of state when Elisha hit, she quickly assumed the presidency.

I'd been holding my breath. Now I whistled it out. A worldwide conspiracy. A real one, not some corncob–pipe dream of raving lunatics.

Rebecca Mack and Candace Bloom. Together. With their secret lab and male monkeys and diseases. "Why?" I said, half to myself.

"Keep reading," Tia said.

Sweat started building on the back of my neck as thoughts swirled inside my head and Tia paged to a bio on Rebecca Mack. A leading authority on viral and bacterial illness, contagious disease, respiratory and cardiac disease, hemophilia, muscular dystrophy, Huntington's chorea, and other gender-linked and chromosomal-based diseases, Mack was a world-renowned epidemiologist and research superstar. "The brilliant researcher with a troubled past," was how one Paris news site described her.

I didn't have long to wonder about her troubled past. Tia's next screen showed an article from the *Seattle Times E-dition* dated April 12, 2035. No photo, but the story covered the outcome of Rebecca Mack's trial in juvenile court: a manslaughter conviction for killing her mother's abusive boyfriend, the man responsible for her mother's death. Rebecca's sentence: three years in the Hillside Correctional Facility for Girls.

"So have you guessed my theory yet?" Tia said.

"Brighter Day caused Elisha," Sunday said. "Rebecca

Mack. The witch went over the edge. She—they—found a way to kill men."

"Males," I said. "Almost all males." A sensation rose in my stomach, like I was going to vomit. I could taste dinner souring just below the back of my throat. I felt duped, half destroyed.

Mack the Knife and Candace Bloom.

My mother. My mother was a part of this.

I was so stupid. Why hadn't I picked up on these clues? The whole idea—the plotting, the execution—was horrible, outlandish, unbelievable. But I believed it.

Elisha's Bear hadn't shown up on its own. PAC wasn't the result of accidental opportunity. Women weren't our benevolent custodians.

My mother wasn't my guardian angel. My mother wasn't even my friend.

My mother was too young to have been involved in big Elisha, but she was involved now. My mother was my enemy.

Tia put her hand on my forearm. "I'm sorry, Kellen," she said.

"It wasn't you," I managed, but right now I felt angry and betrayed. My mother was one thing, but another woman—someone I'd met—had wiped out half my family, without blinking. Half of humanity.

And she was still free, treated like some kind of hero. How many other people had suspicions about her role in the plague?

It's a theory, I told myself, *a kid's theory.* But I couldn't force myself to disbelieve it now. Anderson wasn't a kid. She believed it enough to point us in the direction of this stuff. Before this frightful chilling moment, I simply wasn't tuned in.

"McDonald's and Starbucks," I said. "And the Studfast samples. It was how they distributed the bug, wasn't it?"

"I think so," Tia said. "Mostly, anyway. They could have used other chain restaurants and stores, too, or put it in the mail, sent it on planes, trucks, trains. They could have had women or unsuspecting men carry it into more isolated places. Like the Afghanistan and Puerto Verde Island occurrences. They wanted to test it out somewhere remote first to be sure it worked."

"Why?" I asked again.

"Anderson gave us the clues," Sunday said. "All the cruelty and destruction and chaos in the world. Mostly because of men."

"*Some* men," I said. "What about all the *good* men? What about the *babies*?"

"There's no excuse for Brighter Day," Tia said. "Or PAC. Or whatever Rebecca Mack is up to now."

Rebecca Mack, the savior of the planet. The monster. Downstairs. *In our house. With Mom.* Cooking up the next "epidemic," I realized. Plotting how to capture Aunt Paige. "They're getting ready to do it again," I said. "My aunt figured it out. She figured out that my dad's in trouble."

"Why the Olympic Peninsula?" Sunday asked.

"I don't know," Tia said. "There's a group of throwbacks over there, but there are throwbacks scattered all over the world."

Suddenly, I remembered my history. It jumped out at me like it hadn't before. "Three throwback colonies have been hit in the past," I said. "Three strong ones, trying to flex some muscle. Elisha returned there. Except for a few women and girls, the settlements were wiped out."

"You're right," Tia said. "I wonder how many people made the connection." She got to a website that discussed the 2081 outbreak of Elisha in northern Europe, in the state of Sweden. We read along with her. The male inhabitants of a large village secretly formed a totalitarian government, kidnapped and abused women and girls from surrounding communities, began to arm themselves, talked of rebellion and assassinations. Which is when Elisha resurfaced. The violent crime and rhetoric died with the men.

"I think we've learned enough to know what's happening next," I said. "And now I have to find my dad."

Sometimes, now that late autumn's outstretched shadows
and first snowfall have sugarcoated the bitter landscape of reality,
now that bare dogwood branches tick against the front window
like small knuckles, I imagine you on the porch steps,
bouncing on the soft soles of your sneakers,
Dr. Seuss in your hand, a joyous smile on your face,
waiting for me to answer your home-from-school knock.
Sometimes I go to the door, just in case.

—EPITAPH FOR BASAAM AZIZ (MARCH 3, 2059–AUGUST 11, 2067),
BY HIS MOTHER, LATEEFA AZIZ,
NOVEMBER 27, 2068

CHAPTER NINE

Aunt Paige picked up on the first ring. "I can't talk to you, Kellen," she said.

I listened for background noise, clues to where she was. "I know what you're doing," I said. Tia and Sunday sat up and stared at me. "Tia figured out everything. *Everything.*"

"I love you, Kellen," Aunt Paige said. "Your dad loves you. Stay put." The connection died.

Your dad. Was she with him?

"Where is she?" Tia asked me.

"She cut me off before I could ask."

"They ain't got her yet," Sunday said. "She still has a chance."

"Yeah," I said, but I didn't like the odds. Unless she eluded the pack of dogs chasing her and got to Dad in a hurry, Elisha most likely would come looking for him. And regardless of what happened with Dad, what would they do to her when they eventually tracked her down?

I stood up and zombie-walked to the window. Up and down the street, lamplight glowed from the opposing rows of old two- and three-story homes. Even in this supposedly desirable neighborhood, though, some houses had stood vacant and deteriorating for decades or been torn down completely. Thirty years ago, the Bear had made quick work of their male occupants and sent their female tenants packing. They'd downsized to apartments or moved in with relatives or found rooms, support, and companionship in big houses like ours.

When I was seven or eight, Aunt Paige took me to an Oregon beach, where we discovered a gray whale, dead on the sand, swarmed by gulls and crows. Its plate-sized eyes were crusted over and vacant. The empty decaying houses on our street and elsewhere reminded me of that poor whale.

A woman jogged alone down the sidewalk, ghosting from one pool of light to the next, wearing skin-tight shorts and a workout bra and a carefree expression. Her long dark hair rippled and shone as she moved.

What would she be wearing if men were still around in big numbers? I wondered. *Where would she be? Home, with her treadmill and dead bolts and alarms?*

I opened the window wide and drank in the cooling night air. In the quiet of the neighborhood, I could hear the runner's footfalls. I imagined she was leading a flock of other runners across the finish line of a marathon. I clapped for her, softly I thought, but she looked up at me and smiled and waved and continued on.

No fears.

I glanced at my watch. Just after eleven. After curfew. Without Minders, I wasn't allowed to go out for a run—or anything else—at this hour.

"Aunt Paige told me to stay put," I said, my back still to the girls. I wanted a second opinion, and something told me I could trust them.

"You *have to*," Tia said. "If you try to go to him, you could *both* die."

Not the second opinion I wanted. "Not if I leave tonight. It's not that far. A quick ride to the ferry, a half hour on the boat, a few more hours on my bike."

"How many hours?" Sunday said, giving me a little encouragement.

I tried to picture maps I'd seen. "I'd have to check."

"You might not even *need* to go," Sunday said, withdrawing her support.

"Sunday's right," Tia said. "Your aunt might get through. She might already be with your dad."

"By the time we know, it could be too late," I said.

"I think we'll know soon," Tia said. "Let's go down and see if we can pick up any vibrations."

"In a minute," I said. I was pretty sure I knew the big answers to the *Why?* question, but something was still missing for me. I got up and started for Tia's computer, but my e-spond sounded off. Without checking the display, I answered it, thinking it was Aunt Paige.

"Kellen?" a nervous voice said.

"Ernie?"

"They got Anderson," he said in a half whisper.

"Anderson? Who got her?" Tia and Sunday eyed me, full bore.

"PAC cops. They came to the house a few minutes ago and took her away."

"Where?"

"I don't know. I just wanted to tell you. My mom says she must have done something bad. But I don't think so."

I again recalled Mom referring to Anderson as "unconventional" during our "visit" of a few days ago. Was Anderson already on the PAC hit list then? Did they think she knew too much? "I don't think so, either, Ernie," I said. "Maybe they just want to talk to her."

"Maybe. I'll watch for her."

"You do that," I said. "Let me know if she shows up."

"Okay."

"Thanks for calling me."

We disconnected. "PAC cops arrested Anderson," I told the girls, in case they hadn't already figured that out.

"Because of what she gave us?" Tia said.

I shrugged. "Ernie doesn't know. He just knows they got her." Under a cloud of worry now, I continued on to Tia's

105

computer and touched in the years 2034 and 2035 and the name Rebecca Mack.

An instant later, the screen filled with references, mostly online news stories. I saw the *Seattle Times E-dition* article from April 12, 2035, but I wanted earlier stuff. What had come before the conviction? I sensed Tia and Sunday hanging close as I scrolled to the top of the list.

The earliest mention of Rebecca (Becky) Mack, age fourteen, was a *Seattle Times* story of her arrest on September 29, 2034, for the killing of a man named Chet Durbin. According to the article, Chet Durbin was Becky's mother's live-in boyfriend. A few days later, the *Times* ran a story in which neighbors related a history of domestic disturbances in the house.

Because Becky was a juvenile at the time, little emerged from the trial itself. I was about to give it up when I noticed a junkyarddog item on her from May 16, 2035, which was after she began serving her sentence.

The interview with Becky Mack, on the grounds of the Hillside Correctional Facility for Girls, revealed Chet Durbin's long-standing and continual physical abuse of Becky's mother and sexual abuse of Becky. According to the article, Becky's mother, although battered herself, didn't believe the sexual abuse was happening.

AT THE END OF OUR INTERVIEW, BECKY MACK, HOLDING HER TAT-
TERED BUT OBVIOUSLY BELOVED BIOLOGY TEXTBOOK ON HER LAP
LIKE A FAVORITE TEDDY BEAR, POINTED OUT TO ME A HERD OF

TWO DOZEN OR SO DAIRY CATTLE IN A GREEN FIELD BEYOND THE RAZOR-WIRE FENCES OF HILLSIDE. "THE COWS LOOK CONTENTED, DON'T THEY," SHE SAID WISTFULLY, AND I AGREED. "AND SAFE," SHE ADDED. SHE NODDED IN THE DIRECTION OF A LONE BULL, A HUNDRED YARDS AWAY FROM THE REST OF THE HERD, MUSCLED AND MENACING BUT NOSE-CHAINED TO A THICK POST. "THAT'S BECAUSE THEY LIKE THE ODDS. AND THEY KNOW EXACTLY WHERE HE IS. AND WHERE HE'LL STAY."

Rebecca Mack had had the seeds of Elisha's Bear growing in her when she was no older than I was now. And in a weird way, I understood why. As far as I could tell, she'd never received anything but suffering at the hands of men.

I eased back on my concentration and noticed the girls again, still shadowing me, the ins and outs of their breath and little else. "Let's go downstairs," I said.

In the living room I checked my watch: 11:30, and there was still an old lady in the office. Shouldn't she have been in bed by now? I kept listening for something, one eye on the office door.

But it was the front door that got my attention. Someone rapped, and I jumped up and scrambled to it with Tia and Sunday on my heels. When I opened it, the two PAC cops stood there. They looked much less concerned than the last time I'd seen them. They were almost glowing.

A bad sign.

"Dr. Mack still up?" Stoudt said.

"I think so." I stepped aside so they could come in. "She's probably in the study."

"Did you find Paige Winters?" Sunday blurted out, brassy as usual.

"We need to talk to *Dr. Mack*," Blevens said. By now they knew where the study was. They pushed past us and headed in that direction. We followed, but not so close that we were too obvious.

They knocked. Mom came to the door, then Rebecca Mack. We heard them more than saw them.

"We got her, Dr. Mack," Stoudt said. "She didn't take a ferry. She was driving around the long way, but we nabbed her at a roadblock before she even got in the vicinity."

We? Stoudt was taking a share of the credit, but her wide rear was nowhere near that roadblock when Aunt Paige was arrested. I was in no mood for this overzealous kiss-ass cop. A moment ago I'd been halfway pumped up with hope, but suddenly I felt deflated.

"Where is she now?" Rebecca Mack demanded.

"In custody, ma'am," Blevens said. "On her way to the Seattle office for confinement." I pictured Aunt Paige, in the back of a PAC car speeding down a dark peninsula highway, her hands cuffed behind her back.

"Tell them to keep her there," Dr. Mack said. "No visitors. No communication."

As I started for the stairs, I looked just past Rebecca Mack and saw Mom standing in the doorway of the study. She was giving me this sad-eyed apologetic look, but I didn't swallow it. She'd chosen to be a part of this. She'd chosen to track down Aunt Paige as if she were a criminal. She'd chosen to condemn Dad to his death. I looked through her and away and hurried to my room.

I'd been at my desk for two minutes, searching the Net for maps of the peninsula, when Sunday and Tia pushed open my door and walked in.

"You haven't heard of knocking?" I said.

"What are you gonna do?" Sunday said.

I didn't answer, but it was too late to clear the map from the display.

"You can't go," Tia said.

"I have to," I said. "He'll be dead if I don't."

"He's a loner," Tia said. "He doesn't hang around the throwbacks that much, does he?"

"Not unless he has to. But there's a reason the whole peninsula is being quarantined. You think the Bear will stop with just the throwbacks?"

Someone knocked at the door. I blanked the screen and stood. "Who is it?"

Mom came in with a big green duffel bag, empty. She saw Tia and Sunday standing by the desk and dropped the bag on the floor. Opened her mouth, shut it, opened it again, eyeing me, the girls, me. She had something to say, but she was holding off. Maybe she hadn't expected an audience. Maybe she would have preferred not to have one. But Tia and Sunday didn't volunteer to leave the room.

"No school tomorrow, Kellen," Mom said finally. "I've

already called and let the administrator know you'll be absent. She's sending me your take-homes for the next twenty lessons.

"In the morning you'll get up at the usual time, but instead of jumping on your bike and heading off to class, you'll be going on a little trip. Before you go to bed tonight, you'll need to pack clothes and whatever else you want to take—enough for three weeks—in this bag. Have it and yourself downstairs by eight thirty. A PAC van will be curbside to pick you up."

She said it like it was all decided. Like I had no voice, no choice. "Why?" I asked.

"I want you away from the city for a while," she said.

"That's not a reason."

"There are signs of a recurrence in this area," she said. "Elisha's Bear."

"Signs?" I said, knowing it was all bullshit. "I didn't know Elisha posted signs."

"I wouldn't have you go otherwise."

"Go where?"

"Montana."

"By myself?"

"You'll be accompanied by other boys and some women. You'll be back in Seattle in three weeks. It won't be so bad."

I wanted to argue, tell her what I knew, but what was the point? I'd just make her suspicious and watchful, and I didn't need that. I was going on a trip, but I wasn't waiting for the PAC van, and I wasn't going to Montana. "Eight thirty?" I said.

She smiled a little. "Yes."

"Three weeks without Anderson," I said, dangling the name in front of Mom, wondering how much she had to do with the arrest. "Sounds like heaven to me."

Mom's smile got a little less tentative, a little wider. "I'll see you in the morning," she said, not taking the bait, and backed out the door, closing it behind her.

"Boys are good liars," Sunday said.

"It's what got us in trouble," I said.

"You *go* to Montana," Tia said. "We'll go warn your dad."

"By yourselves? You'll get caught. You'll end up behind bars with Aunt Paige."

"Why would they suspect us?" Sunday asked.

"Guilt by association," I said. "If you go missing, even without me, they'll know where you went."

"*We* won't *die*," Sunday said.

"If Elisha returns in the middle of this rescue attempt," Tia said, "we'll be safe. You won't."

"I'm *going*," I said. "Just don't get in my way. And don't say anything."

"We'll go with you, then," Tia said. "You'd be under suspicion, a boy traveling by himself. A cop magnet."

"And if you're thinking about a girl-disguise," Sunday said, "forget it. You couldn't pull it off."

I figured Sunday was right, but I knew Tia was right, too.

A lone male pedaling away from the city on a bike—even in daylight—would be a lure for the wrong kind of fish—local authorities or state cops or PAC enforcers. Sharks. Predators. Then what? "Why would you? You barely know me."

"We know you well enough," Tia said. "We know what happened to you." She gave me a look, like *Why argue?*

"Okay," I said. "If you also know what you're getting yourselves into." I was sure they didn't, because I didn't know myself, and getting them into this made me feel guilty. But I needed to go. I needed to get to Dad. And the girls were my ticket.

"We know," Sunday said, and I didn't argue with her. My thoughts had shifted to Mom. She wanted to protect me, but what about everyone else? What about Dad?

"You have a plan?" Tia said.

A plan. The pieces of a plan were rattling around in my head along with all the other stuff, but I—we—needed to sort them out and glue them together. I chose a bed and sat. Tia and Sunday bookended me, Tia closer than Sunday. I began to put the pieces into words.

A new basketball — real leather — in my hands, and Reverend King,
stringing up a fresh net on his driveway hoop, waving me over.

—Last words and epitaph of Lonzell Parker
(April 25, 2054–August 10, 2067),
describing what he could see,
by Patricia Parker, his mother,
November 30, 2068

Chapter Ten

I was still awake when my e-spond chirped to life at one thirty. I tapped it off and sat up. A tangle of nagging thoughts had kept me from sleep. Was PAC really going to wipe out Afterlight and who knew what else? Why? What was Rebecca Mack so worried about? Could we—three kids—do something about it?

I didn't want to do anything dramatic. I wasn't enough of a kid to think we could. I just wanted to get Dad out of there.

The house sat quiet. No sounds came through my open window. Streetlights barely made a dent in the darkness.

My door swung open as I put my feet on the floor. The shadowy shapes of Tia and Sunday drifted in. We said nothing. We'd talked all this out. I grabbed my shoes and backpack and joined them. Together we moved out into the hall and down the stairs. In the kitchen we pulled stuff from shelves and the fridge—not enough to raise instant suspicion—and loaded it into our packs.

Outside, nothing moved. We stood over our bikes in a crease of dark between circles of muted lamplight and murmured to each other, checking to make sure we had everything. Then we were off on the bike trail to downtown.

"Time?" Sunday grunted after a few miles of quiet.

I glanced over. Her long blond hair streamed behind her like exhaust. I checked my watch in the next pool of light. "Almost two. We've got a half hour."

Soon, downtown high-rises towered in front of us, their lights reflecting off the surface of Lake Union. We got to the ferry terminal with ten minutes to spare. The rich salty smell of the Sound tugged at my memories—adventures on *Mr. Lucky*, trips with Mom and Aunt Paige. The big blue ferry—not nearly full—was still loading. At the ticket booth we paid our money to a young woman who seemed more interested in her psychology textbook than in us, and then rode onto the ferry, faking casualness.

We parked our bikes in racks near the bow. Most drivers stayed in their cars, dozing, setting their mental alarm clocks for a half hour, the length of the trip. But we headed topside, where more passengers sat in various stages of stupor, heads down on tabletops or bowed into a book or newspaper. Even half conscious, some of the women eyed me suspiciously. I was thankful Sunday and Tia stayed close, not leaving who was in charge of my care and feeding open to question.

We sat by a window. "Three more hours once we dock?" Tia said.

"If everything clicks," I said. "Barring roadblocks and whatever else."

"If we have to go around roadblocks," Sunday said, "it could double our travel time."

"Which means the house will be awake," I said. "Mom and Rebecca Mack will know I'm—we're—gone. They'll know where we went. They'll have Dad cordoned off like a murder scene." I felt my positive attitude falter. Now that we were actually on our way, it was impossible not to worry about roadblocks, the discovery of our absence from the house, PAC cops—*every* kind of cop—on the lookout for us.

"We can't stress about it," Tia said. "We just have to do our best. We have to try, and then we have to get out—get *you* out, Kellen, at least—before tonight. June twenty-first starts at midnight."

"What if they move it up?" Sunday said.

"I don't think three kids are going to make them change their whole plan," I said. "They might not even *be able* to change it."

"The virus or whatever it is has to be on hand," Tia said. "Someone has to be ready to bring it in and plant it wherever they plan on planting it."

"No Starbucks in the hinterlands," I said. "No McDonald's."

"It's a small population," Sunday said. "Judging by what

115

we know about big Elisha, it ain't gonna take much to set the epidemic in motion."

She was right. A few disease-toting "tourists" wandering into peninsula villages, onto the piers where live-aboard boats were moored, would do the trick.

We were the first ones off the ferry. As we moved out, traffic passed us from behind, a steady parade of music and sound effects and tires on pavement. Then we were all alone in the dark, shifting down as we began an uphill piece of road.

We followed the highway north and west across the island through tall stands of trees on either side. We didn't say much, but it felt good having Tia and Sunday near, knowing it was their choice.

Eventually, we approached the bridge that would carry us off the west side of the island and over Eagle Pass. We'd half expected a roadblock here; a gateway to the peninsula seemed like the logical spot for one. But the road was clear.

We scooted onto the bridge, tussling with the grating under our wheels. When we reached the other side, the girls pulled over onto the shoulder. "Break," Sunday said, and although I didn't admit it, I was glad. We all took out water bottles and drank thirstily.

I checked my watch. "Almost three thirty. I think we're on schedule."

"Four hours or so until they start listening for signs of us," Tia said.

"Until the net gets cast," Sunday said.

Motivated by those chilling thoughts, we got back on the road. Everything was going smoothly until we entered a long curve to our right and noticed light filtering through the trees.

We hid our bikes and backpacks and proceeded on foot. I led the way into the underbrush, taking a shortcut to what I hoped was a safe vantage point. My eyes were used to the dark by now, but it was still hard to see and tough to keep from stepping on dry twigs, tripping over downed branches and stubborn shrubs, and making noise.

The lights brightened. Some of them flashed, sending weird diffused rays of red and blue into the trees. I heard women's voices. Half crouching, we crept to the edge of the forest, hid behind thick rough-barked trunks, and peered out.

We'd found our roadblock.

Two state police cars were angled halfway across the highway, their noses just far enough apart to form one narrow lane. Their roof lights were on, spinning. Another car, a plain sedan with the familiar giant-woman, midget-man insignia on the door, was parked on the shoulder. To the west of the police cruisers, two state troopers stood, flashlights in hand, pistols holstered. So far. To the east were two other troopers. Two PAC cops paced the pavement. They were all women, but their intuition wasn't working. None of them looked in our direction.

Next to me, Tia breathed—slow, shallow, almost silent. I forced myself to exhale. Inhale. Rich dank smells rose from the crushed plants at our feet.

A car approached from the west. The state cops waved it down. The PAC cops strolled over, examined the driver's papers, had a discussion, and backed away. The state cops motioned the driver—a woman—through. It wasn't a full quarantine.

Elisha hadn't been unleashed.

"Let's get moving," Sunday whispered, and we did.

We collected our backpacks and bikes and struggled back through the woods and out, well beyond the roadblock, unnoticed. We pedaled away, not wasting our breath on talk. I left my hood up, trying to be inconspicuous. A few cars passed, going our direction, then a couple moving the other way, toward the roadblock.

We arrived at the Hood Canal Bridge. No roadblocks, but behind us the sky was lightening. I checked my watch. "It's almost five," I said, and without discussing it, we picked up our pace, flying across the long, floating span. The dark water, stirred up by a northern wind, smelled of salt and sea life.

A half hour later we reached Highway 101, the route to the remains of Port Angeles, to the settlement of Afterlight. We stopped and slipped off into the woods for a pee break and out again for water, cheese, apples, and more pedaling.

At almost six o'clock, a car came up behind us and slowed. Fake engine sounds disrupted the quiet. Headlights illuminated the still-shadowy road in front of us. We went into single file, the girls in front, to let it pass. But it didn't.

Lack of sleep had caught up with me. I felt myself getting

irritated, and I turned to stare down the offending driver. But as I did, the car pulled parallel to us, and the passenger motioned us to the shoulder.

A familiar logo—big woman and tiny man—decorated the car door.

We stopped. My heart pounded. I put on my innocent look, hoping we could remember our story and tell it with a straight face.

The PAC-sters got out. They were both youngish, but they looked dowdy in their dumpy, drab, retro uniforms. The driver clicked on a flashlight, even though the sun was nearly up behind the trees and I could read the words on her name tag from fifteen feet: CLARK, MONITOR. The other one was Bellows; she was an INVESTIGATOR.

Clark shone the flashlight in my face. "Going somewhere, throwback?"

"I'm not a throwback."

Clark and Bellows exchanged a smirk. "ID?" Bellows said, fingering the handcuffs that stared hungrily up from her leather belt.

I handed over my card. She slipped it into her pocket scanner and studied the screen. "Seattle?" she said. "How'd you get through the roadblocks?"

"Roadblocks?" Sunday said. "We've been over here since Tuesday."

"We're visiting Kellen's dad," Tia said. "Our uncle Charlie. We're just taking a ride while he's out fishing."

"He's a throwback?" Clark said. "At Afterlight?"

"A loner," I said. "His boat's moored near Afterlight."

"You're Kellen's Minders?" Bellows said, eyeing Tia, then Sunday.

They nodded.

"ID and credentials?" Bellows said. She gave my card back to me and took two each from Tia and Sunday. Again, she slid them through her scanner and studied her screen. Birds were awake now, greeting the morning. Cars passed occasionally, their drivers giving us curious looks.

"Your Minders' credentials are in order," Bellows said finally. "But you're a long way from Nebraska." She returned the cards to Tia and Sunday.

"We're visiting," Tia said.

"How much longer on the Peninsula?" Clark said.

"Just until tonight or tomorrow," I said.

"Good luck on that," Bellows said. "There's a quarantine drill in the works. There may be more roadblocks going up ahead of you. If you get stopped, give them this." She wrote something on a stiff paper form and handed it to Sunday.

The cops got in their car, made a U-turn, and headed off.

"We did okay," Tia said as we climbed back on our bikes and wobbled away.

"I guess nobody's sounded an alarm yet," I said.

"But now they know who we are," Sunday said. "And where to find us."

We accelerated. We were running out of time.

What color did you see last?
The melancholy blue of afternoon sky?
The jelled-puke beige of a cinder-block wall?
Prison isn't a place to die.
I'll miss you, Mikey, shortcomings and all.

—EPITAPH FOR MICHAEL BALDERSON
(JUNE 12, 2048–AUGUST 10, 2067),
BY KAREN BALDERSON, HIS FAVORITE (AND ONLY) KID SISTER,
DECEMBER 3, 2068

CHAPTER ELEVEN

We kept moving. Here the highway was once divided into separate belts of two-lane concrete. But what had been the eastbound lanes was now in ruins. Its surface was heaved up and fractured, and vegetation—everything from dandelions to blackberry bushes to forty-foot-tall alders and firs—reached skyward through the jagged, widening cracks. The westbound lanes accommodated two-way traffic with no worries of congestion. On both sides of the old thoroughfare, abandoned buildings shed layers of paint and façade as they crumbled and settled and faded into the backdrop of greens and browns.

Nature, resurrected.

As time moved us deeper into morning, we came across travelers—all men and boys—on bikes and motor scooters and muscle-scooters and skateboards and skates. Bare-bones transportation. If these guys cared about status, they must have looked for it in intangibles. Most of them waved to us as they passed. Our brothers. I thought again about the Fratheists, gliding along in their flowing crimson robes, treating me like I was someone special.

We were getting close, but we were closer to seven o'clock. We sped downhill and around a curve and in front of us, too late, we saw another roadblock. Four sets of eyes took us in as we kept pedaling.

"What if they know?" Tia said without moving her lips.

"Cross your fingers," Sunday said.

We braked to a stop. I took it as a good sign that they hadn't jumped us and put us in handcuffs yet. Sunday handed the free pass to a PAC cop, a tall, square-jawed woman with friendly eyes. She looked over the form, me, Tia and Sunday, me again.

"Trials soon, Kellen?" she asked, handing the paper to her partner.

"Three months," I said.

"You studying hard?"

"Night and day."

"You Dr. Dent's—Heather Dent's—son?" the other cop asked. She was older, shorter, and had eyes like a cod—round and cold and emotionless. And, suddenly, I was sure we'd had it. All the congeniality had just been preliminary crap.

"Yeah," I said casually. I looked for an escape route. Could I make a break for it? Crash off into the woods? I didn't think they'd shoot me. I could maybe get the rest of the way to Dad by foot.

"I met her once," fish eyes said. Her name tag read PELLEUR, INVESTIGATOR. "She gave a talk to a group of us a while ago. A smart woman."

"Kellen's smart, too," Tia said. "He's going to ace his trials."

"Wonderful," the tall one—MILNE, INVESTIGATOR—said. "Then you won't have to bother these young women to escort you around anymore."

"We don't mind," Sunday said. "He's our cousin."

"That's generous," Milne said. "But I'm sure you have better things to do." She handed the form back to Sunday and gestured for us to continue on.

The pleasantries were genuine after all. But I kept my mouth shut. Better to keep a low profile. I'd been dislodged from the conversation anyway. And we'd been dismissed. We mounted our bikes and moved out. "Study hard," Pelleur said to our backs. "All of you."

Another close call had given us a little rest. But how much longer before Mom discovered we were gone and every cop on the peninsula knew? The adrenaline came roaring back. I had no problem keeping up with the girls as we topped a hill and raced down its windward slope.

Ten minutes later we caught our first glimpse of the Strait of Juan de Fuca, blue, flecked with white, its landmasses rising in the distance. Vancouver Island was one of them. It was once part of Canada, a foreign nation. Now we were all united on this continent. Unless you were a guy who hadn't passed his trials, you flowed freely everywhere, even across those arbitrary borderlines on PE maps.

We reached the fringes of a town. Clumps and rows of houses and other buildings rotting under the weight of neglect and weather began to appear on the sides of the highway and down intersecting roads that had decomposed into haphazard patterns of pavement and dirt. The skeletal remains of traffic lights and streetlights and billboards materialized in the distance.

We passed a battered road sign. Under the words PORT ANGELES, the word POPULATION could still be deciphered. After it, someone had painted over the number, whatever it was, and printed neatly: *Only God Knows.*

We passed another sign, handmade: *Afterlight*, it read.

So we'd arrived. But I didn't know where, exactly, Dad kept his boat.

The water was to our right, to the north, a half mile or so beyond what was now a dense dilapidated collection of houses and other buildings.

A few people, mostly men, walked the streets. I pictured them gasping for breath, falling, lying still. Guilt laid a heavy hand on my shoulder, shouted in my ear: *They deserve to be warned.*

I ignored the words. Dad was my priority; he was the only one who counted right now. But I couldn't help comparing myself to Mom, who would have gone to any length to get me out of Elisha's path but wouldn't consider alerting anyone else.

Even Dad.

"See if you can see anything that looks like a marina," I told the girls from landlocked Nebraska, pedaling determinedly just ahead of me. "Masts, or a sign sticking up above the roofs."

Sunday, sitting on the front seat of the tandem now, looked behind us. A frown darkened her face. "Let's get off this highway," she said, and turned down a lumpy side street. We worked our way toward the waterfront and along it. But there was no moorage in sight, and we were nearly out of town again.

On the side of the road, a prehistoric blue-and-rust pickup truck idled. Genuine engine sounds escaped from under its hood and all along its ancient exhaust system. Behind the pickup was an empty salt-corroded boat trailer, and an old guy messing with the hitch and chains. In the back window of his truck hung a rifle, something I recognized only from photos.

Tia and Sunday stopped. I stopped. "Are you going somewhere to get your boat?" Tia asked the guy sweetly. It sounded sweet to me anyway.

He looked her up and down. He wasn't as old as I'd first thought. He'd just let himself go—oily ball cap, dirty tattered clothes, unruly grayish-brown beard. What showed of his face was red, maybe from weather, maybe from drink. "Gotta get her in for some bottom work," he said. "Even old girls need their babying. And fishin's about to get hot."

"Where do you keep her?" Tia asked.

"Second-Chance Marina," he said. "Just outside town."

"The direction we're going?" Sunday said.

"A mile or so," the guy said. "Why?"

"We're looking for someone," I said. "A fisherman. You know a man named Charlie Winters?"

"He a loner?" he asked. "I know a loner fisherman named Charlie."

"Yeah," I said. My heart thumped at the possibility of good news. "You know where he moors his boat?"

"Right near mine," he said. "Slip C-forty-four."

"Is he there now?" Tia said.

"Don't know. I been away from the docks for a bit, doing my security job."

"Thank you," I said. "We'll go take a look."

We pedaled away. I could feel the guy's eyes on our backs, boring in. What would he tell the cops if they stopped and talked to him the way we did? "I'm glad you asked him, *Tia*." Despite all that was going on, I recalled Sunday's advice.

She gave me a fake annoyed look, but I detected the unmistakable hint of a smile at the soft corners of her mouth, in the deep brown of her eyes. "It's really true," she said. "Guys never stop to ask for directions."

"We were getting there," I said.

"Maybe," Sunday said. "Or maybe we would've gotten discouraged and wandered around and around in a circle for an hour."

I didn't argue with her. She could have been right. I pedaled harder, following this waterfront road as it snaked through the outskirts of Afterlight. The pickup truck passed us, its empty trailer bouncing and rattling along behind it, and the guy gave us a toot and a wave. The rifle barrel glinted in the morning sun.

To our right, a hill cut off our view of the water. On top of it stood an old lighthouse, striped in red and white like an antique barber pole. Beyond the dirty glass of the windows that surrounded the watch room, there was no sign of light or life.

Ahead of us the pickup slowed. One broken brake light flashed on. The truck turned right, just as a forest of masts appeared through a clump of evergreens and above a shallow layer of morning fog.

I scanned the marina entrance as we got nearer. "I don't see any cops there yet."

"Could be at his boat already," Sunday said.

We arrived at the gate. It was permanently open, lying twisted on the ground; no one was around. Beyond the opening was a short weedy gravel road that forked in the directions of the main dock and a launch ramp where the familiar pickup truck and trailer were backed up to the water's edge. The old guy was already making his way down the dock.

The marina was big, a crossword puzzle of docks and boats with a rock breakwater in the distance. A storage shed stood just inside the gate. It was open and apparently empty. "Wait in there with the bikes," I said. "I'll go the rest of the way on foot and see what I can see."

"Forget it," Sunday said. "We can be as sneaky as you."

"Why should all of us get caught?" I said.

"We're in this together," Tia said. She laid her hand on my arm, my left forearm, right on my skin, and let her fingers rest there for a moment, raising my temperature and pulse and anxiety level. Her big eyes were serious, all business. "They won't do much to us, anyway, even if we get caught. They'll put us in handcuffs, maybe, and take us back to Seattle in the back of one of their cars. It's you who has to worry. You and your dad."

"Okay," I said. "But let's hurry."

We ditched the bikes in the shed and hustled onto the main dock, following the route our friend the fisherman had taken. There was no sign of PAC cops yet, but we kept checking ahead of us and behind, scooting stealthily from piling to piling, hull to hull, shadow to shadow. Far ahead of us, the fisherman took a left and headed down a side dock. We hurried on; no one was between him and us.

We stopped. A half dozen slips away from us the fisherman was untying his bowline. He tossed it on his deck and disappeared between boats. A moment later his ancient tub backed out of its slip. The rumble of its engine changed pitch, and the boat headed out as we continued on, passing number C-39. Peering anxiously ahead, I got a bad feeling. I didn't glimpse anything that looked like Dad's boat.

A few seconds later, we were there—C-44.

It was vacant. I looked around, hoping we were at the wrong space or he was nearby, on his way in or out.

But there was no *Mr. Lucky*, there were no boats moving, nothing familiar anywhere.

"What do you want to do, Kellen?" Tia said.

"Maybe he's coming right back," I said.

"Maybe," Sunday said. She left the alternative unsaid: *Maybe not.*

"We should wait awhile for him," Tia said. "We have

some time before the quarantine." She left the reason for the quarantine unsaid: *Elisha's Bear.*

"We can't wait here," Sunday said, and I agreed. It was after eight o'clock now. Mom expected me downstairs by eight thirty. So far we'd been blessed, but we probably had only a few more minutes before the cops came calling.

"But somewhere nearby," I said. "A place where we can keep an eye on the marina."

We started back, jogging. "The shed?" Tia said.

"Too obvious," Sunday said as I looked around for other options. "It's right on the way in. They'd look there first."

We reached the main dock and a space between boats. For an instant, I saw the shoreline, old buildings, the road, and a quarter mile away, maybe, a candy-striped tower. "The lighthouse," I said. "Maybe we can get up in the lighthouse."

"You think it's open?" Sunday said.

"We can try," Tia said, and we continued running, eyes mostly on the road, ears tuned to the approach of cars. But as we dashed toward another boat, this one an antique wood cruiser that someone had converted into a commercial trawler, I noticed something behind its dirty windshield.

"Just a minute," I gasped as I hurried down the finger pier. I gazed inside. Everything was dusty and cobwebby. No one had been here for a while. I scrambled over the side and landed on the deck. It was slippery with morning dew, and I half skidded to the cabin entrance.

The door was unlocked. I swung it open and stepped down into the cool staleness of the cabin and spotted what

I was looking for. Just above the steering wheel a battered pair of binoculars gathered dust and salt. I snatched them up and headed back out to rejoin the girls.

We took off again. I half expected a lecture about thievery, one of the curses of man. But Tia just smiled. Sunday flashed me an appreciative grin. They both knew what we needed to do. The binoculars could help.

At the shed we collected our bikes and checked the neighborhood and approaches for cops once more. Still nothing.

We pedaled through the gate and out onto the road. An old car headed our way, then a couple of guys on bikes. Nothing that looked like cops. We got curious stares from everyone we passed. We were an oddity, I knew, especially Sunday and Tia—girls in man-country. I'd seen kids since we'd arrived, but they seemed to be even less common than the adult females who were here for a variety of reasons—adventure, escape, independence, rebellion, loyalty, love, lust.

I wondered how nervous Sunday and Tia were about being here in this man-world. So far no one had bothered them, but the possibility had to be on their minds, especially when they looked at my skinny self. What could I do to protect them?

The lighthouse loomed on our left, far off by itself, perched in the middle of a mound of greens and yellows long in need of cropping. A chain-link fence had once enclosed the grounds, cutting them off from the road, but the fence was now shredded and leaning. Its gate was open and hanging by one hinge. A mottled gray seagull, its feathers fluffed up and unruly like a bad case of bedhead, stood on a metal gatepost and scolded us as we rolled through the opening.

It felt good to get off the road, out of the spotlight. We left what remained of an asphalt driveway and angled off through the unkempt grass and up the hill toward the lighthouse, then around it, to the water side, where we couldn't be seen from the road. Here a red door stood brightly shedding its paint, framed by the candy-cane stripes of the lighthouse itself.

We went to the door. A rusted latch and padlock held it in place. I rattled the door in frustration. It moved half an inch back and forth but no farther.

When I turned back to Sunday and Tia, they were already hurrying toward a downed section of fence. Girls of action. I decided just to watch, breathe in, breathe out, waiting for the rubbery feeling to leave my legs, as the girls worked a half-fallen bare metal pole out of the ground. They lugged it back, one on each end. The base of the pole—Sunday's end—was buried in a ball of concrete.

"I've seen this in old movies," Tia said. "SWAT teams used battering rams to get into locked places." I didn't know what SWAT teams were, but I'd take Tia at her word.

With me facing the girls, we cradled the pole close to the cement blob at hip height—the height of the lock—and from six feet away made a run at it.

We smash-bashed into the door. I felt the thud all the

way into my bones. The noise was loud, sending seagulls screeching into the air, warning one another of earthquakes and tsunamis and toppling lighthouses, no doubt.

The impact had been a bit high. But we'd put a nice dent in the metal door, a good sign of things to come. So we backed up and gave it another go and this time we were on target. We hit the lock and latch. Neither of them broke, but the collision pulled one set of bolts halfway out of the building.

We adjusted the height of the battering ram once more and retreated and charged forward and hit the latch square. And this time the bolts wrenched all the way out and dropped to the ground. Rust shavings fell like bloodstained snowflakes. The latch dangled freely, fastened only to the door.

Using the knob of concrete, we gave the door a nudge. It swung in, creaking piercingly although not nearly as piercingly as everything else we'd done. But after we finally dropped the pole I moved to my left a few feet, anyway, nervous, and peered toward the road.

"Success," Sunday said just as Tia gave me a quick half-hug, but instead of enjoying it I looked past a wisp of her dark hair and spotted a state police car racing down the road toward the marina. No sirens, but its lights were flashing. An instant later another car followed, moving just as fast. Plain gray sedan, insignia on the side.

Big woman, little man.

I long for a conversation, a real one,
full of give-and-take and laughter and memories and plans,
not an urgent, gasping, prayerful dirge, you propped up on a pillow,
coughing out frightened good-byes,
me a mute lump, bathing your face in my tears.

—EPITAPH FOR JOHN MATSUMOTO
(SEPTEMBER 8, 2034–AUGUST 11, 2067),
BY SANDRA MATSUMOTO, HIS WIFE,
DECEMBER 5, 2068

CHAPTER TWELVE

"Cops," I said. The girls joined me in shrinking back into the shadow of the lighthouse. A moment later, poking our heads around cautiously, we were in time to see a second PAC car race past.

"Inside," Sunday said, but we were already pulling our bikes through the door. We pushed it shut behind us. The only light filtered down from way overhead somewhere and from a few small dirt-stained windows that followed the upward spiral of a long circular staircase.

I grabbed the binoculars. With Sunday leading the way, we began climbing. The sound of our footsteps on metal echoed all around us.

The staircase disappeared through a round opening in

the ceiling and into the sunlit chamber above us. We hurried up the last few stairs and stepped onto the lantern deck. But the lantern or whatever electronic gadget might have taken its place was gone. The room was empty, except for four unexpected items. Near the center of the enclosure stood a grand piano, its horizontal surfaces covered with a clean white sheet. Leaning against its bench were two violin cases and a cello case.

Perplexed, I looked around the space, unsuccessfully searching for a bigger entrance, an elevator. A freight elevator.

"How did this get up here?" Tia said, laying her hand on the sheet.

She got no answer. I was sure she didn't expect one. She opened one of the violin cases and studied its contents while Sunday did the same with the cello case. The instruments were beautiful—richly polished patterned wood.

Nestled into each case, snug against its instrument, was a bow, waiting for the touch of a hand. Neither Tia nor Sunday touched anything, though, and I wondered for just a moment if they knew how to play, but the way they gazed at the instruments made me believe it wasn't love at first sight, that it was a long relationship renewed. I'd dabbled with the violin and cello before I moved to music that wasn't imposed by my mother. Someone else's music, booming through my headphones.

Tia and Sunday closed the cases and joined me in looking around at the rest of the room.

Most of the windowpanes that formed a circle around us were fractured and filthy. But the view, even through the cracks and grime, was wondrous. We stood shoulder to shoulder and stared out at the blue waters of the strait, the islands, boats spewing out white wakes. To the west, the Olympic Mountains were capped with the milky remains of winter snow. I scanned the water to see if any boats were returning to port.

None, at least that I could make out.

The best part about the view was what we could see of the marina: *everything*. From this bird's-eye vantage point, the docks looked like a cornfield maze. Every finger pier, boat, empty space, was visible.

And so were the government cars that had just arrived at the marina entrance.

I lifted the binoculars to my eyes and adjusted the focus. I could read the names on the boats. I could see the frowns on the faces of the PAC cops as they strutted toward the dock, confident they'd find a bad guy, maybe two.

I was confident they wouldn't. Not right now anyway.

I didn't recognize two of them; the other two I did: Pelleur and Milne. The state cops stood near their car, talking but vigilant.

I handed the binoculars to Tia. Dozens of boats continued to cross the strait, but not one approached the marina. Now I was praying Dad stayed away, at least until the cops gave up.

"They're talking to the *fisherman*," Tia said. She handed the binoculars to Sunday.

"I can practically hear that old loner singing from here,"

Sunday said, peering through the lenses. "Now they'll never leave."

She gave the glasses back to me. Pelleur and Milne had stopped the fisherman's truck on his way out from the launch ramp. He stood outside his pickup door. I could see his head nodding, his lips moving. I knew he was spilling his guts to the cops. And why not? We were just outsiders, trespassers on Afterlight's land and ideals.

The old guy got back in his truck and closed the door, but the cops kept jawing at him through his open window. Finally, they stepped back and he drove off. Pelleur took out her phone and touched some numbers, and out on the dock, heading toward Dad's slip, one of the other two PAC cops lifted her phone to her ear. But she and her partner continued on.

Why had they just kept going? Wouldn't the fisherman have told Pelleur and Milne Dad's boat was gone? Wouldn't they have passed that along to their buddies?

Maybe none of them trusted him.

He was a man, after all.

"They're gonna stake out your dad's slip," Sunday said, and as if confirming that, Pelleur and Milne resumed marching toward the dock.

"How long does he stay out?" Tia asked me.

"It depends. Sometimes he fishes the strait. When he does that, he might be gone for just the day. Other times he heads for the coast, fishes the ocean, harbors the boat at Neah Bay or La Push. He might stay gone for days."

"Does he ever head north?" Tia asked. "Vancouver Island?"

"Wherever the fish are," I said. "He goes north sometimes, and if he's not coming back today, I hope that's where he is. If Elisha returns, I hope he hears about it and doesn't come back." I tried to remember what he'd told me of his plans the last time I talked to him, but that was weeks ago, and Dad lived pretty much for the day. He got up in the morning, studied the tides and sky, listened to his radio for fellow fishermen's lies, and decided on an itinerary.

I realized I was wearing out. My eyes were heavy. I felt like lying down somewhere. Anywhere. And the girls looked like I felt. "Why don't you two get a little sleep?" I said. "I'll stand guard. If anything happens, I'll wake you up."

"You're sure?" Tia said.

"An hour," Sunday said. She was already stretching out on the scarred wood deck. "Wake me in an hour and I'll take over."

"Then it's my turn," Tia said.

Five minutes later their eyes were closed and they were breathing the deep breaths of overdue sleep. I walked around the perimeter of the watch room, looking down and out. I stopped to peer through the binoculars at the PAC cops haunting Dad's slip, the state cops minding the marina entrance. They looked as if they were ready for the long haul. I wondered if someone else was out looking for us.

Minutes passed. I circled the room again and again,

breathing in the musty mildewy smells of the old lighthouse. Nothing changed, except the sun rose higher in the sky, the breeze increased in strength, stirring up more whitecaps. No boats broke off from the distant parade and approached the marina. The cops had gotten comfortable—sitting, standing, leaning. One of the state cops lit a cigarette and exhaled a cloud of silvery smoke.

The minutes turned into an hour. I was about to wake up Sunday when two of the PAC cops—the two I didn't know—abruptly left Dad's slip and headed toward shore. Once they got there, they talked to the state cops for a minute, then took off in their car. A moment later, the state cops got in their car and left. No lights, no sirens, no hurry.

I touched Sunday's shoulder. She didn't stir. I shook her. Hard. Finally, she woke with a start and sat up, rubbing her eyes. "Four cops took off," I told her. "Maybe looking for us. Milne and Pelleur are still at the slip."

Sunday struggled to her feet and went to the window to look for herself. Tia didn't move. She was on her back, her arm shading her eyes from the bright sunlight. Her chest rose and fell like a listless ocean swell. Sunday picked up the binoculars from the window ledge and raised them to her eyes. She aimed them in the direction of the two cops before panning out to the water.

"Get some sleep," she murmured. "If those two leave, I'll wake you guys up."

"Then what?" I said. "I don't know what to do if Dad doesn't come back."

"Does he ever dock the boat anywhere else around here, I wonder?"

"Nowhere I know of. Nowhere near enough for us to get to anyway."

"We wait, then," she said. "We wait till we can't wait any longer, then you'll have to make a break for it. You'll have to get out of the quarantined area, because if Elisha's really coming tomorrow, the cops will be watching everything. You can't afford to be caught and turned back."

"What about you and Tia?"

"We ain't in any danger. We're untouchable. We laugh at the Bear. We'll stay right here as long as we can. If the cops give up, if your dad comes ashore, we'll be there to meet him and warn him away."

"We'll see," I said. "Maybe it won't get to that." Sunday was right about Elisha's Bear. She and Tia could laugh at it; I couldn't. But I couldn't imagine running off by myself and leaving them here to face whatever was about to happen.

I took the binoculars from her. Something out on the water had caught my eye. Something was moving on an angle in our direction.

I focused. It wasn't *Mr. Lucky*. It wasn't even a fishing boat. It was a Coast Patrol cutter, big and white and green. And fast, I knew, although right now it was just cruising.

"What is it?" Sunday asked.

"Coast Patrol." A hundred yards behind the cutter was another boat—about the same size, plain gray, the number 9 on its bow—and as the white-and-green boat turned to starboard and began cruising west and parallel to the shore-line a half mile out or so, the gray boat followed. "That gray one's trailing it. Maybe PAC has its own boats. Or maybe it's navy."

"A naval blockade," Sunday said. "History repeated."

"How's he going to get back now?"

"Get some sleep," she repeated, and I lay down near Tia. I tucked a corner of my backpack under my head and rolled on my side, away from the light, which seemed to be everywhere. But I closed my eyes and a moment later, I was gone.

The next thing I knew, Tia was in my face, inches away. "Someone's coming," she hissed. Disoriented for a moment, I bolted up to a sitting position. Tia was kneeling next to me. Sunday was squatting at the top of the stairwell, staring down into the gloom.

I heard footsteps, clattering on the metal of the stairs. Whoever it was wasn't trying to be sneaky. It sounded like only one person.

We were trapped. We couldn't go down the steps, but there was no other way out of here. Why hadn't I thought of that when we'd settled on this place for a lookout?

Tia and I got to our feet. Sunday continued to squat and squint into the murk. She put her finger to her lips, warning us to keep our mouths shut.

We waited. Tia took my hand. My heart pounded.

"Hello, young lady," a voice said. A man's voice. A familiar voice. An instant later, a head emerged from the circular hole in the floor.

Sunday stood and stepped back. "Mister—"

"Gunny," he said. "Just Gunny." The fisherman. "I figured you'd migrate here when you didn't find him," he said, all the way up in the room now. "Should've given you the key, saved you some trouble. And my hasp some wear and tear." He stepped to the windows that faced out on the strait. He was carrying a big canvas bag. He set it heavily on the floor. "Great view, isn't it?"

"How did you know?" Tia said.

"It's a pretty obvious choice if you're looking for an observation point to watch for someone coming in," he said. Suddenly, I wondered why the police hadn't come here already.

"We saw you talking to the cops," I said. "What did you tell them?"

"I don't have a soft spot for cops," he said. "None of 'em, especially the PAC fascists. I told them I hadn't seen any kids."

"Thank you," Sunday said. "Did they ask you about Kellen's dad?"

"'Barely know him,' I told 'em. 'Seen him around some, though. Think he's out on a long-term trip.'"

"Is that true?" I said. "You think he is?"

"Don't have any idea. That was just my story."

"They half believed you," I said. "Four of them left."

"The one with the dead eyes stayed, didn't she?" he said.

Pelleur. I knew he was talking about Pelleur. I nodded.

"She didn't buy my story. I could see it on her sour face. I just figured, screw her."

"She can't stay forever," I said.

"Maybe long enough, though," Gunny said. "I get the feeling you're trying to reach your dad in a hurry. And now that the cops are involved, I smell trouble."

I felt the girls' eyes on me. Gunny seemed like a good guy, but how much could we tell him?

He smiled a little. "Anyway, I'm thinking maybe you want to get ahold of your dad sooner rather than later. So I brought this from my boat." He crouched down, reached in his bag, and pulled out a battered black box loaded with dials and switches. Mounted on one side was a microphone. He flipped a switch and turned a dial and the radio hummed to life. He turned another knob and static and voices wandered in and out. Another switch. The voices died. "Private line," he said.

"You know how to get my dad on that thing?" I said.

"I've done it before," he said. "You wanna give it a try?"

Decision time. What would I tell Dad? If I told him the whole thing, or most of it, Gunny would hear it. And then what? But what choice did I have? "Okay."

"You got something confidential to say to him, I can take a hike," Gunny said.

"It's no problem," I said. "You should hear it, too."

Gunny raised his eyebrows. He raised the microphone to his mouth. "*Mr. Lucky*, come in," he said. "*Happy Hour* to

Mr. Lucky, come in. Charlie? Gunny here. Come on in."

He waited. I waited. The girls waited. The only noise in the room was the hum and static of the radio as it sat on the floor, and Gunny knelt over it. He looked like he was praying.

"*Mr. Lucky* here," a voice crackled. Dad. "Down stowing some kings in the cooler, Gunny. Hit it big today. You should come on over."

"Where are you, Charlie?" Gunny said.

"Not far," Dad said. "Halfway to Sekiu." I knew where that was. *Not* far. He was right off the peninsula, just a few miles west of us.

"Got someone who wants to say hello," Gunny said. He handed me the mike.

"Dad?"

"Kellen? What are you doing there, Kellen?"

It spilled out of me. I sat on the floor and told him everything. Gunny didn't take his eyes off me the whole time, but he seemed to take the news calmly. I ended my story with, "You've got to get away, Dad. You'll be safe if you get away."

"No can do, Kellen. I'm not leaving you there. And I can't run even if I wanted to. I'm low on fuel, and those boats you mentioned—the Coast Patrol cutter and the destroyer—there are more of them everywhere. They're not letting anyone in or out. No outside boats are allowed to come closer than two miles from coastal settlements, and anyone who tries to leave the two-mile zone is getting turned back. I've seen it happening. I just couldn't figure out why. They didn't bother me because I was minding my own business, catching fish, staying around my own little hot spot." For some reason, Dad—like Gunny—didn't sound surprised by the whole thing.

"If you come back here, they'll get you," I said. I stood up and looked out. "They're still waiting at the slip."

Silence from the other end. "I tell you what," he said finally. "If Gunny will help us out, I think I've got something that might work."

"Anything," Gunny says. "Us loners have to stick together." Which sounded like some kind of oxymoron when I thought about it, but I was glad to have him on our side.

Dad told us his plan, or at least the first part of it. My heart was drumming so loud I thought Tia, who was hovering nearby, was sure to hear it.

CHAPTER THIRTEEN

An unresolved question had been squirming its way from a back corner of my mind toward the front, but when the three of us finished going over our part of Dad's getaway plot, Sunday beat me to it. "How'd the piano get up here?"

"That is a puzzle, isn't it?" Gunny said. But he didn't seem to be in a hurry to solve it for us. We had some time to kill before we met Dad, and this was as safe a place as any to kill it.

We waited patiently for him to go on. Even Sunday kept her mouth shut.

"My friend Carlos," Gunny said finally. "We played together in a small orchestra when we were barely out of diapers, relatively speaking. On a cruise ship, the *Starry Night*. Out at sea when Elisha's Bear came rushing out of hell."

Gunny paused for a long moment. I glimpsed memories dancing behind eyes squinted against the sunlight. "Anyway, Carlos was from Seattle originally. We tried living there for a while but it was too confining for us. We ended up here, a pair of almost-loners, living in an abandoned house, resurrecting an abandoned fishing boat, just the two of us and our instruments.

"We visited this place a lot, admired the view and the acoustics. One day he got the bright idea of disassembling his piano and putting it back together up here. I was foolish enough to agree to help him. So painstakingly, carefully, we pulled it apart, sawed it apart, hauled it up here in pieces small enough to fit through the hatch, and screwed and drilled and dowelled and glued and clamped and wished it back together. I was mostly the mule. He was the detail guy, the piano man, the perfectionist."

Sunday whistled admiringly.

"Where is he now?" I asked.

Gunny looked at me as if he hadn't understood the question.

"Carlos," I said. I would have liked to have met the man who had the great idea of bringing a grand piano to the top of a lighthouse, who could take apart such a complicated instrument and put it back together. "Your friend. Where is he?"

"Gone," Gunny said hoarsely. "Went overboard one night while we were fishing up north. I didn't realize it right away. I searched for him for hours in the dark, but it was futile. The water's deathly cold and quick up there. Unforgiving."

"Sorry," I said, and the girls echoed me. Gunny lifted the edge of the sheet, the lid, exposed the keys, touched a chord. The room filled with sound, deep and drawn out.

"Wow," Tia said as I circled the room nervously, peering down at the surrounding grounds. How far could that kind of sound travel? But no one was around to hear it.

"Requests?" Gunny said. "I play a little piano."

I remembered a piece of a story Dad told me once, and then at my request, several times after that—music on the radio long ago, intruding into the mountain air then, into his memory forever. "'Brahms's Lullaby,'" I said.

Gunny nodded. He sat. He played. Nursery-room notes spilled out, swirled around us, hung in the warmth.

The piano sounds died. "Anyone else?" he said, and I figured he meant does anyone else have a request, but Sunday thought differently.

"I'm a cellist," she said.

"Violinist," Tia said.

"I've had affairs with both," Gunny said, and I assumed he meant instruments and not players. "Can we do something together?"

He didn't have to ask twice. Cases opened. Instruments and bows emerged. Even the sounds of tuning and warming up were unlike anything I'd ever produced on my best day. I was glad there wasn't another string instrument around. I had a feeling in this company I'd stand out like a pig dancing ballet.

But I could listen.

Gunny lifted his eyebrows and looked from girl to girl, questioning silently, as the room quieted.

"Samuel Barber?" Tia said. "His *Adagio for Strings*?"

I knew the piece—not well enough to play it, but I knew it.

Gunny smiled. "Wonderful choice, uh . . ."

"Tia," Tia said. "And this is Sunday." She glanced at me. "And Kellen." I was sure Gunny knew who I was by now, but I was glad Tia included me in the introductions. The sound of her saying my name gave me the warm tingles.

"Good to officially meet all of you," Gunny said, looking like he meant it.

We nodded, returned his smile, told him we were glad to meet him, too, and I really *was* glad.

Sunday sat on the piano bench. Gunny and Tia stood on either side of her. I hung out near the window, one eye on them, one on the marina and beyond. Ears wide open.

Sunday began, low and mellow. Tia and Gunny took their cue and joined in seamlessly. Whispered notes slipped sadly out of all three instruments, melted together, climbed high and wide and dangled in the air while other notes built and joined them. Somehow, without sheet music or rehearsal, Gunny, Tia, and Sunday were more than doing justice to this beautiful lament to the human condition.

How much *didn't* I still know about these girls?

I'd never been to Nebraska, but as the music continued to flow and ebb around me, I pictured myself a couple of years down the road, after the trials and the driver's license and the loosening of the leash, driving through the vast flat corn-fields of that state with the windows down and heat pouring in and all of my car's sound effects off, and I round a slow bend in the highway, and on both sides of me now, instead of tall stands of corn, are clusters of beautiful brown-skinned white-gowned barefoot Nebraska girls, violins and violas and cellos in hand. Heavenly music permeates the heavy air; I can hear it, smell it, feel it seeping in through my soul.

I didn't want this moment to end. But it had to.

I had a mission.

Pelleur and Milne were still waiting at the dock when we left the lantern deck forty-five minutes later. We made our way down the stairs and warily out into the sunlight. Gunny's pickup was parked on the road; he hadn't wanted to draw attention to the lighthouse.

Cautiously, we skirted the wide expanse of grass, sticking close to the tall evergreens on our left, scuttling through their shadows.

We reached the road, lingering for a moment by the last of the trees to make sure no cars were coming. Then we hustled across the cracked pavement and dove into the bed of Gunny's trailer-less pickup. He threw a tarp over us and slammed the tailgate closed and suddenly everything was dark and stifling.

We were safe for a moment. For some reason—stress, fatigue, whatever—I started to laugh. It must have been contagious. Tia followed me. Sunday joined in.

It felt good. We kept it up until exhaustion took over. Sunday dropped off to sleep, then it was Tia. I tried to stay awake, curious about the twists and turns of the road and what lay ahead. But I didn't last long.

◆ ◆ ◆

I woke to sunlight in my eyes. The tarp was lumped in the

corner of the pickup's bed. Tia was pressed into me, and I thought about how cool it would be if we could just stay like this. But Gunny was here, too, pulling down the tailgate, and the screech of metal on metal got Sunday and Tia stirring and me sitting up.

We were parked away from the road in a thin grove of cedars. Through them I could see water, and in the distance a familiar boat: green hull, white cabin, teak trim, outriggers angling skyward.

I peered through the borrowed binoculars. The name of the boat leaped into focus: *Mr. Lucky.*

By the time we got to the beach, *Mr. Lucky* was nearing the center of the bay, moving closer. I could see Dad's silhouette behind the glare of the cabin windshield. He was at the helm, working the controls and wheel.

I waved, the girls waved. Dad waved back. Gunny, standing at our side, saluted. A long stone's toss from shore, *Mr. Lucky* cruised to a stop.

The engine cut off. Dad appeared on the stern deck. He lowered *Mr. Lucky*'s wooden dinghy into the water from its spot on the boarding step. In a moment, he had the oars unstowed and he was rowing expertly right at us.

After Gunny and I pulled the dinghy's bow high and dry, Dad jumped out, carrying a big dirty pack. Thrusting out of a gap in its top flap was the butt of a rifle stock. He smelled like fish; he hadn't shaved; his dark hair poked out of his knit cap in different directions like strands of seaweed.

He hugged me, lifting me off the ground like a baby. I hugged him back, trying to outdo him. It felt good.

"You're getting so big, Kellen," he said in my ear. "I can't believe you're thirteen already."

"*Fourteen,*" I said. But he was right about my getting big. I was approaching six feet, only two or three inches behind him now.

"*Fourteen,*" he echoed, reddening. He shook his head. "Where have *I* been?"

I could hear the husky embarrassment in his voice. I didn't want to make it worse. I let his question search for its own answer.

I introduced him to Sunday and Tia. He gave me this knowing look—raised eyebrow, little grin—that said he suspected some kind of romantic thing was going on.

"You shouldn't have come here just for my sake, Kellen," he said. "You've done a good job of tracking me down, but now what? Now we're both standing too close to the fire, and PAC's about to throw gas on it." He gave Tia and Sunday a worried look. "You shouldn't have brought your friends."

We started for the truck. "I didn't have a choice," I said. "About you or my friends. They insisted on coming."

"We made him bring us," Tia said.

"He needed Minders anyway," Sunday said. "And we ain't in any danger here."

"Not from Elisha's Bear," Dad said. "There are other risks, though." He turned to Gunny. "How was the road?"

"Two PAC cars and a state cop just between here and the marina. Luckily, they didn't hassle me. Maybe because I already talked to some of 'em this morning."

"So you think we can get to the access spur?"

"We put all four of you in back, they see just me in the cab, I think we'll be okay," Gunny said.

Dad frowned. "They're not going to let us through the roadblocks now," he said to the girls. "And getting around them would be tougher than it was this morning. Impossible, maybe. So if PAC really does bring Elisha here, the only way for Kellen, Gunny, and me to avoid the bug is to go into the hills and hide out for two weeks or more. If you go with us, you'll be there that long, too. Your mothers and the authorities will be going crazy. And I don't know about our supply of food. Gunny has some; I have some." He patted his pack. "But five people can eat a lot in two weeks or more."

"We have more food," Tia said, and I did a mental inventory of what was left in our packs. Enough for a day, maybe.

"We don't eat much," Sunday said. A lie, based on what I'd seen so far.

"There's another option," Gunny said. He glanced toward the cab of his pickup. All I saw there was his rifle hanging in the back window.

"I've thought about it," Dad said, making me suddenly curious about what "it" was. "We need to tell them what's happening anyway," he continued, making me even more curious about who "them" was. "But I don't know if they'd let us all in, especially for that long. Another reason, maybe, for not taking the girls with us."

"You can't just abandon us here," Tia argued. "You said there are *risks*."

"She's right, Charlie," Gunny said. "There's some fellas over here I wouldn't trust around two young girls on their own. What we should probably do is get on our way—all of us—and check in with the boss first thing. Maybe just seeing us anxious characters will chip away some of that crusty surface of his and he'll invite us to stay. If he says no, we can keep on going into the boonies."

Dad looked at me. He looked at the girls. I could have tried to convince them to remain behind. There was a reasonable chance that after Dad, Gunny, and I got far enough away, Tia and Sunday would be able to just walk out to the highway, flag down a PAC car, and be back in Seattle in a few hours. At least we had some idea of what it was like here. I, for one, had no idea what we were heading into. Who was "the boss"?

But I couldn't just pretend Dad hadn't mentioned risks, and Gunny hadn't gotten more specific about what they were. The girls might not be in danger from Elisha, but this was throwback country. Besides, it really didn't seem fair to just ditch them. Not after all they'd done for me.

And then there was the way Tia made me feel when she was near. And how I knew I'd feel if she wasn't. "I don't think it's safe to just leave them by themselves, Dad," I said.

"It won't be easy," he said.

"We don't care," Tia said.

"We won't be a burden," Sunday said. "You might need us."

From somewhere Dad produced a feeble grin. He hoisted his pack into the truck. "Let's go, then."

CHAPTER FOURTEEN

We got into the back of the pickup, and Gunny covered us with the tarp.

Tia was on my side of the truck bed again, but it was so crowded now, I had an excuse to stay close to her; she had an excuse not to move away.

"Where are we going?" I asked, loud enough for everyone to hear over the squeaking and clattering and engine noise as we moved off.

Dad didn't answer for a moment. "There's a place up in the hills, back in the woods, at the end of an abandoned logging road," he said finally. He hesitated again. "It's a lab. Foothills, it's called. Gunny and I both do security work for the people who run it."

"Security work?" I said. "You're a *fisherman*."

"Mostly." He was almost yelling above the motor and road racket. "But I need money to work on *Mr. Lucky*. Gunny's been working security for the lab for a while, and he told me they were looking for more help. So I joined up. For now, I fish around my work schedule."

"What kind of security work?" I said, recalling Mom and Aunt Paige's conversation about Dad's involvement in that mysterious something.

"Outside. I watch the perimeter of the grounds, patrol the woods and trails, make sure no one comes close who's not authorized."

"You carry that rifle?" I said.

"I haven't had to use it."

"Does PAC know about the lab?" Tia said.

"I didn't think so before today," Dad said. "Now I do. If the Bear's coming, I think the lab is the reason."

"What kind of stuff are they doing?" Sunday asked.

"Huge. Covert. Strictly outlawed." He paused again. "If PAC knows about it, it's an automatic and immediate target."

"They'll kill every male on the peninsula just to shut down a lab?" I said.

"I'm sure they would," Dad said. "But that's the ironic part. Several people working on the project are women. So even Elisha might not halt the operation. PAC is going to have to come in with old-fashioned methods—guns and bombs and bulldozers and whatever else they have at their disposal—if they want to stop what's going on."

Guns and bombs and bulldozers. To me, a place that might attract that kind of attention didn't sound like the best choice for refuge-seekers. "So tell us why we're going there," I said.

"It's a lab, but it's also a well-designed fortress," Dad said. "And there's food, water, places to sleep."

"What *is* going on there?" I said. Sunday never got a real answer to her question. It was everyone's question now.

We turned right, almost stopping as we moved from pavement to what must have been shoulder, then rough, rutted surface. Gunny accelerated, and we started uphill. Even with the almost-opaque cloth of the tarp over my head, I could tell that we'd moved from sunlight to shade. Instantly, the temperature dropped.

Finally, Dad answered me. "I guess it's not a secret now," he said. "I've never been officially told, but Gunny's done some inside security. He's seen a few things and snooped for others."

The truck bounced through a washboard curve, and Dad raised his voice. "He told me the lab is developing a vaccine for Elisha's Bear. If it works, and Gunny says it's a whisker's breadth away from completion, they can vaccinate every male on earth. Women will still have the upper hand, but they won't be able to stage these accidental outbreaks anymore."

"A vaccine," Tia said. "They wouldn't allow it."

"They couldn't use Elisha as a weapon," Sunday said.

"How did they find women who would do the research?"

I asked, wondering how long Dad had known about, or at least suspected, the original conspiracy.

"They had to look for brilliant women who were sympathetic to the idea," Dad said. "They searched for those few who were qualified to do the work and who didn't believe in what PAC was doing. *Had* done. The Fratheists were helpful in singling out scientists who could be approached safely. Gunny says it took a long time to recruit all of them."

"How did they develop the vaccine?" Tia said.

"I'm not a scientist, Tia," Dad said. "But I know they got their start by exhuming bones and tissue from some of the mass grave sites."

"With more help from the Fratheists?" I said. "At Epitaph Road?"

I felt him shrug. "Maybe."

"Can they immunize you and Kellen?" Tia said. "And Gunny?"

"That's crossed my mind," Dad said. "But I don't know if they've reached the point where they can try it on humans."

The truck continued to bounce along, twisting and turning, mostly uphill.

Finally, it stopped. I heard Gunny's door open, and an instant later he was dragging the tarp off of us. "I think you're okay without this now," he said. "Ride up front, Charlie?"

In answer, Dad jumped over the tailgate and landed softly on the stripe of greenery that marked the center of the road. "I think I've bored these guys enough," he said. "And my bones are ready for a rest."

Dad and Gunny climbed into the cab and we started off again. It was good to breathe fresh air, but now that there was no excuse for being hip to hip with Tia, staying close felt awkward. She must not have seen it that way, though. She stayed put. Our hips continued to enjoy each other's company. Mostly.

Just when I thought this road couldn't get any skinnier, we left it, taking another turn onto what was not much more than a path, an almost-accidental serpentine channel through tree trunks and underbrush. The stubborn growth pressed in, twanging past the mirrors, scraping against the sides of the old pickup. Sunday, Tia, and I stuck to the middle of the bed, where low limbs and whiplike twigs wouldn't take a toll on our skin.

After another ten minutes of wooded twists and turns and bumps, we moved out into a clearing. The truck stopped, but Gunny and Dad stayed put. So we did, too. Gunny honked his horn three times.

A moment later, from an opening in the face of a giant pumpkin-shaped outcropping fifty yards in front of us, a man emerged. He was dressed in camouflage—browns and greens and tans—head to toe. He carried a rifle, angled across his chest. At least it wasn't pointed at us. Yet.

Eighty-four years old, but he still had life by the jewels.

—EPITAPH FOR GLENN SORENSON (APRIL 21, 1983–AUGUST 9, 2067), BY CHANDLER FOX, AURORA BLAIR, MISSY CONNORS, AND KELLI SPALDING, HIS DAUGHTERS AND GRANDDAUGHTERS, DECEMBER 12, 2068

CHAPTER FIFTEEN

Camo-guy marched over to the truck, eyeing us the whole time. A step away from Gunny's window, which was rolled down, he stopped. He was short but built like a block. "Gunny," he said. "Charlie."

"Miller," they chorused.

"What brings you up here on your own dime?" Miller gave us—especially the girls—a long and suspicious look, as if we were spies. "And what about the kids?"

"Long story," Dad said. He gave Miller a short version, but enough to let him know that we weren't junior moles.

"Unbelievable," Miller said, but he looked like he believed it. "You think it's really going to happen?"

"Cops are everywhere," Gunny said, "and I'm not talking about our little constables pedaling around on their bikes. Something's up. These kids have probably saved your life."

Miller studied us again, but this time there was more to his expression than hostility and suspicion. He looked almost grateful. "You'll want to talk to Wapner, then," he said, stepping back. "Go on ahead. If he won't take you in, let me know. That means I won't be welcome in there, either. I may just want to grab some supplies and follow you into the hills."

"We'll do that," Gunny said. He started the truck forward again. We moved across the clearing and approached the crack in the outcropping. Moss and lichen covered most of the stony surface. Far back, the cleft widened, then narrowed to the black crease of a cave entrance. Next to that opening I could just make out what appeared to be a metal box mounted on the rock. It was the same gray color as the stone that surrounded it.

We skirted the wall and more house-sized rock formations, slowly half circling into deep shade. Ahead of us, in front of a dense barrier of evergreens and bookended by two soaring cliffs, a low cinder-block building came into view.

Could this possibly be the lab, the *fortress*?

Gunny drove past the entrance and stopped at the side of the little building. He turned off the engine, got out, and unlocked the door of a red metal box mounted on a thick pole. Inside was a phone. He picked it up and punched a series of buttons. "Gunderson," he said after a moment. "I need to talk to Dr. Wapner." He listened for another moment. "I'd prefer he come out," he said. "I have Winters with me, and as I'm sure you've seen, we're not alone."

Dad stepped out of the truck. "Stay where you are for now," he told us. Gunny replaced the phone, locked the door of the box, and joined Dad nearer the front of the building, waiting.

In less than a minute I heard the clicking sounds of opening locks. And then a man—Dad's height, thin, receding gray hair buzzed a centimeter from his scalp—appeared from around the corner.

"What is it?" he said impatiently to Dad and Gunny. "I have work." He had an accent, but I couldn't place it.

"My son and his friends brought us some news we thought you'd want to hear, Dr. Wapner," Dad said.

For a moment the doctor turned his attention to us, to Tia and Sunday especially, before refocusing on Dad and Gunny. "What is it that couldn't wait, that told you it was permissible to bring *outsiders* here?"

Dad explained the whole thing, most of it anyway, from our arrival on. He carefully left out anything about the work of the lab—the vaccine. Officially, it was still a secret. The doctor asked us questions from time to time. He seemed to be warming to us.

"We wanted to warn you," Gunny said. "And we wanted to ask you for refuge from the Bear."

"I appreciate the warning," the doctor said. "If they know where we are, if they're aware of the nature of our research—and this quarantine decree tells me they may well be—they could come here with their plague. They could try to do us in with it, put an end to everything we're doing.

"Your coming here tells me one other thing: neither of you is the person who tipped them off. Because I'm certain someone *did* tip them off. But who?"

It was a rhetorical question. Dad responded with a functional one. "What about allowing us to stay?"

"Do you know what we're doing here, Winters?" Dr. Wapner asked. "Gunderson?" When their only answer was a half-guilty, half-embarrassed silence, he continued. "I suspect just the fact that we have this research facility where it is may have given you some idea of our work."

"I've had my suspicions," Gunny admitted. "I've kept 'em to myself, except for Charlie here."

"That's commendable," Dr. Wapner said. "But what are they?"

Gunny told him what he "suspected," but he didn't mention snooping around for his information. He told the doctor he just put two and two together.

"You're exactly right," the doctor said. "We've developed a vaccine. We're also developing a treatment for unvaccinated males who are exposed to Elisha."

"You haven't said whether you'll let us stay," Dad said, not letting loose.

Dr. Wapner eyed the girls again. His expression made me want to keep right on going, into the farthest hills. "Certainly. But if we're going to add you five and be under siege for two weeks, we'll need someone to go back to town to get food and supplies."

"The cops are on the lookout for Charlie," Gunny said. "They don't care about me—I've already passed under their microscope. I'll go."

"You're sure?" Dad said.

"Perfectly," Gunny said.

"I'll be the real hero, then," Dad said. "I'll haul the stuff in when you get back."

"And we'll help," Sunday said.

"Come with me," the doctor said.

We followed him through the door. The walls, with open, half-empty shelves here and there, were simply the interior faces of the exterior's gray block walls. Just inside was a cabinet filled with flashlights, headlamps, night-vision goggles, binoculars, a spotting scope, radios, talkalouds, and other electronic stuff I didn't recognize.

There were no people here, no computers, test tubes, books or papers, no jars of mysterious fluids, no monkeys—northern owl or otherwise—in cages, electrodes planted in their shaved skulls or jammed down their throats, measuring their lung function. The doctor closed the door. The only light came from overhead tubes.

Dr. Wapner printed out a supply list and handed it to Gunny. "I've modified the amounts to reflect a three-week period and twenty-one people," he said, "in case the rest of the security staff chooses to stay. Use our usual account number at the co-op."

"Right," Gunny said.

"What about the vaccine?" Tia said. "You said you've *developed* a vaccine. Could you give it to Kellen and his dad, and Gunny before he goes to town? The PAC women might bring Elisha early if they think word is getting out."

"We have a vaccine," the doctor said. "All of the male scientists of Foothills have injected it in themselves to determine if there are adverse effects. Three days later, we're all still standing. What we don't know is whether it will be effective against the full-blown disease. The women we have

working here are trying to replicate Elisha in its most virulent form, and they're close. But until they do, until one of
us is exposed, we won't know for sure."

"Would it hurt to give it to us?" I asked him.

"Not based on our experience."

"Can you do it, then?" Dad asked.

"I don't know why not," Dr. Wapner said. "It may not
provide you with any protection should Elisha's Bear find
us, though."

"We won't expose ourselves on purpose," Gunny said.
"But we've got nothing to lose, as far as I can tell."

"Let's proceed, then," the doctor said. His expression
brightened. He went to the middle of the room, where a
large multicolored rectangular rug that had seen better days
lay at an angle. He bent down and swept it back. Underneath
it was a square door made with the same unfinished wood as
the floor. He lifted the door as we gathered around. Gunny
hung back. He'd been down there before, I decided. Inside
security. Snooping.

Descending from the floor was a steep wooden staircase.
At the bottom was another floor—smooth pea-green concrete, well lit—but that was about all I could see. "Wait
here," Dr. Wapner said, and started down the stairs agilely
as if he'd done it a thousand times.

He disappeared. We waited. I thought about getting
jabbed with a needle. But then I thought about Gunny
going to town to face the cops and maybe Elisha's Bear on
the loose. I thought about being totally helpless should the
Bear penetrate the lab's defenses, about dying an agonizing

death, and I decided a needle wasn't a big deal.

Voices rose from the depths: the doctor, a man or two, a woman or two. I couldn't make out the words. They sounded foreign, like something from an ancient movie about Nazis.

A moment later, Dr. Wapner was on the stairs. He arrived in the room with a small plastic box holding three hypodermic syringes. The needles looked like tree trunks. Was I really going to just let this guy—doctor of *what*?—stick one of them in me? Was Dad okay with it?

The doctor set the box on the desk. "Who's first?" he said, and Gunny rolled up his sleeve and offered his arm. Wapner rubbed on disinfectant, then plunged in the needle and emptied the syringe. Dad was next. He got through it without a grimace and gave me a reassuring smile. At least that was what I thought it was. I stepped up, trying to appear brave for the girls. But I couldn't help squinting my eyes, looking away, waiting for the jab. It was done before the temptation to run took over. I imagined weak or dead (I hoped) little Elisha bugs beginning their journey through my body.

"I'm on my way," Gunny said. He hugged the girls, he shook hands with Dad, and he shook hands with me. His grip lingered, and I became more and more aware of his scars and calluses and beneath them, his strength and warmth.

"Beware of strange women," Dad said as Gunny went out the door. Gunny didn't respond. He pulled the door shut behind him, and we were cut off again from the outside air, the sunlight. In here, it smelled of disinfectant and sweat and fish.

Dr. Wapner locked the door. "We have showers downstairs,"

he said as if he'd noticed the smell, too. "If you want fresh clothes, I believe we have something that will fit all of you, and a washer and dryer for the clothes you're wearing."

"Really?" Sunday said as if he'd just offered her a trip to an exotic tropical island. I thought about Puerto Verde and Grand Cayman and another lab—Brighter Day—and those northern owl monkeys again. How different from those monkeys were we? I felt a chill.

Sunday began moving toward the opening in the floor. Tia followed, I followed. I didn't care that much about a shower or clean clothes, but I was definitely curious about what was down those stairs. I rubbed my arm where the giant needle had entered. It was a little sore, but when I looked I didn't see any sign of damage—no bruising, no blood vessels pulsing with tiny foreign bodies.

"The rifle will have to stay up here, Charlie," the doctor said, sounding friendlier now. "No arms in the lab area, security or not."

Dad gave him a look, like he was ready to protest, then shrugged and took the rifle out of his pack and leaned it against the wall. It was short-barreled but mean-looking, all black, a magazine big enough to hold dozens of shells. I'd never seen Dad shoot a gun of any kind—I'd never even seen him with a gun—but he looked comfortable with this one, reluctant to let it go. He'd told me once about pirates, men who "catch" their fish by stealing from other boats. Dad got his rifle after a friend's catch was pirated at gunpoint.

I was surprised by what greeted us at the bottom of the

steps. The staircase ended in the middle of a small room, but long, well-lighted corridors branched off from it in four directions like the spokes of a wheel. They reached much farther than the perimeter of the room we'd just left. I realized that the upstairs building was just an entryway, a false front for the real thing.

Doors, most of which were closed, lined the hallways. Dr. Wapner shut the overhead hatch, bolted it from the inside, and moved around us to lead the way down the corridor that lay straight ahead. An *A* was painted above its entrance. The other hallways, in clockwise rotation from where we were standing, were *B, C,* and *D.*

"Where does the air come from?" Tia asked, and I could see why she was curious. With nothing but dirt and rock and roots over our heads, with no windows and a single door leading out of here, I had this claustrophobic feeling pressing in on my chest.

"We have ventilation to and from the outside world," Wapner said. He pointed to a grilled opening high on the wall. No light showed through. "Of course, everything is filtered to screen out the finest dust, the most microscopic forms of bacteria and viruses and toxins."

He stopped at the first open door and invited us to look in. It was a big bathroom, three toilet stalls on one wall, three shower stalls on the other. Sinks and mirrors lined the remaining two.

We continued on, passing a laundry room, then a kitchen with the latest in appliances, a bar in the center, and a long table near one wall. A couple of plates with half-eaten sandwiches sat on one end of the table. I realized I was starving. I was tempted to walk over and wolf down the leftovers. "You're all welcome to return here as soon as we finish our little tour," Dr. Wapner told us, apparently reading my mind. He seemed relaxed, almost carefree. I wondered if he knew something I didn't. Besides all the obvious scientific stuff, of course. "There are provisions in the refrigerator and cabinets."

We doubled back along the corridor, got back to the hub, and took a right down another hallway, corridor D. The sign on the first closed door said LAB ONE. We passed it by and went to LAB TWO. The doctor gave the door a sharp rap, and a moment later the latch clicked and the door opened. And the tour group was face-to-face with a woman. She smiled, but she didn't look happy. She looked harried.

She also looked familiar, in an everyday-face-in-a-strange-place kind of way.

"This is Dr. Margaret Nuyen," Dr. Wapner said, and instantly I knew why she looked familiar. Just as it jarred me breathless, she focused in on me and it hit her, too. I could see it in her eyes. They widened and then went into communication mode. And the message she was sending me was *Don't. Don't say anything.* And to verify the message, just in case I had any doubts, she gave her head a whisper of a shake, a bare side-to-side twitch.

"Dr. Nuyen is one of our lead scientists," Wapner said. "She's as responsible as anyone for the vaccine you just received. I told her about the news you've brought us, and she agrees with me that we need to show you every aspect of our hospitality."

While Dr. Wapner introduced the girls and Dad to Dr. Nuyen and they exchanged canned pleasantries, I found myself staring at her face and imagining her a year, then twenty years, younger—I saw her daughter Merri in her—and pretending not to stare at the same time. Why had it taken me more than a second to recognize her? She looked pretty much the same as the last time I'd seen her, when she was my housemate. She still had an Asian face, she still spoke English with an Aussie accent. She even *sounded* like her daughter.

For a long but too-short moment I thought about Merri. Up-close body-to-body amorous visions danced in my head.

I was introduced. I nodded hello, as if Margaret Nuyen was someone I'd never seen before today, a stranger. But what *was* she doing here? And why didn't she want anyone to know we'd met? It wasn't like I really knew much about her. She was a scientist. She had a daughter a couple of years older than me. She used to live in the same house I lived in. Oh, and there was the breathing problem. That was about it. Anything incriminating there? Anything Dr. Wapner didn't already know? I doubted it. But I'd go along with her. I had no reason to rat her out or whatever. Not to Wapner anyway. Not yet.

Thank you for not fixing that leaking bathroom faucet
before you left me;
now I lie awake at night,
listening to the ∂rip-∂rip-∂rip of our lives,
thinking of you.

—EPITAPH FOR RANDALL RESER
(AUGUST 21, 2010–AUGUST 15, 2067),
BY CALLIE RESER, HIS WIFE,
DECEMBER 14, 2068

CHAPTER SIXTEEN

Behind Dr. Nuyen, Lab Two didn't look much like a lab, at least not the lab I kept seeing in my head. In the murkily lit room were desks, tables, computers, papers strewn about and taped to the walls or tacked to bulletin boards. Not much else. Which in a way was a relief. At least there was no chance of renegade Elishas escaping from test tubes or canisters and floating over to the door, where we were still standing.

Neither doctor invited us in for a closer look, and a moment later we were moving again, proceeding down the hall. I gave Dr. Nuyen what I hoped was a reassuring backward glance, and she tried to smile. The smile wasn't convincing, which made me think of something Dr. Wapner said when we were still outside, his rhetorical question of who tipped off PAC about the work this lab was doing.

Was Dr. Nuyen the spy? The traitor?

It would make sense. She was a well-known medical research scientist and she knew my mom, an upper-echelon official from PAC and soul mate of the angel of death herself, Rebecca Mack.

A coincidence? I found myself doubting that.

I needed to talk to Dr. Nuyen, I decided. I needed to give her a chance to tell me if she was involved in leaking information, or at least look her in the eye when she heard my question and came up with an answer, whether it was the truth or a lie. But could I find her again? And get her alone?

Our next stop was a closed door marked SECURITY. The doctor hesitated for a moment, then turned the knob and cracked the door wide enough for him to peer in for a long beat. Finally, he motioned for us to follow him through, managing to casually get his hand on Sunday's shoulder as he herded us inside. I was surprised when she didn't recoil.

A youngish red-haired guy sitting at a console in the center of the room nodded in our direction. "Dr. Wapner," he said, and went back to his work.

Three walls were alive with monitors. Those on the wall to our left showed interior shots—several rooms in the lab, men working in some, women in others, a couple of angles from inside the little upstairs room.

Lab Two—Dr. Nuyen's space—wasn't showing.

Across from us were monitors displaying outside views:

the exterior of the building from all sides, the rock outcroppings, the spot where the narrow road emptied into the clearing, a variety of shots of the surrounding forest.

The screens on the third wall, behind us, monitored the logging roads on the way in, beginning with the turn from the highway. As we watched, Gunny's rusty old truck appeared on a screen and disappeared again. I realized they'd known someone—Gunny, at least—was coming the whole time we were on our way in.

"Everything okay, Jimmy?" Wapner asked the security guy.

"Smooth," Jimmy said.

"You've alerted all outside personnel? Scrambled the sleepers?"

"Twice, just to make sure."

"Can you go vertical with half of the outside building cameras?" Wapner asked, but it wasn't a question, it was a directive. "And switch all interior shots to exterior feeds?"

"Sure." Jimmy fidgeted with some controls, and the first four screens on the opposite wall segued from clearing to trees to mountains to broken clouds as the cameras panned skyward. On the wall to our left, the views of inside rooms vanished completely. In their place appeared new scenes of the grounds—woods, open areas, roads—in the vicinity of the lab.

"Good," the doctor said. "Leave everything as is until further notice."

"Will do."

"You've got the whole horizon and above on those four monitors?" Dad asked, studying the screens on the opposite wall. He seemed as interested in this stuff as the rest of us were. It was obvious he hadn't been in here before today.

Tia and Sunday were transfixed, too. I'd never been around them when they were this quiet. But in addition to their being wrapped up in the technology and our surroundings, I had a feeling Wapner's attention had them dampened down—nervous and uncomfortable. And I didn't blame them.

"I've gone to wide-angle," Jimmy said. "We've got one-eighty coverage in all directions. A seagull comes over the treetops, we'll have its picture."

While everyone else was studying the monitors, I glanced over at the wall to our right. Except for two more screens mounted high and showing what looked to be highway approaches, it was mostly bare. But below the monitors were four full-sized metal doors with locks and latches and small single windows, their thick glass crisscrossed with heavy wire. A faint light showed behind the window of the door in the far left corner. I casually sidled in that direction, hoping for a peek inside, picturing imprisoned monkeys.

But Wapner caught me. "I'll save you the trouble, young man," he said sharply, and I felt everyone's eyes on me. Jimmy tensed in his chair, as if I was about to do something drastic. "Those are holding cells. They're vacant. For now."

His last two words sounded like a threat. I nodded and moved back to the group, wondering why the light was on in one of them if they were all vacant. The creepy feeling I was getting wasn't helped any by the fact that just as we were leaving the room, I swore I heard a noise coming from the direction of the far door. A muffled voice. A human voice. A woman's. Or girl's. I looked around at the other faces, though, and saw no reaction. Had I imagined it?

We returned to the hub of the underground, and Dr. Wapner took us down hallway C, another corridor full of closed doors with different lab numbers on them. "There are scientists at work behind some of these doors," he announced, breaking off a murmured conversation with Dad, "but it's necessary to maintain sterile conditions in all of them and quarantine in some. So you'll have to use your imaginations. Think of a group of dedicated people working sixteen hours a day for little remuneration but the eternal thanks of society."

"If PAC really knows what's going on here," I said under my breath to the girls, "this place has a short life expectancy. Maybe we should think about leaving, going on up to the mountains, where we wouldn't have a target on our backs."

"It looks like these guys are prepared for anything," Sunday said, and I guessed that was her vote for staying. And in a way I could see why. Here there were comforts and food. Out on the trail we'd have little of either. Tia looked less sure about this place, but I knew she wouldn't leave Sunday here by herself.

"Women's sleeping quarters," Wapner said, turning back to us and gesturing to a half-open door on our left. "There are two unclaimed bunks in there, all made up and waiting for you young ladies." He gave them the closest thing to a smile I'd seen from him so far. "And right here," he said, pointing to another half-ajar door directly across from the first one, "is the men's sleeping area. Plenty of room in there for you and your dad, Kellen. But he won't be joining you for a while."

"Dr. Wapner has asked me to take on some security duties, since I'm up here anyway," Dad explained to me. "There's no point in me just hiding out when I could be on the grounds, watching for intruders." He sounded as if he was trying to convince himself.

"What if PAC comes?" I said. "You'll be safer down here."

"It's my job, Kellen," he said. "And I'll be okay on top. I'll keep my distance from any strangers. If Gunny's got the balls to go off to Afterlight by himself, I can at least go up and scout out the woods."

Gunny. So that was it. When Gunny had volunteered to go I could tell that Dad felt like a shirker. Now he wanted to make up for it. "Gunny doesn't have a kid," I told him, before I realized that Gunny could have twelve kids and I wouldn't know it.

"Your father's not going topside because of what Gunderson is or is not doing," Wapner said. "Your father has a duty. He wants to help protect what we're trying to accomplish here."

Dad nodded. Halfheartedly, I decided. But he set his backpack inside the men's bunk room, gave me a quick hug, and headed down the hallway and toward the stairs. "I'll see you soon, Kellen," he said over his shoulder.

"I must get back to my work," Wapner said to us. "You're free to return to any of the rooms or spaces I've shown you. Those that are off-limits will be locked, so you don't have to worry about accidentally going somewhere you're not wanted. You can shower, rest, eat, whatever. If you go outside the antechamber upstairs, however, your safety will be much more precarious than it is in here. Especially yours, Kellen. If you leave the premises, I'm afraid you're on your own."

"We're not leaving," Sunday said.

Wapner gave her another smile, creepy this time, and she actually smiled back. Like she wasn't repulsed. But nearby, touching me, Tia cringed. "I'm happy to hear that, my dear," he said. He turned on his heel, strode down the corridor, turned right, and was gone.

"Lecher," I said, picturing the Wapner leer.

"What?" Sunday said.

"He's a dirtbag," I said, and Tia stuck out her tongue and scrunched up her nose in disgust.

"I thought so, too, at first," Sunday said. "But now I think he's just a weird scientist. I think he's nice underneath. He's letting us stay."

"Maybe," I said absentmindedly, still distracted by my run-in with Dr. Nuyen and the question of what to do about her. Should I tell the girls? What exactly *was* there to tell at this point? So far, all I had was a handful of suspicions.

I decided it would be better to talk to Dr. Nuyen before I

said anything to anyone, but to do that I had to ditch Tia and Sunday. I needed to get back to Lab Two. For my own curiosity's sake, at least, I needed to find out if Merri's mother was the spy. After that, I'd have another decision to make.

Fortunately for me, I didn't need to figure out how to get away by myself. The girls were both eager for showers—before getting something to eat, even—and they said goodbye and closed the door to their sleeping area in my face.

I threw my backpack in the men's sleeping quarters and headed down the hall and back to corridor D. The door to Lab Two was closed when I got there. I tried the knob. It turned, and the door opened.

Across the room, Dr. Nuyen sat at a desk, studying me. "I thought you'd return," she said. "Either you or Wapner. Close the door, please."

I eased the door shut behind me. She motioned me nearer, until I was standing by her desk. I glanced around at the walls and ceiling and spotted what looked to be a couple of small cameras mounted in upper corners of the room. I already knew they weren't being monitored, but I couldn't help being apprehensive.

"No worries," she said. "The cameras are lit when they're transmitting."

"Why are you here?" I said.

"Sit," she said, gesturing to a nearby chair.

I pulled the chair closer and planted my rear. "Where's Merri?"

"Safe. Nowhere near here."

I felt relieved by a fraction. "Are you the spy?" I said. "The one who told PAC about this place?"

"They've known about this place for a long time, Kellen," she said. "PAC has eyes and ears at Afterlight and every other throwback settlement. They sent me here because of what they knew."

"Why didn't they bring in Elisha when they first heard about it?" I asked. "Or they could have just blown up this whole complex and everyone in it."

"That's not PAC's style. We wanted to monitor the research. We wanted to see if a group of ragtag men and a few gullible women could really develop a vaccine."

"And now you have."

"Yes."

"And you've given it to us."

"You think so?" I recognized her expression. It was the one she'd worn whenever she saw Merri and me together and pitied me for believing her mature sophisticated daughter was actually interested in me. "You think your friend Dr. Wapner is really looking after you, protecting you from Elisha's Bear?"

"He said you haven't tested it against the real disease yet, so he can't be sure it will be effective."

"That's true," she said. "But now he'll have his opportunity to find out."

I nodded, not sure what she was trying to tell me.

"You don't understand," she said. "PAC is about to present us with an unexpected opportunity to test the vaccine under the actual conditions for which it was developed. The good doctor is outside now, inoculating the rest of the security people, just as he did you and your dad and Gunderson. Except only half of you will have gotten the vaccine. The rest of you, *the control group*, will have to settle for only an extra few milliliters of saline passing through your bodies, at least until the next time you relieve yourselves. Or the Bear arrives. Whichever comes first."

"Half?" My mind raced to register what she'd just told me. "Which half?"

"Only Wapner knows."

"Dad could be in the control group? Gunny?"

"Either. Both. Neither."

"Me?"

"Yes."

"But I'm inside. I can't be in the test. Wapner says bacteria and viruses can't get in here."

"True. Unless the filters are sabotaged, or PAC, as you suggested, simply blows up the place. And don't let him send you outside on an errand, or psych you into going out on your own."

"He just told me to stay inside, where I'd be safe."

"And he had your trust, didn't he? Wapner is a fanatic, but he knows human nature as well as he knows human disease."

The room suddenly seemed colder. I felt chilled, outside and in. My stomach rolled from hunger and lack of sleep. And terror.

Rain still falls, night still descends,
sun still rises over fertile front-yard beds,
rosebuds still dilate, exhaling familiar perfume,
Mrs. Sims still totters by, filling her withered chest,
and peers around the yard for a sign of little Billy—
a flying ball, a cloud of dust, an infectious smile.
Everything is the same.
But nothing is.

—EPITAPH FOR ARMY CORPORAL WILLIAM (BILLY) BODINE
(JANUARY 8, 2047–AUGUST 9, 2067),
BY LISA BODINE, HIS MOTHER, AND PATRICK BODINE,
HIS FATHER (DECEASED),
DECEMBER 16, 2068

CHAPTER SEVENTEEN

"What's going to happen now?" I asked her.

"That's partly up to you," she said. "If you tell Wapner what you know about me, I'm sure he'll lock me up. At the very least. I haven't done anything to impair what's gone on here, but he'd be afraid of that, afraid of me cooperating further with PAC."

I allowed her to stew about what I was going to do. I didn't know myself. "What *about* PAC?" I said. "When are they coming? And why is Wapner acting as if nothing is going to happen, as if he'll just be able to carry on?"

"I'd like to know the answer to that last question. But I know he has confidence in the security of this place. And if it looks as if it's going to fail, he's got two secret backdoor escape routes."

"Where?"

"Doors hidden behind panels at the ends of corridors A and C. I used the C door to get out at night and make my calls to PAC. To your mother."

My mother. In it up to her ears.

"Which brings me to your other questions," she continued. "I don't know exactly when PAC is coming. It's not easy for me to get away discreetly. I haven't talked to your mother in more than a week, when I let her know that it was now or never. That the vaccine, as far as I could tell, was ready to step out on its own and change the world. But from what she told me then, and what you've said, it sounds like tomorrow. Possibly sooner."

Sooner. And Dad was out there, fully vulnerable, maybe. Dr. Nuyen didn't look afraid of what I might do with what I knew, but I decided to reassure her anyway. "Wapner's a creep," I said. "I'm not telling him anything."

"Thank you," she said. "That makes my life easier."

"The damage is already done anyway."

"*Damage?* You've studied history, Kellen. Would you really want to live in a world where men were in charge again?"

"You think *women* are perfect? Your *big boss*, for instance? And a vaccine wouldn't put us in charge. It would just make it harder to slaughter us."

"It would be a giant step in the wrong direction." She

labored to take a deep breath, trying to hide her efforts with a mask of calm even while that mask colored. Her eagle eyes remained on me. "Women are far from perfect," she continued. "Some individuals have done unspeakable things. But women haven't—and won't—put all of humankind in jeopardy. Men, on the other hand, took this planet and its inhabitants to the brink of the abyss. Dr. Mack and her PAC mates found a difficult and painful way—but the *only* way—to bring us back." Her eyes shifted from me to her watch. "But I don't have time to debate you. I'll just thank you again for not saying anything. If that's still your intention."

"I'm doing it for Merri, not you."

"That's fine." She considered me again. "She really liked you, you know that? I didn't think so for most of the time we were all living together; I thought she'd just discovered a new toy. But she was upset when we left so abruptly, and the main reason was you."

I was halfway surprised, even considering the note on the wayfarers' wall. Part of me wondered if the doctor was telling the truth. She could be lying to keep me on her side. But it didn't feel like a lie. I decided to believe her story. This one, unlike Wapner's tall tale about the vaccine, wouldn't cost me. Or Dad. "Girls," I said. "They just find me irresistible."

Dr. Nuyen managed a smile. "Like the young woman you arrived with, for instance?"

"Tia."

"I was thinking of the other one. Sunday. She couldn't take her eyes off you."

Sunday? And this woman was supposed to be brilliant? But I remembered the library, the conversation when Sunday and I were alone, her sticking up for me later, volunteering to come along with me on this crazy dangerous journey. I thought she'd become just a friend. Just a loyal friend. But maybe the doctor knew what she was talking about. For a moment I questioned my feelings toward Sunday. But I didn't need another complication right now.

I decided to get back to what really mattered. "Is there a way I can communicate with my dad?"

"I'm sure he took a talkaloud with him. You could get him on that. But the frequency is unsecured. Anyone on the lab network, including Wapner, can listen in."

"How did you call out?"

She glanced at her watch again. "PAC set me up with a satellite phone in the woods. I sneak out, take a short hike, walk up to a big cedar, reach inside a hollow space in its trunk, and pull out a phone. It's like something from an old spy movie."

"So we wait?"

"You wait. I have work to do. The other women are expecting me to help them put the finishing touches on more vaccine and get it ready to move if we have to, along with data and instruments."

"You'll still help them?"

"It's why I was hired, but from here on out, what I do for Foothills is strictly for show. My job is to help PAC bottle up this threat." She gathered together some papers and headed out the door, leaving me alone and pondering what to do next.

I noticed her computer screen was still alive. It was cluttered with icons, most of which were numbered and lettered with meaningless (to me, at least) labels. In the top right corner, though, was a mound-shaped icon I could at least make some sense of. It was labeled FOOTHILLS PROJECT.

I touched it. An organizational chart with names and titles and photos and contact information appeared. Dr. Wapner headed the chart. Below him were three sets of people: Team T, Team V, and Security. Four male scientists and a male lab assistant were on Team T. Four female scientists, including Dr. Nuyen, and a female lab assistant were on Team V. Dad's name and photo were included on the ten-man security team roster. Gunny and Miller were also there.

At the base of each lab team grouping was a label: GENERAL INFORMATION. I touched the one for Team T. In its place a small padlock appeared, along with the words PASSWORD PROTECTED, FORMULA T TEAM ACCESS ONLY, and a box for password entry.

I left it and pressed the Team V GENERAL INFORMATION label. Instantly, it was replaced with the words CURRENTLY LOGGED ON, and a moment later the screen filled with a page of notes, headed with the word VACCINE. I skimmed through it. It was the introduction to an article on the origins and objectives and parameters of the project. I scrolled to the last page. At the bottom was the word DATA. I touched it. Another padlock icon and the words FURTHER ACCESS SECONDARY PASSWORD PROTECTED, FORMULA V TEAM ONLY appeared.

I didn't have a password, secondary or whatever; I wasn't on anyone's team. I wouldn't be going any further. But I'd learned something. I knew who belonged where. I knew Team V—for *vaccine*—was made up of females only, which made sense. It would be dangerous and probably deadly for males to be exposed to Elisha's Bear during research. I wasn't as sure why Team T—for *treatment*, I supposed— was all-male.

Before I left the desk, I navigated back to the screen Dr. Nuyen was showing when I'd started snooping. The spy might not appreciate another spy.

It was too soon for the girls to be done with their showers. I slipped out of the room and headed down the corridor, trying to act cool, like I wasn't doing anything wrong. And I wasn't. Yet. Nobody was around to check out my act anyway. I took a right at the hub and hurried down corridor C until it dead-ended.

I didn't see a panel. But according to Dr. Nuyen, a door should have been hidden here someplace. So I began looking for secret buttons, levers, compartments, openings. I waved my hands, hoping to trip a sensor. Nothing.

I looked up. Mounted high in the corner, too high for me to reach, was what looked to be a lens of some kind. I retraced my steps, opened the first door I came to, and peered inside. It was a small storage room. On all four walls, floor to ceiling, were shelves, filled with boxes. In one corner stood a broom. I grabbed it and returned to the end of the hallway.

Waving the business end of the broom in front of the lens, I hoped for something to happen.

Nothing did. At first. Then I heard a click, a whir, and overhead a panel slid back, a metal ladder descended and unfolded. I waited, but not long. In a few seconds the base of the ladder was on the floor and the panel was all the way open. I couldn't see anything but weak light beyond the gap.

I was tempted to go up; I needed to talk to Dad, to let him know he was being used as a lab monkey. But was that what Wapner wanted? Me wandering around up there with no clue of where Dad was? Was Dr. Nuyen in on the whole thing? And what about the girls? They wouldn't know where I'd gone.

I waved the broom in front of the sensor again.

Click. Whir. The ladder retracted. The door closed. I was standing alone at the end of an empty hallway with a broom in my hand. I needed to get moving. I needed to *do* something.

I stashed the broom back in the storage room and hurried to security. The door was open; I went in. Jimmy was at his console. He was intently eyeing the screens, all of which were still monitoring the exterior, and he didn't notice me at first.

"You're back," he said finally, after I was halfway across the room. His gaze swept from me to the monitors and back and forth across them. He was expecting something.

"Do you know my dad's location up there?" I asked.

"I know where almost everyone is," he said. "Come here."

I stood by Jimmy's side. He touched an eyeball icon on his screen. A numbered grid appeared. Inside it was an irregular outline, nearly the boot shape of what once was Italy. Spread around inside the boot were eight pulsing dots, each a different color, each with a small number in its center. Jimmy referred to a card taped to the top of the console desk.

"Your dad's the green one," he said. "Number three."

As I watched, the yellow dot, number two, began creeping from left to right. "How do you know?"

"They each have a GPS, transmitter, and identifying color code and number. The rest is just up to the computer."

"So where is he?"

Jimmy studied the screen. "Sector J," he said. "Inside the cleft in the big rock, I'd say, or possibly up higher where he can see better. Right above the fail-safe box, maybe. Elevations aren't precise."

"Fail-safe box?"

Jimmy gave me a look, like I was pressing my luck. "I don't know how much of this I'm supposed to tell you," he said.

"Dr. Wapner gave us the run of the place."

"Not exactly," he said.

I held my breath, hoping not to tip the scales in the wrong direction.

"But I guess the cat's kind of out of the bag now," he added.

I breathed. "It is."

"Besides the door you used to enter this place," he said, looking almost grateful for the chance to talk, "there are two other entrances, or exits. One of them leads to a tunnel that eventually opens up at a spot deep in the woods. The other one goes to a tunnel that terminates inside a cave."

"The cave inside the cleft."

"You saw it on the way in?"

"Yeah."

"Did you notice the box?"

I nodded.

"It's locked—you need the combination to get in—but inside it is another touch pad. Hit the right numbers and a button, and this whole place implodes, the cliff collapses. It's to prevent anyone from getting at the work that's been done here. Strictly as a last resort, of course."

"The other back entrance—it has a fail-safe box, too?"

His eyes stayed mostly on the walls, dancing from screen to screen. "It's the other option, depending on which way people get out. But they both touch off the same explosives. You wouldn't have a prayer if you were anywhere in this complex, the tunnels, or the topside building."

"Dr. Wapner showed us one of the doors," I lied. "The one at the end of corridor C. Where does that one go?"

"Deep woods. About four hundred yards of tunnel to get to the opening. The door in corridor A leads to the cave. But it's six hundred yards to the door out, and you'd be more exposed once you leave the cave."

"Who has the combinations?"

"Not me. Nobody on the security team, as far as I know. Wapner for sure and maybe one or two of his trusted people."

"So if I left by the door at the end of corridor A, I'd end up out by my dad?"

"Within shouting distance. As you can see," he said, pointing at the moving yellow dot, "some of the guys are on patrol, but Charlie—your dad—is a static sentry. He'll be there until I get orders to move him."

"Is Dr. Wapner out there?"

"Could be. But I couldn't tell you where. He's got a GPS but no transmitter. He doesn't like to be monitored. He's kind of like a god—sees all, hears all, knows all, but elusive and shadowy and defined mostly by his deeds. And the faith of his followers."

"Will Gunny appear on the screen once he gets back on the grounds?"

"He'll be a red dot, number four, going pretty fast, but he's not here yet."

I glanced up at the two monitors showing the cutoff from the highway. No sign of Gunny or anyone else. Below the screens the four cell doors were still shut tight. But someone had turned off the light behind the window on the far left, and for some reason that gave me an unsettled feeling in my gut.

"You going out there?" Jimmy said.

"I need to talk to my dad."

Jimmy handed me a talkaloud. "This will do it."

"Face-to-face." I tried to hand it back to him.

"Keep it. You may want it later. And if you decide to go out, take the main door. I don't think the doctor would appreciate your using the other ones."

"Okay."

"But I don't think leaving here is a good idea. PAC could show up anytime."

"We've got the vaccine now," I reminded him, knowing I was only half right.

He shrugged. "The Bear may not care."

I hurried out and made my way to the girls' bunk room. I knocked. Sunday came to the door. She was dressed in someone else's clothes—shorts and a T-shirt. Her hair was a shade darker, still wet. Scrubbed free of sweat and grime, her face shone. Only her earrings—thin silver hoops with tiny blue stones—looked the same. Behind her Tia sat on a bunk, pulling on her shoes. She smiled.

"Where you been?" Sunday asked. Was I imagining the concern in her voice? How would I feel if she or Tia disappeared, even for a few minutes?

I walked in, closed the door behind me, and began telling them everything they'd missed, starting with my visit to Dr. Nuyen.

"I guess I was wrong about Wapner," Sunday said when I got to the part about half of us getting fake vaccine. "He *is* a dirtbag."

She didn't need anyone saying "I told you so." And I

didn't have the time. I went on, covering the rest of it—the secret door, Jimmy—as fast as I could.

"You can't go out," Tia said to me.

"He's my dad."

"He left you—again," Sunday said.

"You could be in the control group," Tia said, pacing now. "Your dad might have gotten the real stuff."

"I'm *going*," I said. "If I get out and back before PAC shows up, it doesn't matter who's immunized. I can save both of us."

"I'll go with you then," Tia said. "You might need some help."

We both looked at Sunday. Her jaw quivered but set. "You ain't smart after all, Kellen," she said. "And I ain't putting my kiss of approval on your idiot plan. Besides, I'm hungry." She turned and stomped out of the bunk room, heading for the kitchen. I was tempted to follow her. My stomach was achingly empty, but more than that I was confused and pissed. Why had she picked now to go off on her own?

I didn't have time to chase after her. Tia and I moved toward the hub. "What's with Sunday?" I asked.

The olive skin of Tia's face reddened a little. She shrugged. "She's . . . worried about you."

Maybe. We climbed the stairs and tried the door. It was unlocked on both sides, almost as if Wapner had issued me an invitation to get out and go for a walk.

No one was in the upper room. Everyone was busy, concocting or watching or scheming. Outside, daylight faded. June 21 got closer.

I had to find Dad.

Tia and I hurried away from the little building. It felt good to be moving, breathing fresh air, but I couldn't help nervously scanning the woods, the hills, the sky above them, for some sign that the Bear was coming early. PAC knew what was going on here; they knew where *here* was. Whether they showed up in five minutes or five hours, I knew they'd come soon. The stakes were way too high for them to stay away for long.

I didn't see any sign of intruders.

"It's quiet out here," Tia said.

"Like a funeral," I said.

We rounded the stone wall and kept going another quarter mile or more, heading for the opening between the outcroppings. I moved out a bit so I could spot Dad or he could spot me if he was somewhere above the cave, keeping watch from the trees.

At a place directly out from the gap, we stopped and stared up at the rock, the trees and undergrowth above it. I couldn't see anyone; the woods were in shadow now. They looked like an impenetrable fence. I waited, hoping Dad would step out and call my name. I fingered the talkaloud in my pocket, wondering if I should try it. But I didn't want Wapner and everyone else listening in.

"Can we get up there?" Tia said.

"Dad might have, according to Jimmy's grid. I don't know how, though. I don't see a trail or anything."

"Should we try?"

"He could be somewhere down here, too, back in the opening or the cave. If we go up, we could miss him."

"What do we do?"

I stared into the breach, at the surrounding stone, the trees. "Dad!" I yelled. "Dad!" My voice echoed and hung in the air. I wondered who, if anyone, had heard it.

I only wondered for a moment. An egg-sized rock landed in the dirt at our feet and bounced away. We looked up as another one arced out over the outcropping and touched down nearby, raising dust. A moment later, Dad stepped out of the trees and waved. He was above us and maybe forty yards away. He raised a finger in a wait-a-minute gesture and disappeared into the woods to his right.

We went to the entrance of the narrow canyon, where I felt a little less vulnerable. The air had grown chilly. Tia moved nearer, nudging into me, and I managed to put an arm halfway around her waist. Suddenly, I no longer felt the cold.

A minute later, Dad appeared from out of a small fissure in the rock right near us, a fissure I hadn't even noticed. His rifle was slung across his back. I dropped my hand from Tia's side. I didn't want to invite any crap from him.

"What are you two doing out here?"

"I had to talk to you." I told him why, with Tia filling in the blanks when I took time to catch my breath.

Dad's face darkened as he listened to our tale. "The PAC tyrants murdered my dad," he said. "And billions of others. They locked up Paige. They're planning on wiping us out. Wapner's doing something important here. Something that could change the world. And he's always been straight with me before."

"How would you know?" I said. "And why would Dr. Nuyen lie?"

"Look, Kellen, I appreciate your coming out here, but I knew when I volunteered to do this today—Gunny, too— that there were no guarantees on the vaccine. We've got sentries all the way to the highway. If someone heads this way, I'll hear about it. I'll have plenty of warning. If the wicked witches show up, I promise I'll run to the lab for shelter."

"What if they sneak in through the woods?" Tia said. "Kellen says they know where everything is."

"They're so blinkin' comfy here they've installed a *phone* in a *tree*," I said. "They probably know every square yard of this *whole compound*. They could be watching you *now*. We still have time to take off for the hills. PAC wouldn't come after us. They're coming for the Foothills Project and its scientists. For Wapner."

A little grin appeared on Dad's face. A hint of brightness. "You inherited your mother's fire."

"It's not funny," I said.

Dad's gaze lifted to the distant peaks. "There are no guarantees up in those hills."

"Elisha's coming *here*," Tia said.

"I know these woods pretty well myself," Dad said. "And even though it looks like the bad guys are on their way, I'm confident they're not here yet."

Something beeped insistently. Dad reached in his pocket, took out a talkaloud, raised it to his face, and pressed a button. "Winters."

"I'm back," Gunny's voice said. "I just turned off the highway. But PAC picked up my scent. By the time I got to the cutoff, there were two PAC cars and a cop car in my rearview mirror, trying to look inconspicuous."

"Did you get the supplies?" Dad said.

"Yeah. No worries there."

Another voice cut in. "Where are you now, Gunderson? And where are the authorities?" Wapner.

"I'm stopped, a hundred yards off the highway, waiting to see if they follow me in. So far, they're not coming."

"Proceed to the lab," Wapner said. "We'll deal with them if they start up the road."

Another voice—Miller's, I thought—broke in. "They're not moving in," the man said. "I've got my glasses on 'em, and they're setting up a roadblock at the spur. Four cars now, and what looks like an armored vehicle under a tarp on the back of a transport truck. They're getting ready to off-load it."

"Affirmative on that." Jimmy's voice this time. "I've got 'em on the monitors. No turning back, Gunny."

Wapner swore, un-scientist-like. I took out the talkaloud Jimmy had given me and touched the power button. It came alive. Now I could practically feel the anger in Wapner's voice. "Are all the mines in place?" he demanded.

"Buried," said Jimmy. "I'll arm them as soon as Gunny

passes. I'm monitoring the cameras at all three sites."

"If anyone besides our team members ventures up the road," Wapner said, "at your first opportunity, blow them back to creation."

"Yessir," Jimmy said.

"Are you moving, Gunderson?" Wapner asked.

"I'm on my way."

"Anything else to report?" Wapner said. "Anybody?" He paused. "I shall see you at the building, then, Gunderson. In ten minutes. The rest of you continue your diligence."

I formed a picture in my head of the mad scientist creeping through the woods. "How about now?" I said to Dad. "Will you come back now?"

"They're not moving in yet," Dad said. "They're just making sure no one leaves. And Wapner wants us out here. Regardless of his methods, if there's a way to salvage the work he and the other scientists are doing, I think I should help."

He didn't allow me another chance to argue. He gave us a quick hug and slipped back into the fissure.

On our way back there was no sign of Wapner or anyone else. I wondered if he'd be disappointed that I wasn't staying outside long enough to field-test his vaccine. I wondered if he was watching us right now.

Nothing had changed in the upper building. We'd left the door unlocked; it was still unlocked. No one was inside, and the hatch to the lab area was still open. We closed it behind us and descended the stairs. Nobody was in the hub or hallways.

What now? I was starving, but Wapner's little speech about blowing people back to creation had me feeling even more ambivalent about him. I wanted to be in the security room, studying the monitors, letting Jimmy explain to me what was going on.

"Can we get something to eat?" Tia said.

"Sure. Something quick, though."

"Let's check with Sunday first."

We went to the bunk room. Sunday's stuff was there, but there was no sign of her.

"Maybe she's still in the kitchen," Tia said.

But no one was in the kitchen. We could see that from the doorway.

"Where else could she be?" Tia said.

"Bathroom, maybe?"

We hurried to the bathroom. It was empty. I was beginning to feel like we were the only ones here. Every door we passed was closed. And locked.

We ran to Lab Two. It was locked. I knocked. Loud. No answer at first. Then a voice—Dr. Nuyen's. "Who is it?"

"Kellen," I said. "And Tia. We're looking for Sunday."

The door clicked and opened. Dr. Nuyen slapped a magnetic QUARANTINED sign on the outside of the door and pulled us inside. Tia's face was pale. I took her hand and gave it a squeeze.

Dr. Nuyen headed toward her desk. "When did you last see her?"

"Half an hour ago," Tia said. "Maybe a little longer."

"We went outside to talk to my dad," I said. "Sunday stayed here to get something to eat."

"I haven't seen her," Dr. Nuyen said, sitting down at her computer, touching a screen to life. "I was hoping someone on Team T would let his guard down once the excitement and panic levels rose over Gunderson being followed. So I came back here. And I was right. I was able to fish out a password to access Team T data."

"Why?" Tia asked.

I inched closer to Dr. Nuyen and her display, wondering what she was looking at or for, and like Tia, *why* she was looking.

"Curiosity, mostly. I wanted to tie up a loose end before I lost the opportunity."

"You need some help?" I asked. "Tia's good at worming her way into files."

I expected her to say she was a scientist, she didn't need help from kids, but she just mumbled a distracted "no thanks" and something about too many cooks.

"Why is Team T all male?" I asked, half-afraid Dr. Nuyen would wonder how I even knew about the makeup of that team. Tia gave me an impatient look and a tug back toward the door.

"Good question," Dr. Nuyen said. "Availability, maybe. Coincidence, maybe. I hope to have answers soon." She was concentrating now, barely glancing toward us as we edged toward the door.

"We have to go," I said. Now I knew what it felt like to

lose someone I cared about—even for a few minutes—and I didn't like it. I wanted to find Sunday.

"Set the lock," Dr. Nuyen said, still staring at her screen. "And leave the sign up."

Out in the corridor I glanced left and right, hoping for inspiration.

"Can we try the kitchen once more?" Tia said. "She told me she was starving."

"Why not," I said. "Maybe she was just on her way from one place to the next when we were there."

The kitchen still appeared empty, but it was a big room with a corner we couldn't quite see from the doorway, so this time we went all the way inside. Nothing. Nobody. I was getting jumpier by the second, not quite believing she'd be this hard to locate.

Tia picked up an apple from a table and nibbled at it. She took a step. "Yuck!" she said, staring down at her feet, where a half-peeled banana was squashed against the concrete floor. Part of it—a blob the color and texture of pus—clung to her shoe. "Why don't people pick up their messes?"

I didn't answer her. Something else had grabbed my attention. Something silvery and blue, near the banana but under the table where Tia couldn't see it.

I walked over and picked up Sunday's earring and showed it to Tia. "Maybe the banana's hers, too," I said, imagining lots of things, all bad.

"It could be someone else's," Tia said.

"The earring or the banana?"

"Both?" It wasn't even convincing for a question. I let her think about it, though.

"She left here in a hurry," I said after a bit, trying not to let anything scary come out in my voice.

"*We* need to hurry," she said, tugging me toward the door.

"Security," I said once we were back in the hallway. "Sunday must be in with Jimmy, watching the monitors." Anything was possible.

The security door was unlocked, which was a relief. And Jimmy was there, still at his console.

But Sunday wasn't.

"Have you seen Sunday?" Tia said. Her voice had tears at the back of it.

"The other girl?" Jimmy said. "Not since you were all here together."

"Not even on the monitors?" I said.

Jimmy shook his head and gestured toward the walls, reminding me that the screens were all tuned to outside cameras.

I wondered if that had been the case the whole time we were outside. "But where could she have gone?" I said.

Jimmy shrugged, trying to look unconcerned. Instead, he looked jumpy.

"Can you switch some of the monitors back to inside views?" Tia said.

"No."

"Why?" I asked.

"Dr. Wapner's orders. And anyway, there's secret stuff going on in the labs."

"How about the corridors?" Tia said. "All the rooms that *aren't* labs?"

"You're welcome to check those yourself."

I was about to ask him once more if he'd seen her on the monitors if not in person, maybe following us outside, when I heard a noise. Tia heard it, too. I could see it on her face. It was the same kind of noise I'd thought I heard earlier, coming from the holding cell at the end of the room. A woman's muffled voice. I looked. Dim light filtered out from a window again, but it wasn't the one on the far left.

It was the window on the far right.

"Who—?" Tia began, but at that moment the room erupted with sound: first a horn, then a stranger's voice, bloated with excitement, over the sound system.

"Helicopters! Three helicopters, crossing the perimeter at high speed. Heading your way! ETA less than three minutes!"

"I'm nearly back!" Wapner's voice, urgent. "I'll secure the main door. Jimmy—check all other openings, airways, and filters. All personnel on outside security, disperse immediately. Get as far away from the lab as possible."

Jimmy sprang up and raced out the door.

A heartbeat later a thunderous explosion sent a shudder through the room. The floor quaked and rolled. The walls trembled. Debris sifted down from the ceiling. Were the helicopters here already? Had someone set off a mine?

Tia's fingers dug into my arm. Dust dulled her dark hair. I

was wobbly but frozen, thinking of Dad, closer than anyone else to the lab. If the helicopters were still on their approach, he had less than three minutes to get his stubborn ass out of harm's way. But Wapner would be securing the door, shutting out Dad and everyone else. Could Dad make it to the cave in three minutes?

What about Gunny?

The door swung open, and for an instant I was wondering how Jimmy had gotten back so quick. But it wasn't Jimmy; it was Dr. Nuyen, breathing hard. She was covered in chalky grime. She was wearing a small backpack, also covered.

"What was the explosion?" I asked.

"Me," the doctor wheezed. "I blew the filters. You two have to get out of here. *Now.*"

"You *blew* the *filters*?" I said.

"We can't leave Sunday," Tia said.

"You can't *help* Sunday," Dr. Nuyen said. Her eyes shifted to the end of the room, the far right holding cell. "You need to get *out.*"

We didn't get out. We sprinted to the cell. Tia pounded on the door while I twisted and pulled futilely at the doorknob. Over our noise, I heard something from inside the chamber. Tia continued to pound while I kept turning and tugging and Dr. Nuyen tried to pull us away.

A palm pressed firmly against the inside of the wire-crossed glass. The top of a head appeared. The blond hair was matted down but familiar.

Too familiar.

Sunday's face rose above the bottom of the window frame. It was pasty-white and sweaty. Her green eyes were teary and terrified. A silver hoop earring with a small blue stone hung from her left ear. Her right earlobe, empty, was smeared with dried blood. She mouthed a word, and even if I couldn't have heard her frightened voice through the sealed door, I'd have had no trouble deciding what that word was.

"Run."

Her face disappeared. For a moment her hand lingered, pressed against the glass, as Tia sobbed and my stomach tightened into a throbbing knot.

"What's *wrong* with her?" Tia wailed.

"I'll tell you," Dr. Nuyen said. "On the way *out*."

God's hand is mighty, and to our dim instincts, indiscriminate;
it sweeps away fine grain as well as useless chaff
and disease-ridden vermin,
leaving behind bare fields and pregnant seeds
and the smell of rain on the horizon.

—EPITAPH FOR FATHER TERRANCE FITZGERALD
(JULY 21, 2003–AUGUST 14, 2067),
BY SISTER CECILIA MARIE SANDUSKY,
PRINCIPAL, ST. JOSEPH ACADEMY,
DECEMBER 17, 2068

CHAPTER EIGHTEEN

Dr. Nuyen dragged us away, and a blood-chilling moment later we were running out the door and down the corridor, Tia crying and me sick. And scared. What had happened to Sunday? What was happening outside?

We reached the hub just as the hatch opened and someone started down. I looked up. It was Wapner. We accelerated, angling down the C hallway. Smoke hung in the air. Debris covered the floor. And I realized where we were heading: the hidden exit to the tunnel that ran to Dr. Nuyen's forest phone booth. I slowed down long enough to scoop up a long piece of twisted metal framework.

When we got to the end wall, I waved the strip of metal

in front of the lens, hoping the explosions hadn't wrecked the mechanism.

They hadn't. The overhead door opened, the ladder began to drop. Slowly. Too slowly.

"*Margaret!*" It was Wapner, hurrying down the hallway. "What happened here?" he shouted.

"Get back, you monster!" Dr. Nuyen yelled. "I have a gun, and I'll use it!"

I'd seen no gun, but something in her voice made me believe she had one. Wapner hesitated, long enough for Dr. Nuyen to boost Tia onto the descending ladder and make sure she started up. I was next. I scrambled on and up, pushing Tia ahead of me. Before my head reached the ceiling, I looked back and saw Wapner start toward us again, then stop as Dr. Nuyen reached in her backpack for that gun.

I kept moving. I heard our rescuer behind me. Tia leaped onto the floor above us and I rolled after her and stumbled to my feet. The light was feeble here, but I could make out a square of rough wood flooring and two lamps marking the perimeter of the little room we were in and the entrance to a narrow tunnel.

Dr. Nuyen popped through the opening. She punched a button and the ladder began to move up.

"Go!" she ordered, and we did, racing for the tunnel with her on our tail.

"What about *Sunday*?" Tia cried over her shoulder.

But before Dr. Nuyen could respond, my talkaloud crackled to life. "Dr. Wapner!" an unfamiliar male voice said.

"Nash here. Dr. Nuyen's trashed the computers. She's left with all the backup data on Formula V."

"*What?*"

We kept running. Overhead bulbs gave us just enough light to avoid tripping. Jagged watermelon-sized rocks lay on the rough floor of the tunnel, forcing us to weave and jump, splashing up cold water from dark puddles. I glanced back, but the curve of the tunnel prevented me from seeing the door. Or anybody climbing through it. Dr. Nuyen had fallen behind. She seemed to be struggling.

"Status on Formula T data?" Wapner demanded over the talkaloud.

"Secure," Nash said. "We have the backup."

"Take the data," Wapner ordered. "Head for the A exit with the other men ASAP. I'll meet you there." His voice came in bursts, as if he was moving now.

"The women?" Nash said.

"Confined, Jimmy?" Wapner said. "Exposed?"

"Yessir," Jimmy's voice answered. "Except for the two on the run."

"They're with the boy," Wapner said. *The boy. Me.* "Who's near the C egress?" he added.

"Through the trees, two minutes by foot." Gunny's voice.

"Get there in *one* minute," Wapner said. "When Dr. Nuyen and the brats emerge—*if* they emerge—take the data. But no prisoners." *No prisoners.* My brain sent a message to my legs: faster, *faster.*

A pause on Gunny's end. The faint sound of a long

breath. Then more purposeful breathing. He was heading somewhere. "Will do."

"You're in the control room, Jimmy?" Wapner said.

"For now. But I ain't waitin' forever."

"What's going on in the sky?" Wapner said.

"Cameras vertical. Nothin' yet."

"Monitor for thirty more seconds. Then join us at the exit."

We kept running while I tried to breathe, while I attempted to digest everything I'd heard. For a long moment all I heard were our footfalls.

I lifted my talkaloud and pressed a button. "Dad?"

Nothing.

Where was he?

"Dad?"

Nothing. Tia reached back and took my hand. We dodged and jumped together, with Dr. Nuyen farther back now.

"Choppers!" Jimmy roared. "Three of 'em. A hundred yards up and dropping. Directly over the building."

"Riflemen nearby?" Wapner asked.

No response.

"Shoot them down!" Wapner ordered.

"They're dumping something!" Jimmy said. "Cylinders!"

"Pan down!" Wapner said.

"They're hitting!" Jimmy said. "Shattering. All over the building. Right above the corridors. They've pinpointed the airways!"

"I'm sure they have," Wapner said. I heard other voices

in the background now, excited male voices. He was with Nash and the other men. I pictured them climbing the other ladder, escaping into the other tunnel.

"Dad!"

Nothing.

A big saw-toothed rock loomed up ahead, right in the center of our path. Tia and I skirted it on either side.

But a long moment later there was a cry from behind us.

We stumbled to a stop and looked back. Dr. Nuyen was down, writhing on the floor. She was holding her leg.

We raced back to her and knelt down. The rocky floor stabbed at my knees but I barely noticed. Even though she was wearing long pants, I could see there was something wrong. Her lower leg was angled, and when Tia pushed up the pant leg, blood flowed everywhere. A sharp spear of white bone protruded from the skin.

"You have to go," Dr. Nuyen said, trying to breathe.

"We'll carry you," Tia said.

"There's no time."

I helped her to a sitting position. I couldn't look at her leg. Even in the gloomy light, her face was already pale.

"Sunday," Tia said. "What happened to *Sunday*?"

"Elisha—the Biblical Elisha—had *two* bears," Dr. Nuyen said, and for a second I was sure she'd gone delirious from shock. *Two bears?*

But she went on, rapid-fire. "Their Formula T—the one the men worked on—isn't a treatment for males already exposed to Elisha. It *is* Elisha." Her voice was weak, but there was weight behind each word.

"But for *females*." Quick breaths, shallow.

I *couldn't* breathe.

"They want to decimate the world's female population. They have to be stopped. *You* have to stop them."

"You didn't know?" I said.

"None of us imagined this. Me. Rebecca Mack. Your mother." Strangled breathing attempt. "If we had any idea, Formula T would have been our priority. I would have gone after it harder. Or we would have just buried this place.

"Just after you left me at the computer, I stumbled across the truth," she wheezed. "And equally terrifying news: they'd moved from lab animals to human subjects."

"Sunday?" Tia said.

"Sunday. Before her, Kate, Team V's little Fratheist lab assistant. Wapner said she'd had a death in the family." She shook her head. "He was right." Her eyes closed. "Now they've exposed the others on Team V."

Below her ankle, her shoe and the ground surrounding it were soaked with blood. I remembered the far left door in security, the light in the little window. I pictured Kate the Fratheist lab assistant dying behind the door.

And Sunday.

The doctor opened her eyes. "Once you get out of here you'll find a fail-safe box on the closest large fir." Deep breath this time. "Both combinations are 8667. You have to push the button. *Fast.* No second thoughts. No hesitation."

She struggled out of her backpack and handed it to me. "The vaccine data is in there. Get it to your mother. Wapner has the Formula T data—and probably the concoction itself—and he's racing for the other exit." She took a shallow labored breath. "It's up to you to make sure he doesn't leave the tunnel." She squeezed my hand.

Tia and I lurched to our feet and took off. I didn't want to look back.

"Tell Merri I love her!" Dr. Nuyen said faintly. Then she urgently added something that sounded like "alone but merry." The confusing meaningless words were the last ones I heard from her.

Elisha turned to the young men who were mocking him,
and cursed them in the name of the Lord.
Then two she-bears rushed out of the woods,
and tore the offenders to pieces.

—2 Kings, 2:24

Chapter Nineteen

Running hard, I fingered my talkaloud. "Dad!" I said. "Dad! If you're anywhere near the tunnel A exit, you can't let Wapner and his guys out. They've got an Elisha formula for females. They killed Sunday with it. *They killed Sunday!*" I hurdled a big rock and stumbled but managed to stay on my feet and keep up with Tia. "But if you're in the tunnel, you have to get out. *You have to!*"

No answer. Where was he? My chest ached, I was exhausted, but I tried to stay focused. I didn't want to end up like Dr. Nuyen.

"No worries, Kellen." Dad. Dad's unreasonably calm voice on my talkaloud. "I'm safe. You find a safe spot, too."

"Where are you?"

"We'll talk soon."

Nothing more. But I felt recharged.

"Planes!" Gunny's voice over the talkaloud this time, excited. "Crop dusters! A whole flock of 'em! Coming in low! Trailing spray!"

Panic raised his pitch. "Overhead! *Overhead* now! *Shit coming down!*" The high-pitched thunder of propeller aircraft poured out of the talkaloud and faded away.

What was waiting for us outside? Elisha's Bear thick in the air, almost for certain. And Gunny, with his orders to take no prisoners. But in here there was no safety, either. If we didn't blow up this place, Wapner would.

And for Tia, there was no dilemma. Her only good choice was outside, where she didn't have to worry about Elisha. Yet.

Just Gunny.

We flew out of a curve. In the dim distance loomed a dirt-and-rock wall, fronted by a ladder.

"Almost there," Tia said. Two words, but I heard relief, hope, fear, sadness.

I felt crowded in by those emotions, too, but shoving them all aside was this big bullying feeling of inadequacy. I was a kid. I hadn't signed on for this junior assassin stuff. Knowing the consequences—death and destruction, never mind that the bad guys, mostly, would be the ones getting buried—how was I going to push that button?

I tried to ignore the feelings—all of them. We kept racing along. My talkaloud stayed quiet. When we reached the ladder, Tia spotted a control box and flipped a switch. Overhead, a door slid away, revealing a tangle of evergreen boughs rising into a dusky sky. I half expected to see Gunny's face peering over the edge, but no one was there.

Tia started up the ladder with me nudging her along. On the way I checked Dr. Nuyen's backpack: a couple of sealed metal containers, several data storage chips in plastic sleeves.

And no gun.

We reached the top of the ladder and stepped into the real world. A small clearing surrounded the exit door. I could hear aircraft not far off. Although the fresh air smelled wonderful and my lungs felt starved for oxygen, I was reluctant to take a deep breath.

Fifteen feet away stood a thick-trunked fir tree, and mounted on it was a metal box identical to the one at the cave. We hurried over, Tia reciting the combination out loud. But it was etched in my brain. I'd seen it in headlines and epitaphs. I'd seen it in my grandfather's. The date Elisha's Bear first charged out of the woods.

Heart pounding, I was about to touch in the combination on a pad of numbers when I heard a familiar voice. "Kids."

Gunny. He was standing on the other side of the shadowy clearing, a rifle dangling at his side, pointed at the forest floor.

I held my breath.

"*Hurry,*" he said. "You gotta nail those guys." I breathed. I punched numbers. The door opened. Aside from a small screen displaying another selection of numbers, the only prominent feature inside the box was a green button.

"I'll keep my distance," Gunny said as I pressed the combination again. "No telling who has what now."

I touched the last number. ARMED, the screen said. Then, ONCE BUTTON IS DEPRESSED, YOU WILL HAVE ELEVEN (11) SECONDS TO CLEAR THE AREA.

I hesitated. I didn't know why. I was a coward. I was a human being. I was a guy.

I pictured the woman jogger in front of my house, carefree. I pictured a giant lake of bodies, women and girls and girl babies this time.

I took Tia's hand.

Together, we pressed the button.

A series of loud beeps began. "Run!" I shouted, and we took off, toward the trees and gloom. We sprinted all out, Tia in front, me on her heels, swerving through trees, hurdling and stumbling over undergrowth. I waited for an explosion, hoping and dreading at the same time.

Suddenly, there was a muffled *whump!* The earth under our feet shook and bucked. Tia went down. I followed. We hugged the ground side by side. Pressed hard against the mossy dirt, I felt the concussion of one explosion after another. My eyes were closed, but I heard tree trunks creaking, branches rubbing overhead. Cones and twigs and needles ticked against my back and the backpack and dropped all around us.

Finally, it stopped.

"You okay, Tia?" I said, opening my eyes, sitting up. A haze of dust hung in the air.

"Sunday," she said. "She's gone . . . buried."

"I'm so sorry," I said, finding her hand and holding on. All I could see was that little rectangle of thick wire-imbedded glass and Sunday's brave terrified face behind it.

"She was dying," Tia said. I knew she was trying to reassure both of us, but I wasn't reassured, and I doubted that she was, either. I should have pushed the button by myself, kept her out of it.

Silently praying that the holding cells were sealed tight, I nodded. "Already dead, maybe." I studied Tia's face for some sign of illness. How quickly did Formula T do its work? When had they given it to Sunday? Not long ago. *Not long.*

But I decided it was too early to tell. If we'd been exposed to Elisha's Bears, it had been within the last five minutes or so.

I took a deep breath, testing my lungs. I couldn't help myself, but I clung to the idea that I was okay for now. The Bear was fast, but not *that* fast.

There was no chatter coming from my talkaloud. Good sign? Bad sign? I pushed the talk button. "Dad?"

No response.

"Dad?"

Why didn't he answer?

We got to our feet and retraced our footsteps. There was no more aircraft noise. Birds were beginning to chirp their quiet evening songs.

A deep depression in the ground marked the middle of the clearing and headed off into the woods. Trees in the cave-in's path were toppled or leaning. The ladderway had collapsed.

I lifted my talkaloud for one more try. "Gunny?"

"Over here," Gunny said. But it wasn't the talkaloud Gunny, it was the in-person Gunny. I stared in the direction of his voice until I saw him, standing in tree shadows and twilight. "The talkalouds won't work now," he said. "You've disabled the base." I could see what I thought was a look of approval. "Good job."

"Dad's wouldn't work, either?"

"Nope."

I felt my spirits rise like warm air.

"But let's go find him," Gunny said. "I've got a flashlight in my hand and a compass in my head. Stay well behind me, but follow the light."

Gunny headed off through the trees. We trailed the dancing beam at a distance. Every few minutes, he stopped and pointed the flashlight in our direction to make sure we were coming. Tia walked in front of me, sniffling back tears. I watched the dim outline of her shoulders rise and fall. I wanted to take her hand, but there wasn't room to walk side by side. Even single file, we were constantly squeezing past tree trunks and low branches and bushes.

I imagined her back on her bicycle built for two, alone, head down, pedaling.

Finally, we came to a familiar clearing. There was more light here, and it was easier to see where the ground had imploded. The trench headed away from the trees, ending in a smoking pile of crushed rock and concrete rubble where giant chunks of the explosive-charged cliff had rained down on the building. What *used to be* the building.

Gunny was standing next to it. "I'm gonna head toward the cave," he half shouted. "I'm guessing that's about where he was when the shit hit the fan."

He walked along the transformed face of the rock wall

and around the corner with us following. I was tempted to yell for Dad, but I was put off by the thought of someone else in the woods. Wapner and his loonies. Women from PAC.

Once we got to the outcropping's cleft, Gunny saved me the trouble. "Charlie!" he shouted. "Charlie Winters!" His voice echoed off the cliffs and died.

"Here." A voice. Dad's voice, coming from the direction of the cave. The voice was distant, or weak.

"Dad!" I shouted as Gunny trained his flashlight beam on the black fissure in the rock.

"Kellen."

The voice sounded closer. Tia took my hand. We waited, everyone holding their positions. And after a long moment, Dad tottered into the beam and stopped, keeping his distance. A gash angled down above his left eyebrow, and a thick trickle of blood skirted the bridge of his nose, detoured around his mouth, and ducked under his chin. He carried his rifle in his right hand, but his left arm hung straight down, limp.

He squinted into the flashlight beam, and Gunny moved it slightly off him. "Kellen?" Dad said.

"Gunny here." He swept the beam onto Tia and me. "Here's your boy. We're traveling separately until we find out who's hot and who's not."

"You're okay, Kellen?" Dad said. "Tia?"

"We're okay," I said.

"Sunday's really . . . ?" Dad studied our faces across the murky expanse. "I'm beyond sorry. Way beyond."

Next to me, Tia swallowed a sob. "What about you?" I asked.

"Mostly fine. I was in the cave, making sure Wapner didn't get out of the tunnel. Some rocks shook down on me, did a little damage."

"You were in there when the helicopters came?" I said.

"Not quite. By the time the crop dusters got here, though."

"Nobody got out?" I said.

"The door started to open, then all hell broke loose. Nobody got out. You two did that?"

"We had to."

"How'd you get into the box?"

"Dr. Nuyen." Tia and I gave him and Gunny a short explanation of the doctor's role in this, what happened with her and Formula T and Sunday.

"Sunday was already failing when we saw her," I said. "The stuff they cooked up must've been potent."

"Don't worry," Dad said. "The cockroaches are gone. They're buried under tons of rubble. Them and their plague."

"For now," Tia said.

"The truck's a ten-minute walk down the trail," Gunny said. "I suggest we go there and take whatever we need for the next day or two at least. By then we should know more."

Yesterday I found your car keys in a dark cubby of my dusty desk,
even though I'd sworn to you I hadn't touched them,
the morning you grabbed the spares, annoyed,
and ran out the door on your way to an appointment,
on your way to meet up with a monster.
I wish I could hear you say I told you so.

—EPITAPH FOR CHASE LANGLEY
(NOVEMBER 23, 2035–AUGUST 6, 2067),
BY CHLOE MALDIN, HIS WIFE,
DECEMBER 19, 2068

CHAPTER TWENTY

We should know more.

That's all Gunny said, but we all realized what he meant.
We should know more about who was going to live or die,
who would need food and supplies in another day or two.

Who wouldn't.

"You can walk, Dad?" I said.

"My legs are fine."

Gunny led us to the dirt road and down it. Except for
Tia and me, we must have looked like a short procession of
antisocial strangers—loners—carefully pacing themselves
to avoid contact with one another.

Once near the truck, which Gunny had driven well off

the road and into the woods, he stepped a distance away and told Tia and me to help ourselves first, since we were the least likely to be infected. I hadn't been out in the air when the stuff fell, and Tia of course was a girl.

But so was Sunday.

Under the tarp we found food and water, flashlights, lanterns, batteries, blankets. Tia and I took what we needed and moved away, farther into the forest. We located a small flat clearing within shouting distance of the pickup, turned on the lantern, gathered cedar boughs for a mattress, and laid down our blankets. While we were busy, flashlight beams danced away from the truck in turns. A lantern winked on fifty yards away through the trees; a second one came to life fifty yards in the opposite direction.

"Dad!" I shouted.

"Here!" he answered, and I identified which light belonged to him.

"Gunny!" Tia called. We all knew where he was setting up camp now, but I was glad Tia had thought to include him in our little roll call.

His response confirmed his whereabouts, his health. It traveled back to us from the direction of the other light. "That's me!"

We dimmed our lanterns. Full dark fell all around us. The night had grown chilly.

The hollow *clap-clap-clap* of a helicopter—distant, for a time—disturbed the quiet. The sound got louder, closer. I doused our lantern. Dad's and Gunny's went dark, too. A searchlight probed the trees a quarter mile away, then nearer, as the chopper hovered and moved, hovered and moved, and we scrambled into darker tree shadows and undergrowth.

The copter drifted away. The light disappeared. The noise faded and died.

From somewhere far off came the low growl of an engine, something big and ponderous creeping along the road. I pictured PAC's armored vehicle—the one the sentry, Miller, probably, had described over the talkaloud—coming to assess the damage and do more if necessary.

A minute later there was a shockingly louder noise, startling and explosive, thundering through the forest, echoing off the surrounding hills.

Then it was quiet again—so quiet it felt as if a giant blanket had dropped over us. The engine sound was gone.

"A mine," Tia said. "More killing."

I pictured body parts—flesh and metal—scattered across a narrow dirt road, blasted against trees, hanging from branches. Tia took my hand. We sat, close and silent, on a fallen log. While we downed water, cheese and crackers, dried fruit, and chocolate, I couldn't help wondering if this was my last supper. I tried to lighten that dark thought with a couple of questions: Shouldn't we have some wine? And a few apostles?

The lame attempt at gallows humor didn't work. My mind instantly boomeranged back to other questions, life-or-death ones: The three males in our little group were supposedly inoculated against Elisha, but how many of us were, really? Was the vaccine any good? Had it had time to be effective? It didn't take a genius to realize that one or more of us might not get out of this.

As if she was listening in on my thoughts, Tia shivered, head to toe. "It's cold," she said.

We slipped off our shoes and stretched out between the blankets. I should have felt awkward, maybe, but I was too tired to feel awkward, and by now Tia seemed as if she belonged next to me, her ankle resting lightly on mine. I stared up at the stars, brilliant in the thin clean air, and listened to her breathe, judging the efficiency of her ins and outs. I took a deep breath, then another, evaluating mine.

She laid her fingers, then the soft inner surface of her wrist, on my forehead. She kept it there, which made me nervous for at least a couple of reasons. "Feel okay?" she asked, faking offhandedness.

For a moment I thought about asking *her* to tell *me* how I felt. But I decided I'd rather not know how the temperature of my forehead measured up against the impartial no-nonsense warmth of her wrist. "Fine," I said.

My eyes closed. I felt Tia turn on her side, away from me. I heard her try to stifle a sob, to keep it to herself, and I put my arm around her and pulled her close. She squirmed nearer, her shoulders to my chest, my lips an inch from her neck. I breathed her in and held on tight, experiencing the jerky rhythms of her quiet weeping. I tried not to cry myself.

Despite all that had happened, being this close to her felt vaguely sexy, and I allowed myself to enjoy the sensation for a long moment. The last thing I remembered before I drifted away was touching her cheek, and the heartbreaking feel of her warm tears on my fingertips.

I pray you've stayed far away,
hiked to the highest reaches of what passes for heaven these days,
because although unimaginable evil has arrived here
on a mission from hell,
your absence, the thought that all of you are isolated and safe,
has kept me going (for as long as I could go)
in the middle of this purgatory—
that and a failing heart that still beats with everlasting love for you.

—NOTE FOUND IN THE BOTTOM OF A ONE-OARED ROWBOAT BEACHED
NEAR KINGSTON, ON WASHINGTON'S OLYMPIC PENINSULA, ALONG
WITH THE BODY OF JOSHUA WINTERS,
AUGUST 14, 2067

CHAPTER TWENTY-ONE

A cough startled me awake.

Not mine. Not Tia's.

Somewhere off in the cold dark woods.

Which direction? I sat up. I waited.

More coughing. Then a rapid-fire series of rough, wracking, chest-deep eruptions. And this time there was no doubt about who was responsible.

Gunny.

Tia stirred. She got up on an elbow. "What?"

"Coughing. Gunny."

"*No.*"

Off in the trees, a lantern came on. I finger-nudged Tia's chin in that direction—Gunny's direction.

More coughing. Not mine, but I felt it deep in my chest.

"Gunny!" Dad was awake, too.

No answer.

The lantern moved up, then side to side, as if it was waving.

Then in one more or less steady direction.

It disappeared, appeared again, disappeared, as Gunny walked among the trees.

Gradually, the intermittent lantern glow faded, the coughing quieted. Gradually, I realized what he was doing. He was leaving. Going off to die, like a wounded animal.

The lantern light disappeared. Minutes passed. I felt empty. First Sunday, then Dr. Nuyen. Now Gunny. Tia wept. She should have been out of tears by now. I put my arm around her and looked up into the blackness of the moonless night.

Ursa Major, the Great Bear, looked down on us. The sky was so clear that I felt myself staring past that constellation to other stars, wondering if this nightmare would be as endless as the universe.

"Kellen?" Dad called.

"We're here," I said. "We're okay."

"Say a prayer," he said. "I'll see you in the morning."

CHAPTER TWENTY-TWO

I heard the cry of a bird.

I opened my eyes and blinked out at the glassy gray of the lake. It was early dawn. The sun was still on its way. Low clouds, pillowing against the hills, clinging to the water, would delay its arrival. The resident loon patrolled the shoreline, looking for breakfast, reminding me of my own hunger. I sat up, trying not to disturb the blankets covering Tia, who was still asleep or pretending.

I got up and walked barefoot to the beach. The loon, thirty feet away, didn't alter his course. He was used to me by now. At my approach, a trout swirled in the shallows and headed for deeper water, but the bird, too independent or proud to accept my help, continued on.

I picked up a flat rock and sent it skipping across the surface. Then another. And more. I began to lose the stiffness in my body from another night of sleeping on dirt and cedar boughs. Seventeen nights now, fifteen in this place.

Today we were heading back—hiking to the remains of the Foothills compound, climbing into Gunny's pickup, bypassing the mines, driving to the little bay where we left *Mr. Lucky*, cruising to Afterlight and Seattle and whatever awaited us there.

Dad had led us here—the place where he and Aunt Paige and my grandmother once waited in vain for my grandfather. Dad thought it would be safer in case PAC came calling again with its armored vehicles or helicopters or a second helping of the Bear and plans to finish the job. It was a long two-day trudge from the lab, and for much of the way, even when I was watching and listening for signs of Elisha in Dad and Tia and analyzing my own state of health, I stewed over our decision not to come here earlier, before we ever set foot in the lab.

Sunday would still be alive.

But at what cost? Dad had argued the night we arrived, and even Tia took his side. What would have happened if we hadn't been there to push the button? Would Dr. Nuyen have gotten out safely and in time to blow the place? If not, would Wapner and his men and their Formula T have killed practically every female in the world?

They convinced me, mostly.

But I couldn't forget Sunday's face in that little window.

Or Gunny's lantern fading into the night.

Or Margaret Nuyen's brave farewell from the tunnel floor: *Tell Merri I love her.* I hoped I'd get the chance to deliver that message.

I walked back up the low bank to the campsite. Tia was still sleeping. On the other side of the fire pit, Dad was sitting up, wrapped in his covers. He nodded to me, but he was distracted, studying the area of damp dirt that lay between us.

I followed his gaze.

I saw indentations. Deep impressions in the soft ground. I stepped closer. They were prints, huge ones, dozens of them, crisscrossing the campsite as if the big animal that left them was pacing back and forth, waiting for someone to wake up and give it its proper respect.

"A bear?" I said. Tia didn't stir. She wasn't faking.

Dad nodded. "Big one."

"*Your* bear?"

He smiled. He'd filled my head with images of his bear. "I doubt it. How long do bears live anyway?"

I shrugged. I didn't know. I didn't want to know. I wanted to believe it was Dad's long-ago visitor. "You want to go down to the lake?"

Dad stretched and stood. He shuffled over and settled in next to me, close. He was wearing socks, formerly white, but they were stained the color of the soil under his feet. He had a three-week growth of beard and a head full of tangled hair and rumpled ratty clothes that had been in and out of the lake a number of times.

He looked just right.

"You know when I first saw you and the girls?" Dad said. "When I got off *Mr. Lucky* and you were waiting for me on the beach?" He put his arm around my shoulders and we gazed out at the lake. "And I made the boneheaded mistake of thinking—saying—you were thirteen?"

"It wasn't a big deal. You had a lot on your mind."

"It *was* a big deal. Even with everything else that was happening and would happen, the fact that I didn't even know my own kid's age bothered me the most. It drove me nuts. Especially when I thought about what you'd done for me."

"Now you know. I'm fourteen. I'll be fourteen for a long time."

"I don't want to be wrong again," Dad said. "When you have a birthday, pass your trials, learn to drive, get out of school, figure out what you want to do with your life, I want to be there."

"My life—" Should I tell him I had dreams of moving here—to the Peninsula—when I got older? Living the life of a loner?

Did I, still, after everything I'd learned and seen?

"As soon as I can," Dad continued, "I want to find some moorage for *Mr. Lucky* and me on the Seattle waterfront. I can go fishing from there and still spend a lot of time with you."

My chest filled with something warm. I thought of my long-ago poem, the one on the wayfarers' wall. The words—*thinking of me*—were true, after all. *They were true.* But for a moment I considered telling him not to do it, that it would mean giving up his freedom, being under someone's—*everyone's*—thumb again.

But did he really have freedom here in the hinterlands? In the end, the throwbacks and loners of Afterlight and the rest of the Peninsula had only one freedom—the freedom to die.

And a new dream was beginning to materialize in my head. If Dad came to Seattle, maybe I could live with him on *Mr. Lucky*. Because the idea of moving back in with Mom after all this, even if Aunt Paige returned to the house, even if Tia was still there, felt like a nightmare.

"That would be great," I said. I would bring up my new dream later. One step at a time.

Dad gave my shoulder a squeeze and let me go. I found Tia's hand in the mound of blankets and tugged her to a sitting position. "Come on," I said.

She rubbed at her eyes. "What, Kelly?"

Kelly. Her new nickname for me. A term of endearment, she called it. Coming from her, it was okay; I'd put up with anything that might soften the pain in her eyes.

For more than two weeks Dad had observed and sympathized with that pain, too. He'd decided to team up with Tia, adopting the *Kelly* tag, with only an occasional and secretive twinkle and wink of his eye.

I still called Tia *Tia*. As often as I could.

"We're going down to the lake, Tia," I said. "Take a look for Dad's bear." I gestured at the tracks all around us.

Her sleepy eyes grew wide. She scrambled to her feet, grasping my hand hard, scanning our little clearing for signs of something big and bad. When she was satisfied that the something had gone away, she gulped in a big breath and let it slowly out.

We walked to the water's edge. The loon was out of sight. The morning had grown brighter. I wondered what was happening out in the world. How many throwbacks and loners and innocent kids and bystanders had died from this Elisha? Had the quarantine worked? Or had someone miscalculated? Had Elisha spilled over? How much information had gotten out? We had no radio, no news, true or otherwise.

How would we be treated when we returned?

Dad stared across the water at the opposite shoreline, eyes narrowed against the gathering light. Tia and I followed his lead. Did he see something? A shadow moving through the undergrowth? An image conjured from a memory?

"Sunday would like it here," Tia said.

I felt pain at the sound of Sunday's name. I welcomed it. I wouldn't ever let myself forget that she'd died because of me.

"She'd want to meet this bear," Dad said, making Tia smile.

A breeze kicked up, rippling the lake, reshaping the wisps of fog.

"Will they believe us about Formula T?" I said.

"They *have* to," Dad said.

"Dr. Nuyen said it was up to us to stop Wapner, Kelly," Tia said. "We did it."

For now, I thought, remembering her words from a couple of weeks ago that seemed like a couple of years ago. Until the next wacko scientist decided to even the score. Would someone else be there to stop him?

And what about the world's reigning wacko scientist, Rebecca Mack? Would anyone ever stop her? What was going to happen when old age finally took her? Or someone—a militant Fratheist, maybe—decided to speed her death along?

That idea—putting an end to her—intrigued me for a moment as I once more pictured Gunny slipping away to die and I imagined all the others who were massacred on Rebecca Mack's orders. But would PAC wither up and die along with her? Or would it be like Hercules slicing away at the Hydra— two fresh and fearsome heads replacing her one?

From somewhere far down the shoreline, the loon cried again. The sound, skimming unhindered across the water, was sad but reassuring. It will be okay, it said. *It will be okay.*

I kept staring. On the distant bank, something moved.

The wind, I suspected at first. The wind in the tall spidery bushes bordering the lake.

But I kept my gaze fixed on the spot. I held perfectly still, waiting. And deep into that long breathless moment, I swore I glimpsed a flash of silvery brown, the wagging side to side of a huge shaggy skull, the sweep of a giant paw.

I swore I did.

We'd arranged with the funeral folks for a return to ashes and dust,
imagining our souls rising in pale smoke
to mingle with the clouds and reunite with each other.
But the fearsome mass-killer thing came calling,
and the body I loved so much—yours—ended up
not wafting to the heavens as cinders and grit but here,
decaying in this crowded restless resting place.
We plan in comfort. We learn in sorrow.

—EPITAPH FOR BRANCH CARROLL
(NOVEMBER 23, 1992–AUGUST 9, 2067),
BY KIMBERLY CARROLL, HIS WIFE,
DECEMBER 22, 2068

CHAPTER TWENTY-THREE

The surface lost most of its chop as Dad steered *Mr. Lucky* around the breakwater and into the harbor. From a quarter mile away, Afterlight looked like a ghost town. But as we approached the refueling dock, I saw, through the morning fog and drizzle, a wispy column of gray smoke rising into the sky from the back edge of town. And then I saw people—all females—on their feet, shuffling along, carting stuff from shore to dock to boat.

Dad aimed us at a berthing space. "Half the boats are gone," he yelled from the wheel as he maneuvered us close and I threw a line to a woman standing near the stern of an ancient wreck of a boat. "And I don't think they've gone fishing."

The woman glanced at Tia but saved most of her attention for me, then Dad, as he stepped onto the deck. "Where you been?" she asked him as two girls—nine or ten years old, maybe—emerged from the cabin of the old tub, staring.

"At sea," Dad said. "Up north. What happened here?"

"The Bear," the woman said, blank-faced. She eyed the name on our boat. "You got lucky. Missed the Bear, missed the Coast Patrol."

I leaped over the side, caught an aft line from Tia, and half-hitched it to a dock cleat. Tia, then Dad, followed me over. "The men?" I asked her. "They're all dead?"

"A few took off for the hills once they figured out what was happening. They haven't returned. All the rest are dead, my man included."

"Sorry," we said in unison.

Glassy-eyed, the woman shrugged. "Never should've come here. People said it wasn't safe."

"You buried them already?" I asked, wondering about traces of the Bear still hanging around. I pictured the mass grave at Epitaph Road, even though I estimated the entire population of Brighter Day to be less than a thousand. Much less now. Dad handed me the nozzle end of a fueling hose. I stuck it in *Mr. Lucky*'s filler pipe and started the flow.

"Cremated," she said, and Tia's hand went to her mouth.

The breeze picked up. From *Mr. Lucky*'s hold, overwhelming the smell of diesel, came the stench of rotting salmon. As soon as we'd gotten on board we'd dumped the carcasses and cleaned up as best we could, but the stink hung on.

"Is that the smoke?" Tia murmured, nodding toward the distant plume.

The woman nodded. "The co-op. Old wood. Good for burning. We moved all the stores out, all the bodies in. Then we torched it. If you need food or anything, some women are rationing out supplies near the marina entrance. They'll be surprised to see you, but they'll be generous. Everyone's leaving, heading back to so-called civilization, so there's no reason to be stingy. The stuff wasn't exactly ours anyway."

"You're going to Seattle?" Dad said.

"Soon."

"In that?" I said, gesturing toward her boat.

"It floats," she said. "It runs."

"Anyone else leaving soon?" Dad said.

"A couple of other boats."

"Same shape as yours?"

"About."

"We'll join you," Dad said. "Just to make sure everyone arrives safely."

The woman gave Dad a look, as if she wasn't quite sure about the idea or him. "That okay?" Dad said.

"It's fine," she said. "It's good."

"Elisha's Bear," Tia said. "When did it hit?"

"Going on three weeks, probably. A day, or maybe two

days, after all those cops showed up in town. And the other two."

"You see planes?" Dad asked. "Helicopters?"

She shook her head. "Thought we heard some. Didn't see any."

"Other two?" I said. "What other two?"

"City women, nosing around, acting like they were interested in being here. I think they were just interested in slumming, looking down their noses at us."

"What did they do?" Tia asked, and I got this empty feeling in my chest, recalling the junkyarddog items about women planting the deadly test versions of Elisha's Bear.

"Drove around, walked around, stopped at the co-op, ate at the café, went on a hike."

"To where?" Dad said.

"Rainbow Falls."

Dad shook his head. "More likely the reservoir. The trail passes right by Afterlight's water source. You were drinking it. Showering in it."

"What?" the woman said.

"We'll tell you," Dad said. "Let's all go take a look at those supplies."

How much longer will it last?
Looking for you around every corner, reaching for you in the night,
walking into our apartment after a long day of distractions
and being freshly surprised at the empty cold silence.

—EPITAPH FOR SETH FRANKLIN (MAY 3, 2043–AUGUST 7, 2067),
BY HEATHER FRANKLIN, HIS WIFE OF FIVE MONTHS AND FOREVER,
DECEMBER 23, 2068

CHAPTER TWENTY-FOUR

As our small raggedy fleet approached the marina, the setting sun broke through the clouds and lit up the glass faces of downtown Seattle's tall buildings. I couldn't tell if they looked friendly or menacing. What kind of welcome would Tia and I get? And what had happened here? Had Elisha slipped past the quarantine?

But as we nudged against the dock we saw men, looking healthy and unconcerned.

"Do you think they know anything, Kelly?" Tia said.

"If they don't," I said, looking around at the other boats tying up around us, "they will soon enough."

Dad had to make arrangements for moorage space, and he wasn't ready to take on the city or Mom, anyway, so he gave us money for cab fare and turned us loose. We promised to find him at the marina by the next afternoon.

My e-spond and Tia's were history, destroyed and discarded during our adventure, but we could have borrowed someone else's phone to call my mother—a stomach-turning idea—or hers. We didn't. We decided our first hellos should be face-to-face.

So we climbed into the backseat of the cab without preliminaries. We would show up at our house unannounced, carrying nothing but Dr. Nuyen's battered backpack and its contents—the scary metal containers, the data storage chips. We had to do this, I knew, but my heart pounded. And as Tia pressed up against me, practically pinning me to the door, I swore I could hear hers pounding, too.

Paparazzi, news buffoons, talking heads,
muckrakers and mud-throwers, seeking sensation and spin,
where were you when the devil was devising this sinister story,
dreaming up something substantial and twisted for the world,
full of conflict and consequence and aftermath,
pictures at eleven?

—EPITAPH FOR JATINDRA PATEL (FEBRUARY 6, 2061–AUGUST 9, 2067),
BY MADHURI PATEL, HIS MOTHER,
DECEMBER 24, 2068

CHAPTER TWENTY-FIVE

According to the clock on Mom's desk, it was past midnight. Tia and I were alone again, sitting close together on the couch, waiting for the start of the debriefing or inquisition or whatever it was that Rebecca Mack had in mind when she'd ordered us kept under wraps until she could fly in from San Diego.

I couldn't help picturing her on a broom.

We'd struggled past a tearful reunion with our mothers and a wrenching encounter with Sunday's. Then it was long showers, fresh clothes, and leftovers, all with Mom lurking around like a library cop. Finally, she dumped us in her office to watch over Dr. Nuyen's precious backpack, which Mom had rushed in here earlier, even before the tears dried.

Just for the record, none of those tears came from my eyes. Nothing about our homecoming felt especially warm and fuzzy to me. By now I mostly understood Mom's role in all of this, and seeing her again was way more bitter than sweet. The thought of living with her in this house—even for a short time—made me long for cedar boughs and damp ground and a cold-water lake.

"What are they going to do to us, Kelly?" Tia said. The fresh concern in her voice—fueled by the surroundings, no doubt—put an edge on the familiar question. We'd had weeks to talk over what we would face when we got back, but our fears were still there, ready to ignite. How could they not be, with images of Sunday and Dr. Nuyen and Gunny and smoke rising over Afterlight constantly replaying through our heads?

"I think they need to worry about what *we're* going to do to *them*," I said. We'd had time to talk about that, too, although so far our plans were sketchy.

She barely nodded, maybe not even a little reassured by my brave words.

"Someone has to do something," I said. "And the someone's us. We can't chicken out just because we're within PAC's reach again."

"I'm *not* chickening out," she said. "I just can't pretend I'm not worried about what could happen . . . afterward."

"I'm worried, too," I said, "so I'm trying to concentrate on what Rebecca Mack and her buddies caused. What they set in motion."

"What they did to the people we loved," Tia said, sitting up a little straighter. "And everyone who loved them."

"Exactly," I said. After seeing how Sunday's death had affected her family, I was more determined than ever not to let this just fade away.

We'd barely gotten into the house that evening when we attracted a crowd, including Sunday's mom. For days and days we'd worried about how we would tell her, but we didn't have to say a thing, at the start anyway. She could count to two. She could subtract two from three. Her face told us she knew who'd survived, who hadn't.

One night in the mountains we'd woken up to the chilling cries of a wild animal—a big cat of some kind, we guessed—drifting across the water. Sunday's mom came close to duplicating that mournful sound once we began answering her questions about Sunday's death, even though we left out or altered or sugarcoated the most horrific and revealing and unspeakable of the details.

An explosion, was what we told her. A cave-in. We didn't know the cause. We were outside. Sunday was inside, asleep.

Nothing about the second bear. Not to Sunday's mom or anyone. We'd save that piece of the story for later.

Tia's mom was a mess—overjoyed to see her daughter, crushed by the absence of her niece. The sisters were off somewhere together now, propping each other up.

The door opened. The old lady walked in, followed by my mother, who barely looked my way. After our first long embrace—too long for me—she'd kept her distance. My hostility must have been showing through.

Mom found a chair against the opposite wall; Rebecca Mack took the one at the desk in the center of the room, the center of attention. Fittingly, her perch was higher than the rest. She could look down on us.

"Is that the Formula V material?" she said, eyeing Dr. Nuyen's beat-up backpack. So far she hadn't even said hello, but it didn't bother me. I decided to let Mom answer the question.

"All there, as far as I can tell," she said.

I didn't like the insinuation, like we might have lost something. "Everything Dr. Nuyen *had* in the backpack *is still in* the backpack," I said.

"You and I will take it to San Diego first thing in the morning," Rebecca Mack said to Mom, ignoring me. The old lady's thin hand crept up to her thin neck. She stroked her skim-milk skin. On her third finger was a big blue-green stone. Bones and turquoise.

"I'll call the lab when we're done here," Mom said. "Let them know to expect us."

So far they'd acted like they were the only people in the room, but finally Rebecca Mack turned to Tia and me. For an uncomfortable few seconds it was a stare-down. "You're both heroes, no doubt," Rebecca Mack offered half begrudgingly, breaking the silence. "You've been instrumental in keeping the world on the right course."

She didn't have an inkling of *how* instrumental, not yet.

But I didn't feel like a hero. I didn't want to be one, especially with the recognition coming from her. "Isn't it kind of lame that you had to rely on a couple of kids to get the world out of a jam?" I said. "And that one of them was a *guy*? Your plan mostly sucked."

"As Dr. Mack just told you, Kellen," Mom said, "we're grateful for everything you and Septiembre did." Her tired pale face was taking on a little color.

"We don't want your gratitude, *Mother*. Your boss here had an excuse or two for what she did. What she's still doing. What's yours? Did you know what PAC was all about when you joined up? Did you ever think about leaving?" I got up. Before I knew it I was standing over her, watching her shrink back against the wall. "Did you ever think *I've got a son? How can I do this? How can I do this to my son's father, someone I supposedly loved?*

"And her name's *Tia*."

Mom managed to close her mouth long enough to start a sentence. "Your father wasn't a target."

"Wasn't he?" I said.

"Kellen *heard* you," Tia said.

"Heard—" Mom began.

"That's right," I said. "In your room. You and Aunt Paige and then Mack the Knife here." I glanced at Rebecca Mack, wondering how she liked her nickname. She looked unruffled and half amused. "Plotting. Scheming. Ignoring Aunt Paige begging you to warn Dad or let her do it. You were perfectly okay with letting him die."

"I wasn't *okay* with it."

242

"You *were*! You're a cold-blooded killer, no better than the bad guys you've slaughtered. What about *me*? Would you kill me, too?"

"Your mother was moving you out of harm's way," the old lady said.

"I wasn't talking to you," I said. "Anyway, that was *this* time. What about *next*? If I'm in the way, is it just tough shit? What about all the innocent people who died during this little massacre?"

"The stakes were too high," Mom said. Her voice was barely audible.

"Were they?" I said. "You don't have a clue."

"We could have been better prepared," the old lady admitted.

"Better prepared?" Tia said. "You don't know the half of it."

"Really," Dr. Mack said. Smug. The world's biggest know-it-all.

"Really," Tia said.

"Did you ever have any sleepless nights over what you've done?" I asked Rebecca Mack.

She didn't answer. She looked at Mom, like *Put a cork in this kid's mouth.*

"Did you ever wonder during those sleepless nights I hope you had if there was some guy just as clever and scary-evil as you?" I said to her papery old face.

She frowned, silent. I had her attention. "There *was*," I said.

"Wapner," Tia said. "He killed Sunday. He aimed to kill

you, too. Both of you. Me. Every female in the world."

For the next several minutes Tia and I told Rebecca Mack and Mom the story of Formula T. We told them about Sunday, and Kate the Fratheist lab assistant, and the other female scientists, and Dr. Nuyen, and Wapner, and the fail-safe button.

It felt satisfying to watch the faces of know-it-alls become the faces of know-nothings.

We finished. The room was quiet for a long time while Rebecca Mack and Mom gathered themselves and Tia and I just hung out, empty.

"It—Formula T—is buried?" Mom said finally.

"Deep," I said.

"*Heroes* wasn't a strong enough word," the old lady said.

"There *ain't* no heroes," I said.

"Brighter Day started this," Tia said.

Rebecca Mack lifted her eyebrows. "Not without justification," she said. "The conflict was started long before Brighter Day."

"Brighter Day's goal was to end the conflict," Mom said. "And the ruin."

"It didn't work, did it," I said to her. "Half the world murdered, the other half on some future mad scientist's shit list, Afterlight wiped out on your watch. And you're just going merrily along with the whole thing." She looked beaten. I didn't care.

"A plot like Wapner's won't happen again," Dr. Mack said.

"Who's going to prevent the next one?" I said. "You have some other kids you're going to send out to do your dirty work?"

"Unlike males, we learn from our mistakes," Dr. Mack said. "But to do that, we need every piece of information we can get." She took out a recorder, clicked it on, and set it on the corner of the desk. "I want you to tell your whole story, from the hour you left here until the hour you walked back in."

We told our tale, parts of it for the second time. We made sure to include all the details we'd spared Sunday's mom. We emphasized how ignorant PAC had been, what would have resulted if Wapner had succeeded. Now the clock said 1:25, but I wasn't tired. Hitting Dr. Mack and Mom with a blow-by-blow description of what they'd turned loose was painful but energizing.

"So here we are," I said finally, "waiting for the next chapter."

"There will be no next chapter," the old lady said.

"You need to get back to your normal lives," Mom said.

"There's no *getting back*," I said. "There's no *normal*. I'll be in this house until I can figure out where else to live, and then I'm gone."

"You don't mean that, Kellen," Mom said, acting surprised, acting like I was the irrational one. "You can't just leave."

I returned her hurt expression with a look of my own that I hoped came off as cool and detached even though I didn't feel cool and detached. "Watch me."

"Where would you go?"

"I have options. People who aren't mass murderers." I expected her to react, but she just sat and stared at me. "How could you?" I added. *"How could you?"*

"Paige," Mom said. "Your father. Those are your options?"

I glared back at her. "Anywhere but here."

"You'll throw it all away," she said.

"Ask me if I care."

Tia stood. She paced, ending up at my side. "We know everything," she said. "We could expose you." For an instant my heart fluttered anxiously, but then I decided Mack the Knife and her apprentice wouldn't take that kind of threat seriously.

And I was right. "To whom?" Rebecca Mack said. "Everyone who matters already knows."

"Everyone who matters?" I said.

"Why do you care about Anderson, then?" Tia said. "Why did you arrest her?"

"Ms. Anderson wasn't exactly arrested," Mom said. "She's been detained."

"We feel a certain level of maturity and accomplishment is needed before a person can appreciate our history," Dr. Mack said. "And even after that, we like to be prudent with the dissemination of information. Consequently, Ms. Anderson has been suspended from her teaching position."

"Whispers and rumors?" I said. "That's *dissemination?*"

"Our communication methods have been effective," the

old lady said. "If you two are smart—and I know you are—you won't waste your time trying to undermine them."

I ignored that little warning, if that was what it was. I didn't want to get into a discussion of what Tia and I could or would do about getting our message out. "Have you even told Merri—Dr. Nuyen's daughter—what happened to her mom?"

"She knows her mother is dead," Dr. Mack said. "She was informed earlier this evening. We didn't provide her with the particulars. We didn't *know* the particulars."

"That must have been a real disappointment," Tia said. "You're obviously ashamed of the truth. The whole truth anyway."

"We live with shame," Mom said. "It's part of what we do."

"And what we *did*," Rebecca Mack said. "But like you, we didn't have a choice."

"Wapner and his loonies felt the same way," I said.

Rebecca Mack didn't have a response. Mom didn't have a response. For a long moment we all stared at each other and at the walls and off into the future.

The women were unbending. The walls were closing in. The future still had some promise. I steadied my hand on Tia's shoulder and we walked out.

We met in our favorite coffee shop yesterday,
me in my layers of cold-weather gear,
you in your faded green T-shirt,
the one that turned your eyes the color of thyme.
We talked about the old days,
and although a glance in the tableside mirror
confirmed the presence of new lines and shadows and loss on my face,
I noticed that you hadn't changed at all,
that you still looked exactly the same as you do
in the photo on our piano,
the one with your faded green T-shirt and thyme-colored eyes and
time-frozen smile, the one resting on a tear-stained obituary notice
with the dates of your coming and going.

—EPITAPH FOR BENJAMIN BRADY
(JANUARY 16, 2035–AUGUST 10, 2067),
BY KATE SIFFORD, HIS ONE AND ONLY,
DECEMBER 25, 2068

CHAPTER TWENTY-SIX

At the top of the stairs, Tia and I said good night. She headed to her room, I headed to mine. I had Mom's e-spond and a call to make.

I touched in Aunt Paige's number, willing to risk waking her.

She answered quickly. "I'm not ready to talk to you, Heather."

"It's me."

"Kellen?"

I told her yes. She responded with tears. After she calmed down, I found out where she was—an apartment (her idea, no restrictions, except some suspected surveillance)—and gave her a summary of everything that had happened since I'd left home. Even though I tried to keep it to the basics, she reacted with a million questions and more crying, especially when I told her the part about Dad—her brother—being in Seattle and planning on staying, and nearly an hour passed before the conversation began to run out of steam.

I plugged in a question. "Do you know what they did with Ms. Anderson—our history instructor?"

"I can make an educated guess. A place on the university campus called Harmony Tower. It's a formerly abandoned dorm PAC uses to detain mild dissidents. Until they're re-indoctrinated and deemed safe again anyway. I was afraid they'd send me there. But I guess they considered me mostly harmless. And in a critical job."

"I miss you so much," she added while I thought about what she'd just told me. It was about the tenth time she'd said those words.

"Me, too," I said.

"You have to visit me. And bring Tia."

"I will. Soon. Maybe tomorrow, if I ever get out of bed. Do you know if people in Harmony Tower can have visitors?"

"With some constraints, I'd expect. Are you thinking about visiting her?"

"I want to."

"Give it a try. I think the worst that can happen is that one of the watchdogs there will tell you no. But be careful. You've got some pull with your mom on your side, but you wouldn't want to end up in the place yourself under any circumstances. And you have your trials coming."

My trials. The last thing on my mind. Something else had taken their place.

Before we said good-bye she managed to tell me once more how much she missed me and I promised once more to visit her soon.

Two thirty a.m. wasn't late if you had things on your mind. I carried them down the hall to Tia's room, expecting to have to wake her up. But she was lying in the dark with her eyes open. In the dim light from the window I saw them glistening.

She sat up as I perched myself on the edge of her bed. She smelled of shampoo and soap.

"Can't sleep?" I asked.

"Sunday's bed is so empty," she murmured, and I took her hand. It was cold, even though the heat of a July day still hung in the room. "It all felt like a nightmare at the time, but being away from it—here—makes it seem more real."

"We can't bring her back," I said. "But maybe we can do something that would make us feel a little better when we go on from here."

Even in the near-dark, I saw a question on her face and

in the angle of her body. So I gave her my answer. And we talked, late.

I returned to my room with thoughts of our planning and plotting filling my head, but that would have to wait until the next day. Right now I had something else to do.

I went to my desk and touched my computer to life. I did a search, hoping. And after a couple of tries to find the right spelling combination, I located what I was looking for. NetSketch had a listing for alonebutmerri.

The profile was slim and generic and contained no photos, but I was almost sure I had the right person. So I composed a note to her.

MERRI—I DON'T KNOW WHAT EXACTLY PAC TOLD YOU, BUT YOUR MOM IS THE BIGGEST REASON FEMALES ON THIS PLANET HAVE A FUTURE. SHE'S A HERO. AND SHE GAVE ME A MESSAGE TO PASS ON TO YOU. "TELL MERRI I LOVE HER," IS WHAT SHE SAID.

For good measure I added ALWAYS, imagining that Dr. Nuyen would have wanted me to. I hadn't included much in the way of information, but if Merri felt shortchanged she could get back to me, and maybe by then I'd have thought of a way to blunt the specifics of her mom's death, even if it meant making up something less painful. For Merri. And me.

I posted the note, knowing she wouldn't read it until the next day at the earliest. But at least I'd sent it. And maybe she would respond. It would be good—mostly—to hear from her, even under the circumstances.

Finally, I headed to bed.

251

I've tried three kinds of phones,
a dozen different messages,
and innumerable cries in the dark.
I'm waiting for just one answer.

—EPITAPH FOR JOEY BARROWS, STILL MISSING
(APRIL 11, 2053–AUGUST 2067, I FEAR),
BY MADDIE BARROWS, HIS MOTHER,
DECEMBER 26, 2068

CHAPTER TWENTY-SEVEN

It was almost noon by the time Tia and I dragged ourselves out the front door. At the bottom of the porch stood two new bikes. From their handlebars hung tags, one with my name on it, one with Tia's.

Tia's bike was a single. I could almost see her mind struggling with that thought. Me? I was struggling with the thought of accepting Mom's or Rebecca Mack's or who-ever's thank-you gift or bribe or whatever it was.

I didn't struggle for long. "We don't need these," I said.

"No," Tia said. "We don't."

We left them standing there and continued on to the bus stop. In fifteen minutes we were at the university entrance and a campus map that showed Harmony Tower. On the map it was a different shade of green from the other structures represented—much lighter, as if it barely existed.

Five minutes later we stood in front of the building. It was a poor excuse for a tower—five or six stories of brick. The door was unlocked. Inside, the only hint that this wasn't an everyday dorm lobby was the lack of anyone hanging out except a pasty-faced guard sitting at a desk near a bank of three elevators.

Despite her official PAC uniform, she looked too young for the job, like she could have been a student herself. Maybe that was the reason she was there—to fit in on the campus scene. But she gave us an old lady's world-weary annoyed look when we approached. We just tried to look calm and unconcerned, like we belonged.

"This isn't university property," she said.

"We know," I said. "We're here to see a friend."

"What makes you think your *friend* is here?"

"We were told she was," Tia said. "She's been here a few weeks, probably."

"Yeah? Who told you?"

"Rebecca Mack," I said.

The girl straightened from her slouch. She was practically sitting at attention. "You know Rebecca Mack?"

"We were with her last night," Tia said.

After we mostly convinced the junior guard—her name tag said HILLIARD, CONTAINMENT—that we knew Rebecca Mack and told her who we were there to see and she'd checked our IDs on her scanner, she touched a desktop screen and waited until a voice—Anderson's—said, "Yes?"

"Visitors," Hilliard said.

"John Boyd?" Anderson's voice, even through the tiny speaker, sounded hopeful.

"No," Hilliard said. "A couple of kids. One of 'em's a boy, thinking he's special. The other one's a girl, thinking she's hot because she's with a boy."

Tia and I bit our tongues. Knowing Rebecca Mack hadn't made us immune to abuse, but I didn't want to make the guard's bad attitude worse. We were pretty much at her mercy.

"Do they have names?" Anderson said.

Hilliard told Anderson who we were. Anderson told her to send us up.

"Room 402," Hilliard said. She eyed us while we got on the elevator.

The building was quiet, but as we walked down the fourth-floor corridor to Anderson's room, I heard music from one room, conversation from another. The smell of cooking was coming from somewhere. The door to 402 was open when we got there.

Anderson greeted us just inside. Considering the circumstances, she seemed pretty together. Her eyes looked tired, but not like she'd been sleep-deprived or anything. Her red hair was still frizzy, but there was no evidence of helmet head. Obviously, she hadn't been out riding her bike. "Kellen," she said. "And Septiembre." Her smile was subdued but real. "This is a surprise."

"*Tia*," I said, saving Tia the effort. "She goes by *Tia*."

"Of course," Anderson said. "I remember that now."

She led us in and offered us seats in the small room. In one corner stood a desk with a row of old-fashioned books squeezed between bookends on its back edge, but there was no evidence of anything electronic on the desk or elsewhere. Apparently, PAC didn't trust Anderson to access the outside world except through visitors.

"What have you been up to?" she asked. "And how did you know where to find me?"

For the next hour we answered those two questions and a stream of more from her that eventually dried up as we related the details of the second-to-last part of our journey— the return to Afterlight.

Finally, we told her what had brought us to Harmony Tower. "Rebecca Mack says we can't do anything to expose what Brighter Day did," I said. "What PAC's been up to from the beginning."

"She says everyone who matters already knows," Tia said.

"She's partly right," Anderson said. Her face seemed less animated than when we'd arrived. Her voice was more like a murmur. "Those in power know. From her point of view, they're all that matters. Lots of everyday people—adults, anyway—have figured it out, even though many of them would rather not think about how we got to where we are. They can't change history, and most of them—even some men—believe they've benefited from it."

"Kids don't know," I said.

"Kids matter," Tia said.

"I think so, too," Anderson said. "I want to teach actual history, not a fairy-tale version of it. Or at least give my students the resources to investigate our past before they get so old that they're sidetracked by familiarity and comfort and the belief that the destination validates the journey, no matter how wayward and murderous. Dr. Mack and her crew don't agree with me, obviously. That's why I'm here."

"We want to tell people about it," I said.

"You should."

"Not just kids we know," Tia said. "We want to tell a lot of kids."

"And adults," I said. "We want to reach everyone we can."

"How would you do that?"

"We thought maybe you could get us access to a listing of all the kids in the history classes," I said. "Or maybe all the classes."

"If we had the electronic roster," Tia said, "we could send a message to everyone on it. In no time at all."

"We could tell them everything," I said.

"A summary, of course," Tia said. "But all the important stuff."

"And at the same time we want to put it on the Net," I said. "We want to revive an old website and have the story there for everyone who doesn't know it."

A small grin had appeared on Anderson's face. "Let me guess," she said. "Junkyarddog."

"Can you help us do it?" Tia asked.

Anderson nodded. Her grin widened. "I think they pissed you off."

"We lost people," I said. "Everyone lost people."

Anderson sighed. She swiped at her eye. "See, you can't invoke this kind of passion in us leave-well-enough-alone adults," she said. "How were you thinking of setting everything up?"

"E-spond," I said.

"It can be done, but they've taken mine away," she said. "They've taken away anything I could use to communicate with the world outside my window."

"Can't you just take off?" I said. "That guard downstairs looks like a pushover."

"What good would it do me?" She lifted the sleeve of her T-shirt. A fresh scar, a couple of inches long, angled across her upper arm. In the center of it was a dime-sized lump. "Tracking device. They'd have me back here in an hour, facing more time and scrutiny. As it is now, I'm on my way to convincing them I'll be no problem once I'm out of here."

"We weren't thinking of using your e-spond," Tia said.

"Whose, then? If you use one of yours, they'll know who created the site and sent the message."

"The library's," I said.

"You check out an e-spond and they'll have a record of it," Anderson said.

"We know that," I said. "We're going to borrow it . . . *anonymously*. But can you get us into the school's database?"

"I can do better than that. I can get you into the regional base for trials candidates. Five states. Tens of thousands of fourteen-year-olds. A couple of touches and they'll have your revelation."

"Can they trace your password?" Tia asked.

"I won't give you mine. They might have disabled it anyway. I have a couple of shadow passwords for emergencies, and no one can track them back to me. I'll give you one. I can also show you how to get a basic version of junkyarddog up and running in no time. If you build and trigger it using an e-spond you've borrowed *anonymously*, it can't be linked to you. There's no telling how long PAC will allow it to exist before they take it down, but for a time—enough time, I think—your story will be out there for the world to see."

"When would we know if it all works?" I asked.

"When you try it."

PAC did allow Anderson to have paper and pens. So she wrote down an access code, the phantom password, and the processes for sending our message to the entire list, building and activating the website, and posting the message there.

"What you're doing," she said. "It's worthwhile and brave, but it's bordering on dangerous. You could jeopardize your trials."

"We'll be careful," I said, stuffing her directions deep into my pocket.

We headed for the door, but before we got there, Tia had a question. "Who is John Boyd?"

Anderson's faint smile disappeared. Her eyes filled. For a moment I thought she wasn't going to—or couldn't—answer. But finally she did. "A friend," she said. "Lived in the hinterlands. Near a settlement you've visited . . . Afterlight."

Once outside we headed across quiet campus lawns toward the entrance. I remembered the rumors about Anderson and how she spent her weekends. "John Boyd," I said. "He was more than a friend."

"I could tell, Kelly."

During the short bus ride to the library, my nerves cropped up. Tia pretty much stopped talking, a sure sign that she was nervous, too. Our plan involved more than a little treachery, not a skill for either of us. To add to my anxiety, just as we got inside, I spotted an old friend.

The security cop—the one who had hounded me and called me names and accused me of stealing the last time I'd been here—was standing no more than twenty feet away, suspiciously eyeing patrons as they moved into the checkout line with their books and digital books and movies and recordings and e-sponds. Tia saw her, too—I could tell by the way she froze for a second or two—and together we moved on an angle away from the cop, toward the room where the e-sponds were shelved.

At the last moment, just before we would have been out of sight and safe, she glanced our way. All I could think was *Disaster.* All I could think was that she'd be sniffing along behind me like a wolf after sheep.

All I could think was *There goes our plan.*

But instead of snapping to attention and following us, she got this weird look on her face. It was recognition for sure, but combined with something else. Disgust, maybe. And there was some color in her face, too. It was the pink color of humiliation.

She turned on her heel and walked in the opposite direction. We hurried on before suspicion gained the upper hand and she changed her mind.

I chose an e-spond from a shelf. Tia, who would draw less attention and distrust than I would, took two at a time, and before our jitters got the better of us I threw a quick look around the room and whispered, "Now." She expertly slipped one of them down the front of her shorts. I glanced and detected nothing.

We walked nonchalantly to the checkout desk. The line was short, but it seemed to take forever to get to the terminal and get her e-spond—the one she didn't have stashed away—scanned. While we were waiting, I chanced a couple of subtle looks around the room for the cop, but she was keeping her distance, out of sight somewhere, maybe on the trail of someone else.

We were almost out the door, moving along in a small crowd of people, when the alarm went off.

Tia took a few more steps, getting beyond the range of the sensor, but I stopped. I headed back to checkout, holding up Tia's scanned e-spond and my un-scanned one, pretending to be embarrassed. It wasn't easy. I didn't feel embarrassed, even with all the extra scrutiny from the mostly female crowd and the woman at the desk. "I forgot to scan it," I told her. "My friend did hers, but I was too busy talking."

The woman reached under the counter and touched something. The alarm died. "Happens all the time." She smiled as she checked Tia's e-spond and scanned mine. "Have a good day."

"I'm planning on it." As I walked away I took one more look around. The cop was back, peering across the room for the culprit who'd tripped the alarm. Her eyes fell on me. I nodded in her general direction and headed off, trying not to hurry.

I got through the door without commotion this time and joined Tia at the bottom of the steps. We took off, not looking back. We wanted to put some distance between ourselves and the library.

"Good work, Tia," I said. "Cool like ice."

"You, too, Kelly. I knew you could sweet-talk anyone in there. With that one exception."

"Maybe I'll grow on her."

"Where are we going?"

For a moment I wasn't sure.

Then I was. I didn't know how much we'd accomplish with what we were about to do, but it would be nice to have a witness to it, someone to see that we were trying, at least, to set the record straight. It would be nice to have my grandfather looking over our shoulders. "Epitaph Road," I said.

Ain't no late-night heart-to-hearts,

ain't no summer since you've gone.

—EPITAPH FOR SUNDAY MARIE MCCLOUD
(OCTOBER 11, 2082–JUNE 20, 2097),
BY MARY ALICE MCCLOUD, HER MOTHER,
ABRIL MENDOZA, HER AUNT,
AND TIA MENDOZA, HER COUSIN AND SISTER AND BEST FRIEND,
JULY 17, 2097

CHAPTER TWENTY-EIGHT

Tia and I had been through a lot in the past few weeks. I felt different. I was sure she did, too. How could she not? But Epitaph Road looked the same. The park and the burial site looked pretty much unchanged: sprawling green fields, flaming gas exhaust pipes masquerading as white crosses, mid-afternoon sun beating down, casting short shadows around everything.

But there was no Sunday. And so far, there were no Fratheists.

We stopped at the monolith and waited while an old woman moved out of the way, freeing one of the display screens. I scrolled to my grandfather's epitaph and let Tia read it. "The bear," she said. I'd told her the story of Dad's bear the morning we found the tracks crisscrossing our campsite.

We walked to a quiet spot near the center of the grave-yard and sat down on the warm grass.

"You're sure about this, Tia?" I said. "You could just catch a bus back to the house right now and not be involved. Not even as a witness."

"I'm already involved," she said. "I'm not bailing now. We're partners in this."

"There's a difference between us," I said. "You've got a shining future. Mine's not so shining."

"That could change."

"Maybe. But if not, whether I end up as a second-class citizen or a third-class nobody isn't a huge deal. Not in the big picture. Not when there's a chance to put a hole in PAC's story and a dent in its reputation."

"I have a good feeling, Kelly—we're not going to get caught. Suspected, maybe—most likely—but not caught."

"I have the same feeling—mostly—but I can't help worry-ing about you, the partner with everything at stake. As for me, screw it. I'd be happy catching fish with my dad."

"Too late for worrying." She took out the pilfered e-spond. We began brainstorming. Not far away, a pipe belched fire into the sky. *Grandfather,* I told myself.

We talked and wrote and revised. We knew what we wanted to say, but we didn't know exactly how to say it and how much emphasis and space to give to each item. And we wanted one message we could use in both the mailing to the kids and on the website. So it took some time.

When we'd run out of ideas and cuts and changes, Tia read me what we had.

YOU'RE A SKEPTIC.

IF YOU'VE HEARD CERTAIN THINGS—CONJECTURE, CONSPIRACY THEORIES, WILD-EYED ACCUSATIONS—OVER THE YEARS, YOU'VE MOSTLY SNICKERED AT THEM AND HURRIED BACK TO THE COMFORTS OF WHAT PASSES FOR REALITY. BUT MAYBE ONE RUMOR—THAT DIE-HARD, FAR-FETCHED, ALTERNATE-UNIVERSE ONE ABOUT THE ORIGIN OF ELISHA'S BEAR, ABOUT SOMEONE PURPOSEFULLY UNLEASHING IT—HAUNTS YOU. MAYBE YOU'RE SKEPTICAL INSTEAD ABOUT THE SO-CALLED TRUTH YOU'VE BEEN SPOON-FED FROM AN EARLY AGE—THE IDEA THAT THE BEAR JUST SHOWED UP ON ITS OWN AND TARGETED ONLY MALES.

YOU SHOULD BE.

That was the introduction—the part we hoped would get people's attention.

Tia read on. We tinkered with things a little more, trying to make the information evenhanded and as much like a story as possible. We included a lot of the bad stuff men had been responsible for—wars, terrorism, mass deaths, slavery, human and environmental exploitation—and we wrote about Rebecca Mack's personal experience with abuse and justice. And we documented the history of Brighter Day and Elisha's Bear and its recurrences, including what had just happened at Afterlight.

We didn't mention the Foothills Project and its lab or the smothering of the second bear. We didn't want to inspire more fanatics. Or draw sure attention to ourselves.

Finally, we agreed—it was about as good as it was going to get. I took out the paper Anderson had given me and read everything off while Tia tapped away. In a moment we were into the student database. Simple and mostly sweat-free. She scrolled down a bit and stopped. It looked like a zillion names. She directed our e-script to the MAIL space and chose SEND ALL.

We didn't send it. Not yet. We pulled up another template and followed Anderson's directions again, this time for creating the website. It was quick and easy, even with our nerves on edge.

"Junkyarddog.bites," Tia said when we'd pasted in our message and we were all but finished. "It looks good to see it live."

"Perfect," I said. "Even on that little screen." It was destined for bigger ones.

"Ready?" she said, and I nodded. She took my hand and we let our fingers hover over the e-spond for a few seconds while I thought about the two of us detonating explosions in a far-off forest, not long ago. I recalled sitting in Anderson's classroom—not long before that—and watching the video of San Francisco disintegrating. I wondered what kind of damage this little blast would do. Then I watched Tia tap the LAUNCH icon.

An instant later, a word flashed in the middle of the display: AIRBORNE.

It was done. The wide world had something new to chew on.

Now for our smaller world. Tia shifted back to the MAIL screen. "Your turn, Kelly," she murmured.

I didn't hesitate. With her fingertips resting on my forearm, I touched the SEND ALL icon. A green arrow zipped across the top of the screen. Our message was gone. In a moment the first kids would read it. Then later, tens of thousands more.

I imagined the fallout. I pictured Rebecca Mack and my mother, squirming.

Tia and I shared a hug.

Above us, a flame, nearly invisible in the sunlight, watched over us.